ISLANDS &
BRIDGES

Also by GEOFFREY SCOTT

STEALING HOMER
Rascal Harbor, Book One

KNIGHTS DISARMED
Rascal Harbor, Book Two

ISLANDS

AND

BRIDGES

A RASCAL HARBOR NOVEL

RASCAL HARBOR, BOOK THREE

GEOFFREY SCOTT

PROSPECTIVE PRESS

Winston-Salem

Prospective Press llc

1959 Peace Haven Rd, #246, Winston-Salem, NC 27106 U.S.A.
www.prospectivepress.com

Published in the United States of America by Prospective Press LLC

ƛ TRADEMARK

Islands and Bridges
A Rascal Harbor Novel

Text copyright © S. G. Grant, 2021
All rights reserved.
The author's moral rights have been asserted.

Cover and interior design by ARTE RAVE
Copyright © Prospective Press LLC, 2021
All rights reserved.
The copyright holder's moral rights have been asserted.

ISBN 978-1-943419-88-3

First Prospective Press trade paperback edition

Printed in the United States of America
First printing, December, 2021

The text of this book was typeset in Caslon Pro
Accent text was typeset in Belleza

Publisher's Note

This book is a work of fiction. The people, names, characters, locations, activities, and events portrayed or implied by this book are the product of the author's imagination or are used fictitiously. Any resemblance to actual people, locations, and events is strictly coincidental.

Without limiting the rights as reserved in the above copyright, no part of this publication may be reproduced, stored in or introduced into any retrieval system, or transmitted–by any means, in any form, electronic, mechanical, photocopying, recording, or otherwise–without the prior written permission of the publisher. Not only is such reproduction illegal and punishable by law, but it also hurts the author who toiled hard on the creation of this work and the publisher who brought it to the world. In the spirit of fair play, and to honor the labor and creativity of the author, we ask that you purchase only authorized electronic and print editions of this work and refrain from participating in or encouraging piracy or electronic piracy of copyright-protected materials. Please give authors a break and don't steal this or any other work.

Cover contains an image CC by S. G.. Grant..
Cover contains an image CC by Bev Tabet.

ACKNOWLEDGMENTS

In crafting the fictional lives of my Rascal Harbor characters, I draw inspiration from the lives of those around me. How these folks craft their own lives and loves and lessons fascinates me; the range of personalities that populate my novels necessarily reflects the even bigger range that has filled my life. So, my initial acknowledgment here is to the thousands of people who I have known through their hopes and frailties, their ideas and actions, their ever-present and ever-changing humanity.

Writers write. But they also talk about their writing, and that talk is invaluable. I benefit from talking about and sharing my writing with Anne, our kids, and their partners as well as with a host of friends— Emily Cole, Jean Dorak, Ike Lovelass, Julie Lovelass, Matt McConn, Carolyn Paladino, John Queenan, and Mike Stenger. I much appreciate your time, attention, and insights.

There would be no *Islands and Bridges* without Jason Graves. As editor and publisher, it is Jason's continued support of the Rascal Harbor series and his flexible navigation of the crazed conditions leveled through a global pandemic that have made this book stronger…and now in print. Many thanks, Jason.

To Anne, Alexander and Cassidy, and Claire and Jose.

My best always.

CHAPTER 1

Talk about a tough year. In the previous twelve months, John Louis McTavish lost his wife Maggie to pancreatic cancer, took early retirement from his faculty position at a mid-western university, and moved to Rascal Harbor on the coast of Maine. Oh, and he'd taken away a knife from one man, been threatened with a gun by another…and been almost electrocuted while replacing an old cartridge fuse in a neighbor's breaker box.

For McTavish, a man who was interested in people, but who tried to avoid being involved in their lives, it had been a year of way too much involvement. To make matters worse, the one relationship he cared most about—the one with his college-aged son—proved to be the rockiest. Maggie had always buffered McTavish's general social awkwardness and his particularly awkward connection with his son. Now she was gone and he wasn't navigating the world around himself all that well.

Newly-widowed, newly-retired, and in hopes of restarting his life, McTavish had left his mid-western home to move into the summer cottage he and Maggie owned. He'd loved his time as a college history professor, but he had harbored a long-time interest in living an artist's life. If he'd been thinking clearly after Maggie's death, he probably would have stayed in Indiana to pursue this venture while surrounded by all things familiar. He wasn't and he didn't, and since moving to

Rascal Harbor, a fair amount of craziness had occurred.

At one point, McTavish thought his biggest challenge would be the decision to add color into his artwork. Turns out it wasn't.

CHAPTER 2

McTavish's color dilemma stemmed from his decision to work on his ability to draw as the first step toward his art career. "If I'm to be a proper artist," he said to himself. "Then I need to start with the basics." And the basics, in McTavish's mind, meant focusing on rendering images in pen, pencil, and charcoal.

It wasn't that McTavish feared color or that he'd not had success in the past. He didn't and he had. In fact, his past success gave him the confidence to devote himself to this second career as an artist. But he was a man who took things in small measures and so jumping back into his watercolor box before pushing himself to improve his drawing just seemed wrong.

After moving to Rascal Harbor, McTavish took up human hands as his first drawing project. He'd always thought that faces would be the toughest thing to render well. And they probably were, but McTavish had had some success in his early work on this body part so, to push himself, he decided to focus on hands. What he'd discovered is that hands are every bit as complex a drawing task as the faces that go with them. So McTavish spent hours drawing hands at rest, in prayer, pointing, and working. He'd drawn men's hands, women's hands, and children's hands—sometimes singly, sometimes in pairs—and he was about to pronounce himself a hand expert when it occurred to him to add another element to his drawings.

McTavish still wondered where the inspiration originated to draw rectangles around part of each hand. But the impulse struck and it struck hard. McTavish positioned the rectangles—some horizontal, some vertical—around a section of each hand drawing. Doing so, he immediately realized, created a set of interesting shapes around the hand images. The spaces between, say, the knuckles of a hand and the line in the rectangle above them made for their own kind of appealing shape.

At that point, McTavish recognized what he was doing artistically. Any rendered image consists of two spaces—the positive space of the featured image and the negative space around it. Optical illusions like Edgar Rubin's face/vase print and M.C. Escher's fish and fowl woodcuts are some of the more dramatic examples. But every image that the artist wants us to focus on is defined by the image itself and the space around it. So the rectangles McTavish placed on his hand drawings created a new way of looking at the images. Examining one of these enhanced drawings, McTavish's young artist friend, Jimmy Park, declared "It was there before, but now it's there differently."

Later, on a trip to northern Maine, McTavish began working on another art principle—the figure-ground relationship. Related to the positive/negative space concept, figure-ground represents the element that artists decide to feature—the figure—and what they position behind it—the ground. In Andrew Wyeth's masterpiece, Christina's World, the figure of the woman in the field becomes something more when seen against the background of field, buildings, and skyline.

McTavish's interest in figure-ground relationships ended up developing along two lines—artistic and personal. On the artistic side, he created a series of images where he placed early spring flowers, crocus and daffodils, against backgrounds of dirty snow, rotting fences, and crumbling stone foundations. Doing so pleased his artist's eye, but it also struck him as a metaphor for the idea that life cannot be denied despite the decay, despair, and disorder around it. He liked the many drawings he'd created, but he equally appreciated the insight into his

GEOFFREY SCOTT

own life—the idea that the wreck of his existence after Maggie died could possibly regenerate.

McTavish was reviewing these art/life connections one late spring morning when his son, Noah, came downstairs. Noah was home from college for the summer and the small cottage was starting to prove close quarters.

Though different in many ways, the McTavish men shared a physical presence. Both were tall, though their lean frames made them appear taller than their 5'10" measured heights. Neither was muscular in the obvious sense, but both could split wood for hours and preferred walking to town over driving. It was their faces, however, that cemented their similarities and accentuated their differences. Both had full heads of straight, brown hair and strong jawlines. The differences emerged most notably in their eyes. McTavish's stern eyes could soften, but did so only rarely. Favoring his mother, Noah's eyes presented a more open and inviting quality. Yet that quality could disappear quickly when Noah was angry, especially with his father.

CHAPTER 3

As Noah came down the stairs, he could see his father shaking his head and hear his muttered words. His first thought— Dad's talking to Mom again.

Earlier that spring, Noah realized that his father carried on conversations with his wife even a year after her death. He knew that McTavish found them comforting, for the most part, because he was nowhere near ready to let go of this woman who had loved him in spite of himself. Noah found them frustrating because he could not have his own conversations. He had tried…and failed.

"Who are you talking to, Dad?" Noah asked, as he came up behind his father.

Apparently unaware of his son's arrival and hunched over his drawing table, McTavish looked up with a frown. "What? What? Sorry…I didn't hear you come down," McTavish stumbled, his eyes softening at the sight of his son.

"Didn't mean to interrupt, but I could hear you mumbling and I thought you might be talking with Mom."

"No, not this morning. Guess I must have been grumbling about Ruby's comment about my drawing last night."

"Oh? Did she like it?" Noah asked. Gary and Ruby Park had come to dinner at McTavish's cottage the night before. Noah had worked the dinner rush at Lane's Wharf, then met Gary and Ruby's daughter,

Louise, for a drink. He'd gotten home after McTavish was in bed so had not heard how the evening progressed. "I'm guessing she liked the purple."

"Oh, she liked the purple all right," McTavish said, the mutter returning to his voice. "The purple" referred to the color that McTavish used to emphasize some of the crocus blossoms in his "life amongst decay" art series. Deciding that they needed color, but unwilling to commit to his paint box, McTavish had used a set of variously hued markers to add color to portions of his drawings. McTavish liked the result—within a largely black, white, and gray image of crocus plants clustered against an old stone foundation, he had colored only the blossoms and stigmata of a few plants in the foreground. The effect of leaving the rest of the drawing uncolored, he realized, expanded the figure-ground relationship: The colored plants were the figure, the stone foundation was the ground, and the uncolored plants formed a kind of middle ground—related to the figure by element and to the ground by hue.

None of this figure-ground stuff had registered with Ruby Park. Drawn always to the bright and shiny, Ruby fixated on the vivid purple color McTavish used on one set of crocus blossoms. Pointing and smiling, Ruby said in her pronounced French Canadian accent, "Jesus, John, I am loving to pieces dat color you put der in dem pretty flower leaves!" Then shaking her head so that her hair extensions vibrated, she said, "See, John, see? Dat purple violet is just like my hair pieces!" Just that afternoon, Ruby's stylist Charlotte had interlaced strands of crocus-blossom-purple throughout Ruby's mostly red and orange hair "as accents." Delighted with her "new hair," Ruby was doubly so now that she saw her accent color evident in McTavish's artwork.

If the purple conversation had ended here, McTavish's morning mood would have been fine. What soured him was Ruby's comment later in the evening.

After finishing dinner, Ruby returned to the images. As she reviewed them, she said, "John, I am tinkin' this is some very good work you have made in des pictures. But I wonderin' to myself why is you now drawin' cartoons?"

Taken aback, McTavish sputtered, "Cartoons?"

"Well, yes, John McTavish, cartoons," Ruby said, looking at him seriously. "You did dem udder drawin' pictures of de hands wit boxes all around dem. Dose I liked quite good, even without some color in dem. I really like some of dis color you put in des pictures, John, but dis color is not painting color so my mind is tinkin' dey is cartoons."

Nonplussed, McTavish could only say, "Jesus, Ruby, guess you're right…." At that point, Gary returned from the bathroom, sensed his friend's discomfort, and announced that it was time to head home.

Suspecting that she had somehow hurt McTavish's feelings, Ruby said, "I really do like dem pretty cartoons, John, cross my heart and all." McTavish nodded and smiled his guests to the door, then poured himself an extra finger of Bushmills Irish Whiskey.

Noah's entrance the next morning interrupted McTavish's contemplation of Ruby's cartoon comment and the idea of adding some Bushmills to his morning coffee. He now contemplated how to respond to Noah's question about Ruby's reaction. The part of him that was wounded by Ruby's remark was quickly overcome by the part that saw the humor in it so he told Noah the story.

"Oh, Jesus, Dad, I'm sorry," Noah said as both men laughed softly. "That's an ouch of the first magnitude. What are you going to do?"

"Hard to say," McTavish admitted. "Though I'm thinking about getting new business cards that say, 'John McTavish, cartoonist extraordinaire.'" They both laughed again.

"You know, Dad, Mom might have made the same comment, as a way to get you back to the paints. She loved the paintings you used to do."

"I expect you're right," McTavish said with a sigh. "But she'd have especially loved seeing my face when Ruby called them cartoons. Your mom liked a good chuckle, especially at my expense."

"True, but then you gave her so many opportunities!"

GEOFFREY SCOTT

"Don't you have some work to do?" McTavish said, his chiding good-natured.

"I do, but what about you? I've got my piece for the Arvin Prize just about ready. Hey, are you going to submit your cartoon?"

The Arvin Prize recognized the best-judged piece in the juried portion of the annual Rascal Harbor Art Colony Summer Exhibition. A local Rascal Harbor painter, Mattie Arvin was one of the first Maine women to have a solo show at the Portland Museum of Art. The show in the mid-1950s brought a measure of fame to the reclusive artist and to the Art Colony she founded. After her death some thirty years ago, the Art Colony board voted to create the Arvin Prize to recognize and reward the artist whose work won top billing during the Colony's big summer show. The Arvin Prize offered a $1000 cash award, year-long display in the featured spot at the Art Colony gallery, and the right to call oneself an Arvin artist.

McTavish had not lived long enough in town to achieve resident status when the submission deadline came up the previous year; he intended to make it for this summer's exhibition. Or he did until Ruby Park dampened his spirits. Jesus, he thought, taken down a peg by a woman with crocus-colored hair.

CHAPTER 4

T he Arvin Prize was on Robertay Harding's mind too. Harding presided over the Rascal Harbor Art Colony and had done so for the last ten years. The success of the Colony's expanding membership, well-attended events, and sufficiently filled coffers owed much to her steady, if sometimes heavy-handed, leadership. That said, the fact that the Colony's reach and renown were greater in Robertay's mind than in reality was generally accepted by the town residents, artists and non-artists alike.

A physically imposing woman, Harding was nearly six feet tall with gray curly hair cultivated to wildness for effect. Her booming voice, thick New York accent, perpetually—but artfully—paint-splattered clothing, and self-designed name marked her as "the arty type." Completing Robertay's bohemian look was a bosom of more than ample size and less than ample restriction. Often braless, Robertay's breasts announced themselves boldly and did so to the distraction of the locals, both men and women. Addled men were known to walk into street signs, step on children, and drop their ice cream cones at the sight of Robertay's free-range boobs. Perturbed women stared at and cursed these men, though many also stared at and cursed Robertay. Largely unaware of the ruckus following in her wake, Robertay charged through Rascal Harbor, the Colony, and life with full feathers flying.

Always looking for a way to build the Colony's range and reputation, Robertay had a notion of expanding the pool of artists eligible for the Arvin Prize. To her life partner, Thomas Beatty, she announced, "I am thinking that we need to open up the Arvin competition to non-residents."

Beatty, a burly man of good humor and distracted manner, typically followed a path of least effort: It was far easier to agree with Robertay's ideas and actions than to challenge them. Yet something about this pronouncement provoked Thomas to raise a question. "Oh? Why would that be a good idea, love?"

"It's simple. Allowing outsiders to compete would elevate immeasurably the level of the art displayed, it would bring in considerable bounty in terms of submission fees, and it would lift the profile of the event beyond the local area. It's a brilliant idea!"

"Hmm. I suspect it is. I really do. I do wonder, however, how the Colony membership and townspeople might respond. The Arvin has always been open only to residents—"

"I know that!" Robertay said. "Why would you think that I wouldn't know that! Honestly, Thomas, sometimes…"

"No offense, dear one," Thomas said calmly. "Just pointing out the obvious, I suppose."

"If it's obvious, then it need not be pointed out!" Shifting gears, she continued. "Of course, some of the narrow-minded will balk, but progress is never without casualties. Such a bold move would really put the Colony on the art-world map. I mean, imagine the possibilities. One day, the Summer Exhibition and the Arvin Prize could even go international!"

"You do have vision," he said gently.

"Fucking right I do! I've got vision that even scares me sometimes. But the work I do, the work to which I've committed myself is all for the benefit of the art world, the town, and the Colony. As you well know, I could have stayed in the City and simply dedicated myself to my art. But I'm here and I can build something bigger than myself, a contribution that swells beyond my singular artistic talents."

Pausing for a breath and to see if Thomas was still attentive, Robertay continued. "I have so much to give and I won't live forever, so I have to make moves that may upset a few people. But we must continue on the road to the greater good. People will see that eventually."

Thomas had mastered the art of attentive distraction. Robertay's soliloquies ran a predictable course, so most times he needed to give no more than half an ear to avoid an upbraiding. He had been trying to think through a perspective problem he'd encountered in his own artwork when she started in. He knew Robertay was seeking no feedback on the idea, so he had not had to formulate any response beyond murmurs of agreement. Still, in this instance, he wondered if Robertay might end up pushing too hard and too fast.

CHAPTER 5

Thomas was right to worry. Arts organizations cross Maine communities, big and small. The commonalty is their affinity for promoting art; on every other level—from size of membership to organizational structure to promotion of their efforts—they vary considerably. Actually, they also vary considerably in terms of how they define "art." Some organizations take a liberal view and give space to art of all types while others focus exclusively on one kind of artistic expression or another.

The Rascal Harbor Art Colony, now in its 73rd year, had gone through phases in its history. Originally founded as a group that celebrated all the arts, the troupe had once embraced musicians, dancers, and even poets, along with those in the visual arts. Over the years, however, the visual artists flourished while the other folks moved on or moved away. Mattie Arvin sealed the visual-arts-only focus of the Colony when the only submissions accepted for the juried portion of the big Summer Exhibition took that form. No one much complained, so the decision became a tradition which became the rule.

Even limiting submissions to the visual arts, however, still offered plenty of variety in the works accepted. Oil, watercolor, and acrylic paintings predominated, but pastel pieces, drawings in all media, prints, sculpture, and photography were welcome as well. No one had submitted a video piece yet, but the Summer Exhibition committee had heard that some of the local kids were making videos that they might try to put forward. The committee was ready—no media arts would be allowed.

The visual-arts-only restriction was rigidly enforced by Robertay Harding who also functioned as chair of the Summer Exhibition committee. Robertay was an oil painter specializing in seascapes. Her realist approach, however, competed with her abstract impulses such that viewers of her paintings typically wondered if they were looking at boats at sea, seagulls in flight, or bedsheets on a clothesline. Robertay's appreciation of her own artistic talents outstripped that of others, but her organizational talents were considered first rate by nearly all.

Members of arts groups were typically a bureaucratic-adverse bunch. They belonged to an association, but predictably sidestepped most of the management responsibilities. So when a colleague displayed any sort of leadership and administrative capacity, she or he could generally exert considerable control.

When Robertay first moved to Rascal Harbor, the Rascal Harbor Art Colony president was Timothy Rawling, a watercolorist who had led the organization for nearly a dozen years. Rawlings ruled the Colony with a strong, but fair hand. His downfall came when a Colony member discovered that Rawling's fastidiously precise paintings were the result of projecting photographs onto his cold-press paper, tracing all the shapes, and then filling them in with paint. Accused of being a paint-by-numbers faker during a tumultuous Executive Board meeting, Rawlings quietly resigned. Leading the charge and then assuming the president's spot was Robertay Harding. Her reign had thus far gone unchallenged.

As president of the Colony and chair of the Summer Exhibition committee, Robertay wielded considerable power as the principal member of the Executive Board. Filling out the board were Toni Ludlow in Membership, Jona Lewis for Budget, Regina Baldo coordinating Events, and Thomas Beatty as Administrator.

Baldo was a new addition, rising up from the Colony membership to replace Simon Britton, the former Events chair. The previous fall, Simon had been arrested and indicted for the theft of a recently discovered Winslow Homer watercolor. His incarceration crippled him physically, spiritually, and artistically. His failed attempts at rebounding once freed led him to resign from his Executive Board position.

A photographer of young middle age who'd moved to the Harbor five years ago, Baldo supported Robertay's ambitions for the Colony. Her energy and enthusiasm ran high and, like the Colony president, she was a woman who got things done. Robertay appreciated Regina's efforts, but should they ever threaten the central importance of the Summer Exhibition, she was not shy about shutting them down. Though unorthodox, Robertay had retained the Summer Exhibition chair once she took the presidency. No one had objected, or objected too loudly, so Robertay prevailed.

The other members of the Executive Board were all locals and long-time members of the of the Colony. Toni Ludlow had moved to the Harbor fifteen years earlier; Jona's and Thomas's families were long-time residents. Serving staggered terms, each board member had served at least two years.

Most often the Colony membership and Board members agreed with and acceded to Robertay's plans. They respected her energy and willingness to do the hard work on keeping the association solvent and functioning. Still, a popular game among the membership—and Toni and Jona—was riffing on the phrase, "What Robertay wants, Robertay gets." Among the most repeated replacements for the word "gets" were "manipulates into being," "engineers into place," "throws a tantrum until it happens," and "fucking annoys people until she gets her own way."

The idea of defining who can and cannot participate in an art organization's events was one of the other norms that differed from location to location. Many groups allowed anyone to participate in any of the sponsored shows. Others, like the Rascal Harbor Art Colony, allowed open registration for exhibitions, but narrowly restricted opportunities to compete for juried honors. Of course, organizations could change their rules, sometimes even dramatically. But as a true local—his Rascal Harbor family went back five generations—Thomas Beatty knew that some rules were more important than others. The residents-only restriction around competition for the Arvin Prize seemed like it might be one of those.

GEOFFREY SCOTT

CHAPTER 6

The spread of arts-based groups is pretty uniform across the state. They vary in size, activity, and scope, but most every Maine town and city of any size has one or more organization devoted to the cultured side of life. Less uniform are the ways such groups are perceived both from the inside and the outside.

Some artists perceive their local council as an annoyance, necessary in order to show their work, but a drag on their time and energy. Typically loners, they abhor even minimal obligations to the personal, social, and artistic needs of others. They pay their dues, display their work, and then go home.

Other artists, of course, need the life blood of their associations to feed their artistic and personal souls. These folks find comfort, inspiration, and common cause in the community of their peers. They pay their dues and display their work, but they also attend membership meetings, participate in committee work, clean up the mess after every show, and then they go home.

These two poles merely define the ends of a wide spectrum—individual artists perceive the value of their organizations on the same sort of sliding scale that bowlers do their leagues, chess players do their clubs, and knitters do their circles.

Whatever the type, artists share the same range of generosity, venality, naiveté, kindness, and awkwardness that infects the general populace. Jealousies (obvious and hidden), misbehavior (slight and egregious), and egoism (extreme and more extreme) co-exist with friendship (superficial to true), honesty (sort of to mostly), and caring (obligatory to compassionate). It all makes for a happy stew of complicated and complex relationships, emotions, and involvement.

From the outside, art groups are also variously perceived. In larger localities, with more members and resources, an art association can be recognized as vital to the community cultural fabric. However, the cultural fabric is a lot thinner and more precarious in small Maine towns. The artists in those areas may still think much of themselves and their work, but themselves and their work may be largely ignored. Folks struggling with social and economic challenges may pass on purchasing original artworks for their walls and balk at participating in a debate over whether or not photography is one of the fine arts.

Still, regardless of size, Maine communities tend toward the libertarian line of live and let live. Townspeople may hold stereotypical views of artists in general and they may snicker if an artist bursts into a room with a mane of unruly hair, an article of wild clothing, a waft of body odor, and a display of paint spatter. But unless she or he regularly makes an ass of her or himself, the snickers go largely unheard and life moves on.

Snickers can turn to snubs, however, especially if an art organization holds itself too far above the locals. A group that acts like the savior of all things refined and cultured can find itself dealing with dwindling membership rolls, weak attendance at events, and ferocious gossip.

Although there are lots of ways to avoid such troubles, one is to be more inclusive of the local artists, both part-timers and the less hip.

Such was the Rascal Harbor Art Colony under Mattie Arvin's leadership. As a true-blue local and a quietly effective promoter, Arvin used her talent and fame to build a sense of community among the Colony members and a sense of pride in the Colony among the non-artist residents. Until his disgrace, Timothy Rawlings had largely followed that course. Individual Colony artists might be too much to take, but the group's leader earned and kept covenant with the Harbor townsfolk.

All of this had been explained to Robertay Harding and she had seemed to understand. Still, Robertay's eyes were set on a different horizon. So while the efforts she led were generally successful, Robertay was seen as off-putting and emblematic of the worst artist stereotypes. Perspectives on the art world can vary tremendously. In the case of Robertay Harding, however, that range was pretty narrow.

CHAPTER 7

Although they continued to talk about her idea of expanding the pool of artists eligible to compete for the Arvin Prize, it would be more accurate to say that Thomas talked and Robertay stormed.

"Are you telling me," Robertay said, at one point, "that these people would be against an idea that would only benefit them and the community? Are you serious? Maybe it's you who is the narrow-minded one here. Maybe you don't give the local people enough credit to see beyond their pasts and into their futures!"

"You may be right, dear," Thomas said weakly.

"Of course I'm right! Your provincial attitude discredits you. You and a few others may want to keep the good people of Rascal Harbor prisoner to the past, but you're in the minority and you've got to get out of the way of progress. I'm convinced that the Colony and the townspeople will embrace my plan because they'll see it as one more step into a bright and noble future!"

"You may be right. It's just that—"

"It's just nothing, Thomas! This conversation is pointless. I would have thought you, of all people, would support me in this effort, but I see that you will stay in the shadows of the past. I, on the other hand, have set in motion the wheels of progress."

"What do you mean, dear heart?" Thomas asked innocently.

GEOFFREY SCOTT

"Well, if you ever bothered to check your email, you would know!" Robertay sniffed. "I've called for an emergency meeting of the Executive Board early this morning to begin the implementation of my plan. We've got to act quickly or we won't be able to get the notice out in time to pull in all the best artists."

"Oh. But I was going to paint this morn—"

"Past or future?" Robertay asked. "Past or future? You have to choose!"

With a wan smile, Thomas looked at Robertay and said, "I choose you."

Few smiles greeted Robertay and Thomas as board members Jona Lewis, Toni Ludlow, and Regina Baldo arrived at the Colony gallery. On the principle that food and coffee always smooth possible problems, Robertay had laid out an array of fruit and pastries, and Thomas had the Colony's ancient coffee urn cranked up.

"This better be worth it, Robertay," Jona said as the first to enter the conference room. "I had plans for today." A sculptor, Lewis was a powerfully-built man of medium height and red-haired complexion. Like Regina Baldo, Lewis was in his early thirties.

"Jona, it will. I promise," Robertay said calmly.

"What are you promising?" Toni Ludlow asked as she walked in and went directly to the coffee. Ludlow was a tall, willowy blonde in her late forties who created large, abstract oil paintings.

"Ah, Toni, good to see you," Robertay said smoothly. "I promise this morning's meeting will be worth your time."

"I'm sure it will be," Regina Baldo said, blowing into the room with a smile. "How is everyone doing?" Baldo's short, compact frame and ready smile breathed energy into her artistic enthusiasms.

Greetings of various intensity ensued, none of which dampened Regina's excitement. She, too, had had working plans for the morning, but she took seriously her leadership role on the board and so did not much mind the disruption.

"Well, let's get to it, shall we?" Robertay said a little too enthusiastically. "We've much to do!"

With the group assembled, Robertay described her vision for opening the Arvin Prize competition to artists living outside Rascal Harbor. Somber expressions surrounded the table with the exception of Regina Baldo who began smiling and nodding with Robertay's opening words.

"I just love it," Regina said and beamed. "Think of the publicity this will bring to the Colony and to the town! It could be huge!"

"It could," Jona said slowly. "And it would certainly amp up the level of the work displayed." Pausing, he continued in a confident tone. "I, for one, am not afraid of the competition. I think my work can stand up to anyone's." Pausing again, he added in a more reflective tone, "But there's the logistics to consider. We'd really have to get going soon to get word out—"

"Exactly!" Robertay said brightly. "Exactly right, Jona. We'll have to push, but I have every confidence that—"

Toni said, "Hang on a minute, Robertay. There's a lot to think through here. The logistics are going to be extensive if we're to do this right. But there are other factors that we need to think through. I mean, how is this idea going to play with the membership?"

"I've given that matter my full attention," Robertay said. "And I've concluded that it should not be an issue. I'm fully confident that, once informed, the membership will embrace the idea."

"I think they will too," Regina said.

Jona shifted in his seat. "Maybe they will, but Toni raises a good point. There's bound to be some upset folks for sure. A lot of local artists think they should have been Arvin Prize winners in the past. If we now make the competition even greater, well..." Jona paused, then said, "We could slow down a bit, you know, raise the issue with the members this year, let 'em get used to it, then do it next year."

"I think that's how I'm leaning. I mean, what's the rush?" Toni asked.

Regina jumped in. "But why would we wait? It's a great idea that will certainly give the Exhibition a huge boost in attendance and the Arvin much more attention. I think we should do it."

"I think we should do it, but I'm wondering about the timeline," Jona said.

"What do you think, Thomas," Toni asked.

Thomas, who had been sitting quietly with no expression, now looked embarrassed. "Well, Toni, I… well, of course, I am persuaded that the idea has merit for all the reasons that have been expressed so far. That said, there is the issue of the membership's views—"

"Well, there you have it," Robertay said. "I think we're in agreement."

Toni said, "Wait a minute. I'd like to hear the rest of what Thomas was going to say. Your family's been in the Harbor for a long time, right, Thomas? How do you think this idea will play with them? And your family goes back a few generations, too, right, Jona?"

"Yeah, my family's got lobster bait running through our veins," Jona said with a nod. "I'm the first boy not to go to sea…" Jona hesitated a minute before continuing. "I predict there'll be a split. Some would support it, but I imagine a bunch would be opposed to letting outsiders compete."

"Yes, yes," Robertay said impatiently. "But your family are not artists, Jona. I mean, I'm sure they're lovely people, but they're not artists. This is an art-world decision. Non-artists are not going to understand, though I guarantee you that they'll love the visitors' dollars that will come pouring in."

"They certainly will! The Exhibition is already a big tourist draw so just imagine the economic value that would result from expanding the pool of artists eligible for the Arvin Prize," Regina said.

"I'd still like to hear from Thomas. You've got artists in your family, don't you?" Toni said evenly.

All eyes now turned to a clearly uncomfortable Thomas Beatty. Nervously playing with his pen, Thomas looked at Robertay and then at the rest of the group.

"Well, there are always a range of ways to look at any situation. I can easily imagine my Aunt Lorraine's reaction. She worked in oils for forty years, a good, if not great renderer in the realist tradition, though she began dabbling with Cubism later—"

"For Christ's sake, Thomas! We don't have time for you to review the artistic merits of every painter in your lineage," Robertay said, eyes blazing. "Look, let's do this: Everyone on the board reach out to at least five members of the Colony and do a poll. Tell them that we want to open the Arvin Prize competition to artists outside the Harbor region for all the reasons we've stated. And then, I guess, just ask them if they agree. Okay? Will that satisfy?" Looking around the room and taking silence as consent, Robertay continued. "Right. We'll meet again tomorrow morning to make the final decision." With one last look at the board members, Robertay declared the meeting adjourned.

As they cleaned up the food and coffee, Robertay ranted. "Goddamn it, can't these people see the power of this plan? Do they have to be so goddamn narrow-minded all the time? What is it going to take to lift up this place?"

"I'm not sure that's fair—"

"You heard them, just as well as I did. Their petty little objections, their nettlesome worries. It's death by a thousand cuts! And you were no help at all. Jesus! Your Aunt Lorraine? Really? Couldn't you support me, Thomas, just once?"

Thomas knew this bluster well and that it would take a while to wither. So he continued cleaning up the coffee area, hoping Robertay would calm by lunchtime.

GEOFFREY SCOTT

But then he heard Robertay offer a new and even more distressing twist.

Seemingly talking to herself, Robertay said, "If these people can't get behind this idea, then maybe I'll find some people who can and bring them on to the Board."

Unsure that he should, Thomas nevertheless interrupted, "Oh. That would seem like a drastic step; a problematic idea in the extreme. I can't imagine that."

"Oh, shut up. Please, just shut up! You're just like the others. You can't imagine anything other than what has always been!" Robertay yelled. "I'm frustrated and angry. I want the Colony to do more than just limp along in minor-league fashion. Why in hell can't you and the others see that and support me?"

Back on familiar ground with this comment, Thomas simply said, "I'll go get the car, love."

CHAPTER 8

Small towns sometimes have big ears. In this case, those ears belonged to Larry Court, the spry-for-being-seventy, part-time janitor and all-round handyman at the Colony gallery.

Larry had been working on the boiler that morning and hadn't heard Robertay and Thomas enter the building. As he came upstairs, he noticed the Colony board members walking into the conference room. Curious because there was no notice of a meeting on the gallery calendar, he listened in from a spot just outside the door. He wished he could be surprised by the topic, but Larry had learned long ago that arty folks saw the world a whole lot differently than he did.

Language, meaning, and intention can suffer mightily when messages overheard are then translated to others. Larry got some of the language, most of meaning, and made up his own version of the intention when he later saw Minerva Williams heading into Lydia's Diner to meet with the back-table coffee girls.

"Get over here, woman," Larry yelled to Minerva from across the street. "I got some news for you and the gossip girls."

Walking over to meet him, Minerva cackled and said, "We ain't no gossip girls, we're the 'chinwag chicks'! Same difference, but sounds better!" Retired herself, Minerva had the piss and vinegar of a teenager, the body shape of a chicken, and the mouth of a sailor. "What in the hell can you tell me that I don't already know?" she asked. She and Lar-

GEOFFREY SCOTT

ry had known each other and traded insults for sixty years, so neither took offense at these initial pokes.

"I got something that'll curl your butt hairs, old girl" Larry said with his own cackle.

"Leastwise, I still got some hair to curl, you old cue ball," Minerva said, patting Larry on his bald head. "But for Christ's sake will you get to it? The girls are waitin' and I got a hundred fifty things to do before noon today."

"Fine, Jesus, fine!" Larry growled, angered that Minerva did not seem properly appreciative that he was bringing the news to her first. "Pop the shit outta your ears cause I got a lot to tell and I ain't sayin' it twice."

Minerva muttered, but appeared attentive. Larry offered up a generally accurate, though linguistically enhanced version of the meeting he'd overheard. He knew that Minerva hated Robertay Harding so he played up Robertay's domineering role and her disdain for the Rascal Harbor locals.

"I don't know who the hell she thinks she is," Larry said. "But that bitch is gonna try to take the Arvin Prize right away from the town and give it to the first hoity-toit outsider who shows up with a paintin.' You shoulda heard her, Minerva, she said us goddamned locals ain't got shit for brains, we's all stuck in the past, and we wouldn't know art from architecture. She thinks letting in the shit birds will get the Exhibition more publicity or something. Oh, and get this—if the board don't go along, she thinkin' about bringin' in some that would. Jesus, she's got some nerve, that girl does."

"Nerve and tits the size of Cleveland," Minerva said and snorted. "Sure you wasn't 'mammarized' while you was eavesdroppin'?" Seeing Larry's face color, she continued, "A course you was, but that don't mean you didn't hear what you heard." After a pause, she said, "Jesus, that's some big news, ain't it? I don't know shit about art, but I know a couple of arty gals who won that Arvin Prize and it set 'em up nice for a while. Plus they got a big old plaque to put on the wall. It ain't right

I S L A N D S   A N D   B R I D G E S

27

to be thinkin' about letting outsiders come in and gum up the works for the local crowd."

Gathering herself up and heading across the street to Lydia's and her chinwag crew, Minerva said, "Goddamn, Larry, you might prove to be a useful human bein' after all!"

"Oh, go shit in your hat, Minerva," Larry said irritably, and wondered why he hadn't gone straight to Geneva Baxter, the acknowledged queen of Rascal Harbor gossip.

As Minerva sashayed into Lydia's that morning with news to tell, she saw a place both familiar and strange. Lydia's had the feel of a comfortable old shoe. The narrow diner was done up in every imaginable décor. Nautical gear, needlepoint and cross-stitch works, wall calendars from marine stores and hotels, pictures of employees and their kids, and signs, all kinds of signs, competed for wall space and customers' attention. In fact, it wasn't uncommon during a busy summer lunch rush to hear Trudy Turner, Lydia's owner, snap her fingers under a rapt diner's nose and ask, "You eatin' or gawkin'?"

As she walked to the back table on the right-hand side of the diner, Minerva was greeted with smiles and hellos from those who liked her and grimaces and grunts from those who didn't. 'Bout fifty-fifty this morning, she thought, not a bad day!

All the familiarity—even the scowls—felt good. As most all the summer pukes had yet to arrive, these were her people. But crowding out that generous thought was the news Minerva carried in of a budding war between locals and outsiders. She thought she knew which side she'd take, but then this was a complex topic.

As she walked to the table of her friends, Minerva passed by the "boys' table." Situated on the left-hand side of a short hallway into the kitchen, the boys were a group of retired fisherman. They had been in deep discussion about the low price of lobsters and the hard scram-

GEOFFREY SCOTT

ble their friends who were still in the business were having. Former shrimp boat captain Rob Pownall had just said that Carter Holden hoped to put in an extra fifty traps this season, but was not expecting to make a penny more.

"Economics is what it is, boys," Bill Candlewith said sagely. A gimpy man of short stature and even shorter brain power, Bill repeated, "It's the economics is what it is."

"How they hangin', boys?" Minerva said as she walked past. "Or, should I say, are they still hangin' or did they fall off?"

Ray Manley said, "Why would you care, Minerva? Ain't like you could do anything with 'em." Manley was Bill Candlewith's best friend, though he thought himself superior in the smarts department.

"Hear that, girls?" Minerva called over to her friends on the other side of the hallway. "The boys are challengin' us to an orgy!"

"In your dreams, Minerva!" Bill yelled. Vance Edwards and Slow Johnston, who filled out the complement at the men's table, just smiled.

"It would have to be my dreams, Billy boy, since the girls and I would all be asleep by the time you old roosters could get your cock-a-doodle-doos ready for action," Minerva crowed.

Geraldine Smythe, the tacit head of the ladies' table, called over, "Down, Minerva, down. You keep twitching the boys up and one of them is likely to have a stroke."

"Shit, them boys ain't got enough energy amongst 'em to have a stroke," Minerva said as she settled into her chair.

"Oh, Minerva," Maude Anderson said with a giggle. "The things you say."

"Maudie, I ain't sayin' nothin' that ain't rattlin' around that white-haired head of yours."

Maude, a short, fleshy woman, colored at Minerva's suggestion. Her best friend, June Pickering, did too. Karen Tompkins, the fifth tablemate and youngest of the ladies, grinned.

"But I ain't got time for prattlin' on this morning, girls," Minerva said turning serious. "I got news and it's big."

ISLANDS AND BRIDGES

In light of Minerva's comment to Larry Court about being the "chinwag chicks," none of the assembled thought of themselves as gossips. By contrast, they considered Geneva Baxter a gossip because, once she got a piece of news, she ran all around town with it. She also got most of it wrong. The ladies at Lydia's back table might tell a few people about whatever they discussed, but they worked hard to get the facts right. Thus, they discussed "the news" instead of gossip. The distinction between news and gossip could be a fine one, especially since most of the news discussed was typically second and third hand. Still, the ladies took their conversations seriously, and so Minerva presented her role as reporter in that spirit.

"So here it is, girls," Minerva said in a quiet voice. "Right from the horse's ass, Larry Court." Maude's and June's cheeks colored again; Karen and Geraldine looked impatient.

Oblivious to these reactions, Minerva continued. "So Larry says that Big Boobs Harding is tryin' to change the rules of that big prize they give to the best artist at that summer thing they do. Y'know, the Arvin Prize or whatever it's called. Larry says she wants to let outsiders into the competition!"

"That's the big news?" Karen asked. A trim, athletic, and no-nonsense woman, Karen liked Minerva, but found her dramatics a little over the top.

"A course it is, Karen! Don'tcha see? Letting in outsiders is gonna put the local artists out on their thumbs. Mattie Arvin wanted that prize for a local, just like her."

"What was Robertay's reasons for making the change?" June asked.

"Well, Larry weren't so clear about that. I expect he was half listen' and half dreamin' about Robertay's bumps—"

"Honest to Christ, Minerva," Geraldine said. "I swear you think more about Robertay's chest than all the men in this town do!"

"Well, they're distractin'," Minerva said. "Maybe if she kept harnessed 'em up so they wasn't rollin' and bobbin', and jigglin' around…"

June said, "I'll admit that I can get distracted too. It's like a big,

GEOFFREY SCOTT

old, unruly tide comin' in when she walks towards ya. Ya just can't stop watchin'!"

"Girls, really," Maude said quickly. "Let's get back to June's question. What reasons did Robertay give for wanting to change the requirements for the prize?"

"Larry said it was all about gettin' more artists and more publicity for the group. You know that Robertay would give her left nipple to get her face on the TV," Minerva said.

"Jesus, here we go again," Geraldine said and sighed.

June said, "Doesn't sound like much of a reason to be changing the rules. If the prize was spose to go to a local, then it ought to go to a local."

"I agree," Maude said.

"Maybe…but letting outsiders compete would push up the quality of the art, I bet, and it's bound to bring more people to the Harbor," Karen said.

"Which means more traffic and less parkin' and longer lines at the grocery," June said.

"All true enough," Maude said.

"Right, but it would create more interest in art. Oh, and, if it really worked, then the Summer Exhibition would be bigger news and generate more excitement than the Herrington Arts Festival," Karen said.

"Hmm. You got a point there, Karen," Geraldine said. "Those Herringboners have looked down on us for generations. They think bein' the county seat means—"

"Their shit don't stink," Minerva said.

"Well, I was gonna say something a little more delicate," Geraldine said with a smile. "But that works too."

Minerva smirked. "One more thing Larry said. Old Robertay is so determined to get her own way, that she's gonna get some more board members if the ones they got now won't go along with her plan."

"Can she do that?" June asked. "That don't seem right. She's the president and all, but she ain't God."

"No, she's certainly not God!" Maude said.

Karen leaned in. "Sounds like she's a little power-crazed. She might actually have a good idea, but if she goes about it all wrong, people are going to be upset for sure."

"Might start all kindsa trouble in the town," Geraldine said. "You know locals against out-a-towners and even locals against newbies."

"What's a 'newbie'?" Maude asked.

"Someone who's been living in the Harbor, but not that long," Karen said.

"Okay, but how long is 'long'?" June asked. "I mean that Regina Baldo's only been in town for five years and she seems less of a newbie than Robertay who's gotta be goin' on ten or more."

Karen said, "Good point. But the definition of a 'local' could be a problem too. I mean I was born here, but my folks weren't. They moved to the Harbor when the seafood plant opened. But Geraldine and Minerva, don't your families go back further than that?"

"Ayuh, three generations on my mother's side and four on my father's," Geraldine said.

"And they dug my family out of a clam bed 'round the Civil War," Minerva said.

"So it's clear that an 'outsider' is someone who's not a legal resident," Karen said. "But 'local' and 'newbie' seem a little fuzzy."

The ladies nodded quietly and sipped their coffee.

Minerva slapped her palms on the table. "Well, we ain't gonna solve that one today,, and I got shit to do that I ain't even thought of yet. So I'm off."

Her friends admitted they had to run as well. "Retired" did not mean withdrawn for these women. The checks were smaller and came from different sources and the work was lighter and more diverse, but each woman still put in a full day and found that the next day dawning came too soon.

At the men's table, the conversation was equally as engaged, though the topic differed. They had all left the sea years ago, but it was a subject to which they regularly turned. Rob Pownall knew that fishing the waters around Rascal Harbor was ever changing as stocks of lobsters, shrimp, and the like headed toward depletion. Losing the fishing trade would fundamentally change the character of the town

But Rob also knew that the arts had a long and strong foothold in the community as well. He didn't know or care much about the art crowd but, from the snatches he'd caught of the ladies' conversation, he worried about problems arising there too. He'd experienced enough troubles between fisherman to know that they can get nasty. He wondered if troubles between artists might be as bad or worse.

CHAPTER 9

After sulking over Ruby's "cartoon" comment for a day, McTavish got back to work.

"About time," Maggie whispered in his ear. "I mean, really, John, it was pretty funny. And you know Ruby. She probably wouldn't hang the Mona Lisa in her living room because it wouldn't match her couch."

"That, or she'd touch it up a little by repainting the face to make it 'smilier,'" McTavish muttered.

Maggie laughed. "That's the spirit, boy! Now get back to it and make some more of those 'pretty picture cartoons'!"

And with that exchange, McTavish got back to it.

When he could look beyond the marker-colored portions of his various images, McTavish liked what he saw. Limiting the colored portions to a small area of each piece, meant that they did not overwhelm the white, black, and gray areas of the overall work. Instead, they functioned as a focal point, nestled among but distinct from, the other elements of the image.

McTavish had worked up drawings from about half of the photographs he'd taken in what he now thought of as his "life amongst decay" series. Of these, however, three scenes featuring crocus plants kept pulling at his artist's eye. In one, he focused on a single plant emerging at the base of an old fence post. A second featured one purple and one white-blossomed plant growing in the sun-dappled warmth near a rusted plow. The third, and his favorite, showed a small clump of violet-blossomed plants growing beside a broken, field-stone foundation. The image displayed a side-view of the house wall and foundation on the left side with the colored plants in the foreground, two clumps of uncolored plants in the medium ground, and a portion of a slack-jawed barn in the background.

The drawing flooded his mind with memories of the day he'd taken the photographs and the excitement he'd felt in the realization that, amongst the shattered remains of the houses and barns and fields of his youth, signs of life could still push through.

McTavish then remembered taking other photographs of that particular setting from different vantage points. It occurred to him that one image of the scene was insufficient to tell the story. So he pulled out his camera and pulled up the other photographs of that particular clump of flowers. He'd taken pictures from above, from face on, and from various angles. Although they were clearly the same flowers in each image, they appeared different as sun, shadow, and perspective played out.

Perspective. McTavish found the word lolling around in his brain. It interested him to realize that the plants seemed to change based on the perspective taken. Yet "perspective" was not the right art word.

In the art world, perspective had a particular meaning. At heart, it referred to the technique of creating a three-dimensional image on a flat surface, an image that has the appearance of both depth and space. The technique worked when an artist drew lines from one, two, three, or four points on a horizon line. The classic example of one-point perspective was the road that starts wide in the foreground of a picture and then recedes to a single point on the horizon. Two-point perspective allows an artist to show, for example, the corner of a building where the walls of each side, if drawn to the horizon line, vanish to two points. Three and four point perspective offered artists opportunities to depict images from other angles.

McTavish, like most every artist at one time or another, used perspective to add a more realistic and dimensional quality to his drawings. The side of the house he had sketched for one of his crocus pictures had been formed in just this fashion.

But the notion of perspective that now bubbled around in his brain was more about the vantage point from which a single image could be seen. The side view of the plants and house wall resulted from looking at them from one vantage point. The full-on view resulted from another. And the overhead view appeared from a third. From each of these perspectives, the same clump of flowers showed both similarities and differences. They were the same flowers…and yet they were not the same flowers. The perspective from which one viewed them, changed them.

"Huh," McTavish said to himself. "Might be something there."

CHAPTER 10

The morning after the emergency board meeting at which Robertay introduced the idea of allowing non-residents to compete for the Arvin Prize, the group reassembled in the Colony conference room.

It was a group even more on edge than the day before. First, this was a collection of artists who, except for Thomas Beatty, preferred to work in the morning. Time spent in meetings was time away from their art and livelihoods. Second, other than Robertay, the other members felt unsettled about the proposed change in the Arvin Prize competition. Most volunteered to chair a Colony committee because they supported the organization and saw a benefit to its continued health. None—again, other than Robertay—felt comfortable dealing with conflict. And this Arvin Prize decision had the potential for a lot of conflict. Finally, a couple of the members had heard that word leaked about their meeting and the plan to change the requirements for the Arvin competition. Toni Ludlow and Jona Lewis, in particular, received snarky phone calls from artists who wanted to know "What's up with Robertay this time?"

As Robertay looked around the group, then, she saw no smiling faces. Even Regina Baldo appeared more subdued than normal. Not one to run from trouble, Robertay confronted the somber mood head-on.

"Okay, you all had an assignment to pitch our new Arvin Prize plan to the Colony members. What did you learn?"

"The assignment was to test the waters about a new plan, not to 'pitch our new plan,'" Jona said in correction. Robertay merely nodded while Jona continued. "And what I heard was a mixed bag. I must have talked with ten people, and their responses were all over the place—from pretty excited to pretty pissed off. Richie Connor says he might quit the Colony if the Arvin Prize can go to an outsider. But then Lynn Barnett says it seemed like a good idea to her."

Regina raised her hand to speak. Looking a little annoyed by this schoolgirl behavior, Robertay let it pass and indicated she should talk.

"I'm afraid I found pretty much the same array of perspectives," Regina said tentatively. "I really expected our colleagues to embrace it, but the twelve people I talked with were at odds with one another."

Sensing an opportunity, Robertay broke in. "This is just what I predicted," she said, with more enthusiasm than was warranted. "We've got some immediate excitement about the plan and some growing anticipation. I think this is a very good result."

Toni said, "Wait a minute. I only had a chance to talk with six members, but, like Jona, I had one or two express real anger about opening up the Prize competition. Terrence Calder said almost the same thing as Richie—he'll quit the Colony."

"Jesus, Toni, Terry Calder is nearly dead," Robertay said. "Plus he's just angry that he's never come close to winning the Arvin."

Thomas cleared his throat. "Now, now, Robertay. Terry's an old friend; a long-time and respected member of the Colony. If he feels that way, then there are bound to be others."

"Of course, the old-coot brigade is going to resist any kind of change," Robertay said. "Good lord, some of those people opposed having the gallery open on Sundays and serving wine at the events! Plus, you're never going to get a unanimous opinion about anything, especially among artists. But we've been chosen to lead; the membership is expecting us to lead."

"Actually that's not true," Jona said, correcting Robertay again. "We're all chairs of our committees, but we volunteered for those positions, we weren't elected. Hell, for the most part, we're doing it because nobody else wanted to."

"A technicality does not absolve us of the responsibility of leadership's mantle. This is not a democracy nor is it a dictatorship. We act as proxies for the membership and I believe we have made an active effort to hear their perspectives. We simply cannot let a small group of naysayers—people who refuse to leave the past—subvert the future of the Colony—"

"I'm sorry to interrupt," Regina said quietly, "but it wasn't only long-time locals who were against the idea. In fact, it was kind of a jumble. Some of the folks most opposed were residents who have been here less time than I have, while some of the people most interested are just the kind of long-timers you might think would oppose the idea."

"I didn't do a thorough check," Toni said, "but when I think about who I talked with and how long their history is in the Harbor, I think I agree with Regina's characterization—status as long- or short-time resident doesn't seem to matter all that much."

Jona leaned forward, scowling at Robertay. "I'll tell you what did matter. Somehow word got out about the meeting yesterday. But that's not even the worst part. The worst part is that some folks heard that if you didn't get your way, you were going to add some more members to the board to make sure you got what you wanted. That you had some kind of court packing scheme. I'll tell ya, if they were upset, I'm even more so!"

"I actually heard something like that from a couple people I talked to," Regina said timidly.

"That's nonsense!" Robertay yelled, casting a snarling look at Thomas. "Pure nonsense. I have the utmost respect for this group. I would never try to influence a board decision in that fashion."

Jona and Toni smiled a bit at this declaration, though neither said anything. Thomas looked down at the table, while Regina looked stricken.

"Well, it's going around town, Robertay," Jona said. "And I wouldn't be surprised if a few folks who might have been sitting on the fence, are going to fall off on the side of 'no, thanks' to the change."

Robertay fumed. "Goddamn it! Well, there is only one way to proceed then. Let's vote."

Taken aback by this move, the others all started talking at once. Robertay held up her hand. "Look, like it or not, we are the decision-making body for the Colony. We have a responsibility to introduce new initiatives, consider them thoughtfully, and then decide whether or not to pursue them. We have had a new plan advanced, we've reviewed its merits, and now it is time to ratify or deny it."

"But Robertay!" Regina said.

"I'm calling the question," Robertay said. Looking around the room, she said, "All in favor of the plan raise your hands." Robertay and then Regina raised theirs, although the latter less enthusiastically than the former. Toni and Jona looked at one another. When they turned back to the group, they saw Thomas Beatty slowly raising his hand. At his doing so, Robertay slammed her palm on the table and declared the motion passed.

"Jesus, Robertay!" Toni and Jona said in unison.

"What?" Robertay said in mock surprise. "It passed! Even if the two of you vote against it, it passes." Here, she paused and her face and voice softened. "But look, neither of you is a stick-in-the-mud, you've both got good ideas and are not afraid of change. You'll see. This will turn out to be a watershed day in the history of the Colony. The day when the Rascal Harbor Art Colony broke ground on the future and began asserting itself as a power in the Maine art world!"

Toni and Jona sat in subdued silence. Regina and Thomas tried to smile. Robertay carried on.

"So we've much to do to prepare for the launch of the newly envisioned Summer Exhibition and Arvin Prize. Regina, as Events chair, and I, as the Summer Exhibition chair, will take the lead in drafting the tasks and making assignments. Toni, you'll need to prepare for a slew of new memberships. I've been thinking that we can create a new membership category for non-residents, something like 'an Arvin Prize membership.' It would be a way to signify their affiliation with the Colony and, of course, to put some more money in our coffers. Jona, I expect that will make you happy as Budget chair! And Thomas, our dear Thomas, will handle the publicity for the event and the arrangements for redesigning our space. Oh, friends, this is going to be a marvelous undertaking, one that I'm sure you will be proud of forever!"

As they walked out of the meeting, Toni asked Jona, "Do you think we'll be proud when the membership rides us out of town?"

CHAPTER 11

L arry Court did his best to spread the story of the Colony board's decision, but he had competition from a more legitimate source—the *Rascal Harbor Gazette*, the town's weekly newspaper.

Immediately after the board meeting, Robertay Harding called Nellie Hildreth, the Gazette owner, publisher, and obituary writer.

"Nellie, I've got a hot, front-page story for you," Robertay said breathlessly. "I expect you'll want to stop the presses for this one!"

Nellie admired Robertay's ambitions for the Colony, but she disliked the woman almost as much as she disliked people using hackneyed phrases about the news business.

"I doubt that Ms. Harding, but come on over and we'll hear you out."

Nellie's family had owned and operated the paper for over one hundred years and she was now in her thirtieth year as the controlling force. For the last several years, she'd built a staff she could trust—Rich Reed, assistant editor; Sarah McAdams, chief reporter; and Lindy Strong, budget and advertising director. Nellie no longer had any interest in writing articles for the paper or in handling the daily editing chores. Sarah handled most of the reporting while Rich took over responsibility for the editing, layout, and production of the paper. Nellie focused her talents on writing obituaries.

It turned out that Nellie had a flair for writing about the newly deceased, in part because she brought a flair to each person's life story. Nellie was famous for starting with a version of the dead person's vitals and then adding what she called, "A little touch of creative honesty and reflection." Now tired of answering the question of why she wrote obits as she did, Nellie would say "Look, they had the chance to tell their stories. Now it's mine." And so she wrote stories of the dead.

Nellie's obituaries sometimes functioned as the most interesting part in the paper and, truth be told, some people bought the Gazette for those pieces alone. As Robertay walked into the lobby, Nellie finished an obit for this week's issue:

> Jennifer (Jenny) Twitchell (aged 79) died as she lived, sitting by the phone. She worked for New England Telephone for some 40 years and couldn't break the habit of using the damn thing all day long. She was married to Tunk Twitchell (deceased; real name unknown) for 55 years, but it was the telephone to which she turned in happiness and pain. Somehow a voice on the line carried comfort and care far more than any person sitting in front of her. Daughter Cynthia (William Drummond) and son Albert (unmarried) are unable to attend their mother's funeral. They send their regards to their mother's best friend and blather buddy, Geneva Baxter, who will host a small gathering at her house at 2pm on Tuesday.

Sarah McAdam, the Gazette's best, and only, reporter had been assigned to greet Robertay and show her into the conference room. Normally, Sarah would have taken a potential source over to the alcove where her desk sat. But Nellie told her that Robertay had "Another one of her bullshit scoops," and that they would meet with Robertay together. That arrangement was fine with Sarah. She wasn't afraid of the bombastic artist, she just loved to watch Nellie take on those town folks who thought more of themselves than they should.

Blowing into the lobby in full figure, Robertay announced her own arrival. "Hello all, it is Robertay Harding here to talk with editor Hildreth about the most exciting news!"

Rich Reed, always the peace-maker, was on hand to greet Robertay and helped Sarah show her to the paper's conference room. Nellie followed a moment later.

"Oh, this is most excellent," Robertay said, clapping her hands. "The whole staff—"

"Rich has got real work to do," Nellie said dryly. "So it'll just be Sarah and me. We've got work to do too, Robertay, so let's have it."

A flash of disappointment crossed Robertay's eyes, but she quickly recovered as the enormity of her news re-energized her. "Well, I've got just the most amazing news—" she said breathlessly.

"So you've said," Nellie replied with an edge creeping into her voice. "You've done the wind-up a couple of times now, time to deliver the pitch."

"Right, right," Robertay said, a little unnerved by this spare woman with piercing eyes. "Well here goes! The Executive Board of the Rascal Harbor Art Colony has just voted to change the rules of the Mattie Arvin Prize to allow non-residents to compete!"

"Okay...?" Nellie said.

"Well, don't you see?" Robertay asked incredulously. "This decision changes everything!"

"How so?" Sarah asked.

Sensing that her audience was not yet tuned into the importance of the move, Robertay listed the positives—better quality artwork, more publicity for the Colony, more tourist dollars in the Harbor, greater interest in and appreciation for art, and an edge over the Herrington art crowd.

This last bit struck a note with Nellie. She'd never been much of an art person, but she was a fierce champion of Rascal Harbor. Any opportunity to nudge the snooty Herrington folks off center aroused her interest.

Sarah asked, "Isn't that move going to upset a lot of the Colony artists? I don't know a lot about the Arvin Prize, but I thought it was exclusive to resident artists?"

"It is. That's why this move is so bold. By permitting the rest of the outside world to compete for the Prize, we'll dramatically increase the quality of the work shown and gain immeasurable prestige for the Summer Exhibition. This could be the biggest thing in Rascal Harbor history!"

"I doubt that," Nellie said soberly. "But the idea of pushing Herrington's art show off kilter has some potential."

Excited that she had scored a point with the old editor, Robertay pressed the issue. "Exactly!" she said with a bit too much enthusiasm. "The Herrington Art Festival will seem like a side show!"

"Interesting. Well, Sarah here will write it up. I'm guessing she may want to talk with a few of the Colony crowd and may need another quote or two from you. But I think there's something to run with here."

"I knew I could count on your keen journalistic sense to know a big scoop when you heard one—" Robertay said.

"All right, all right, Robertay, you'll get your story. Now we need to get back to work," Nellie said as she stood. "Thanks for coming by."

"And thank you for your support for the arts and all that they mean for our community. Please know how much your efforts are appreciated."

Once Robertay had left, Nellie said, "Jesus Christ, that woman is about as full of herself as anyone I've ever met. Still, this might be a damn good idea."

"If the locals don't hang her from the first tree they find."

CHAPTER 12

The matter of John McTavish's marital status got its first public airing at the counter of Lydia's Diner. It went about as awkwardly as one might expect.

On the anniversary of Maggie's death earlier this month, McTavish contemplated removing his wedding ring. He'd even taken it off for a minute to see how it felt. The white band of skin underneath and the intense feeling of longing accompanying that action led him to quickly replace it. There might come a day when he would take the ring off for good, but it sure wasn't that day.

McTavish had expected Maggie to comment on the episode. Before she died, she had tried to talk with him about remarrying. Ever and always the practical one, Maggie well understood that her husband needed a partner and she wanted to make sure that he knew that as well.

"Believe me, John, I'm not trying to be a martyr here," Maggie had said to him only a month before she died. "If I had my druthers, I'd wish you never looked at another woman. But you're a man who needs a woman. You're an adult in most ways, but you're an idiot when it comes to the social side of things. You're going to need help, old boy, and I'm telling you to find it after I'm gone."

McTavish knew some or most or maybe even all of this, but he couldn't listen to it then and hadn't been willing to entertain it since Maggie's passing.

It was all too much to think about and, truth be told, the craziness that had surrounded him since his move to Rascal Harbor had pushed thoughts of romantic involvement to the deepest part of his brain. Those thoughts stayed there because Maggie had not resurfaced to talk with him about them, because McTavish had too much to do to manage his life now, and because thinking about them unnerved him.

But others were thinking just such thoughts. Rascal Harbor's population could swell to over 100,000 in peak summer months, but the year-round number was barely 2500. Once the summer complaints had left, the locals took stock of who stayed through the crushing winter months and, with few establishments open, there was a good chance that every resident would see every other resident at one time or another.

So McTavish had been noticed. He was a quiet man by nature, but he'd formed a friendship with Gary Park and his family and they were anything but. Gary introduced McTavish to the men who hung around Gary's garage and Ruby talked about him to all of her friends. The Park kids, Jimmy and Louise, were a bit more discrete, but they talked about "the new guy" and his son in their circles as well.

McTavish would have been noticed, however, even were the Parks not involved. He had tried to downplay his involvement in the theft of the Winslow Homer painting, but he'd become known through that event as well.

And then there was the fact that, although he wore a wedding ring, there seemed to be no Mrs. McTavish on the scene. In a state where there were eighty single women to every single man, such an observation aroused considerable speculation among the eligible and looking crowd.

Julia Nisbett, the long-time morning waitress at Lydia's, was part of the first, but not the second. Now in her mid-forties, Julia had an ex-husband who had long ago destroyed any notion of romance and happily-ever-after for her. She wasn't a man-hater, but her chief relationships now revolved around two male dogs and one male cat. And that was plenty enough of that gender in her mind.

As summer residents for ten years, the McTavishes had often eaten at Lydia's. Breakfast had always been their favorite meal and John found that the slightly greasy eggs, the fresh cinnamon donuts, and the never-empty cup of coffee struck him as just right. Maggie loved the molasses donuts.

Over the years, Maggie and Julia had formed a casual friendship and so Julia knew something about Maggie's illness and her death. Most of what she knew, however, came from Maggie's on-line obituary rather than from her husband. When McTavish appeared alone at Lydia's one morning last year, Julia had only to look at McTavish's face to know that Maggie had died. Seeing that her face registered the news, McTavish had simply nodded. That night, Julia cried as she thought about this strong and active woman taken down by a vicious cancer and about the quiet husband who seemed so deeply in love with her.

After that first Maggie-less breakfast, McTavish preferred to sit at the counter rather than at the front table that he and Maggie had nearly always taken. He had seemed so withdrawn at first that Julia had abandoned her typical patter. She'd served him his coffee and eggs and donuts and let him be. Over time, however, they talked a little and when McTavish's son, Noah, joined him, Julia found herself lingering to talk with both McTavish men. Noah had his mother's engaging personality and Julia noticed that McTavish let the boy carry the conversation with her. Still, when she directed a question or comment at him, McTavish would respond and seemed to appreciate her efforts.

Upon reflection, Julia was not sure why she broached the subject of girlfriends with McTavish that particular morning, but she did. As she poured McTavish's first cup, she said, "I saw Noah and Louise out at the pizza place last night. Looked like they were enjoying each other's company."

Nodding, McTavish said, "They do seem to get along."

"She's a lovely girl and he's as handsome as his dad."

"That would make him an unlucky fellow," McTavish said with a smile.

GEOFFREY SCOTT

"He seems pretty lucky to me. And he seems quite taken with Miss Louise." When McTavish nodded, Julia pressed on. "And what about his dad? Is there anyone he's taken with?"

Julia saw McTavish immediately stiffen and sensed that she'd pushed too hard, so before he could speak, she rushed down the counter to fill more coffee cups.

Elmer Peterson filled the conversational gap. A retired clam digger, Elmer took a counter stool every morning and offered the world his views on whatever topic came to mind. Elmer talked with whomever would listen or sometimes just to himself, but he always had something to say. He and McTavish had chatted a couple of times about the state of the clam season, the Red Sox, and the local economy. Today, however, Elmer pressed on the state of McTavish's heart.

"It's a good question, John McTavish… Is there anyone you're taken with?" Elmer asked with a sly smile.

"No, it's a single life for me, Elmer," McTavish said and drank from his coffee cup, hoping to signal an end to this line of inquisition. No luck.

"Cause if you're not, then I wonder if you want to give my sister a call. She ain't much to look at, but she's gotta heart of gold, my friend, heart of gold."

"Thanks, Elmer," McTavish said, looking around the diner for a way to escape. "I'll keep her in mind."

"Well, you might want to move quick. She'll be turning sixty-five pretty soon. Once she's on the retirement dole, then Christ-amighty, there's likely to be all kinds of fellas ringing her up just to get at that guvment money."

"Good advice," McTavish said noncommittally and looked desperately for Julia to return. She did.

"Good lord, Elmer, you've been trying to marry off Melba for the last ten years. The old gal just isn't marriage material. Now you leave poor John here alone so's he can eat his breakfast without you burning a hole in his ear."

Elmer looked chastened—for a minute—and then was off to a new subject with the man sitting on his other side.

"Sorry," Julia whispered to McTavish with a sheepish look on her face.

"You should be," McTavish said with a wan smile. "Though I suspect Maggie's having a good chuckle at my expense."

"She was a good woman, John. Unlikely you'll ever find another to match her. But if I know her at all, I bet she'd want you to try."

CHAPTER 13

John McTavish's social life was also on the minds of his friends Gary and Ruby Park.

"I is much worried 'bout our friend, John McTavish," Ruby said that evening. "He got dem dreamy sad eyes."

"'Dreamy sad eyes'?" Gary asked, not sure that he wanted to pursue this conversation, but wondering what it was that Ruby saw in their friend.

"Dreamy sad love-hurt eyes. I am noticin' it every time I see him."

"Maybe it's because you called his drawing a cartoon. Maybe that's why he's got 'hurt' eyes."

Missing Gary's point, Ruby continued. "No, he's had dem sad eyes ever since he come to live here in Rascal Harbor, since he come to live here minus Maggie."

"You might be right, but a course he's gonna be sad for missing Maggie. The man's still grievin'. You're not thinkin' that he needs to get married, are you? Cause that seems—"

"No, not married'!" Ruby said indignantly. "But maybe he need a friend, you know, a female woman friend. I am tinkin' of some woman friends of mine who could be a good friend match for John."

"That's dangerous territory, tryin' to fix John up with some of your friends. Some of those girls, all they want is a man to buy the meat and potatoes every week. That's not what John needs."

"No, I am not tinkin' of de meat an potatoes girls who are friends of mine," Ruby said. "I am only tinkin' of de nice ladies, the ones wit de big hearts."

"I don't know, Ruby," Gary sighed. "Some of those big-hearted friends of yours aren't really John's type neither. Don'tcha know anybody who's more like Maggie? If John needs a woman, and I'm not sayin' he does, but if he does, then it's gotta be a woman like Maggie. You know, somebody…tall…and—"

"Tall?" Ruby scoffed. "Honest to Jesus H. Christ, Gary Park, you is tinkin' that Maggie was just a tall woman? A tall woman was Maggie McTavish? Is that de woman you is talkin' so much about so much?"

"Well…" Gary said weakly. "Tall, yeah, but y'know, tall and smart and—"

"Is you now sayin' dat my friends is not smart, Gary Park? Is dis what you are tellin' me now? I have dumb friends who are short?" Ruby was building a decent head of steam. Her fine intentions toward their friend John McTavish were being derailed by her tub-headed husband.

"Jesus, Ruby, calm down," Gary said, trying to get his bearings. "I'm not sayin' nothin' against your friends. Well, maybe against Lillian Pelletier, that woman drives me around the bend. But mosta the others are nice enough, I just can't see any of 'em with John."

At that moment, Louise and Noah walked through the kitchen door. Louise saw her father's face redden when he noticed Noah coming in with her. "Any of who with John?" Louise asked innocently. Then she realized what her father and mother must have been discussing. Turning to Noah, she now reddened. His own realization now dawning, Noah's eyes shifted downward.

Looking up again, his eyes a little unfocused, Noah said, "It's okay. I guess it's kind of inevitable that folks would think about my dad with someone else." His voice trailed off and he again looked at the floor.

Cutting her eyes at both her parents, Louise gently pushed Noah back outside.

"We'll take a little walk," she said to no one and to everyone.

As Noah and Louise walked back outside, she heard her father say, "Jesus, Ruby."

They walked quietly for a while. Louise took Noah's hand and squeezed good thoughts into it.

"They're idiots," Louise said after a couple of minutes. "They mean well enough, but they're idiots."

"No, they're not," Noah said quietly. "They do mean well and, well, I wonder too if my dad will find someone else." Pausing for a couple of minutes, he continued. "It's just that I don't really know how to feel about it. I mean, should I want him to see other women or should I want him to stay true to my mom? And then I think about what my mom might want and, well, I don't know. A part of me, actually a pretty big part of me, thinks that she'd want him to find somebody. I mean she sorta said as much to me once. She knew how much my dad needed her, how much he relied on her. And, I guess, how much she needed him to need her." He paused for a moment, then said, "I don't know what the hell I'm talking about."

Louise squeezed Noah's hand again. "Actually, I think you do. But I expect it's all complicated and it hasn't been that long and people really just ought to mind their own damn business."

They stopped and looked at each other.

"Yeah, probably," Noah said. Then they said together, "But they mean well."

Chapter 14

As Noah drove back to the cottage, his brain swirled. He knew that his father still had a lot of unresolved issues related to Maggie's death. But maybe Noah did too.

Noah looked like his father, and he knew that he drew on some of his father's best qualities. But he'd always thought of himself as temperamentally more like his mother—direct, hard-working, compassionate, open-minded. Louise, however, often said that she thought father and son to be a matched pair. Maybe so, thought Noah, but his father had always felt like a foreign land while his mother had defined the word "home."

Although Noah knew his father was trying to craft a new relationship with him, he resisted on some levels. When he felt angry that his mother was gone, when his longing for his mother left him aching, and when his love for his mother overwhelmed him, he just didn't know what to do with these feelings. He suspected it wasn't fair, but he sometimes lashed out at his father. When he did, he did so less in anger than in a sort of unfocused plea for understanding and love. Knowing that only made him feel more conflicted and confused.

Nearly a year after Maggie's death, Noah and his father still clashed, or more accurately, he still clashed with his father. For his part, his father just seemed to absorb Noah's anger and hurt and frustration. It was like McTavish offered himself up as big pillow onto which Noah could throw himself kicking and screaming until exhausted. McTavish didn't get mad, he didn't push back, he just took it all. Noah had hated this reaction/non-reaction at first; once, he mockingly called his father a "silent presence." He still didn't understand his father's response, but he had to admit that it had, at times, offered him a measure of calm.

That calm had taken a hit tonight. He really wasn't surprised to hear that Gary and Ruby Park had been talking about another woman entering his father's life. He and Louise had not broached the topic until this evening, but he'd known that they would. He trusted Louise and he knew that, when he was ready, he'd bring it up and they'd talk it through together.

So now it was out there, or out there with the Parks anyway. And if the Parks were talking about it, then he expected a lot of people in town were doing the same. As he neared the cottage, he resolved to talk with his father. He just wasn't sure what he'd say.

In the end, Noah decided to follow his mother's typical impulse and just get to it.

"You'll never guess what Gary and Ruby were talking about when Louise and I walked in tonight," Noah said as he entered the cottage.

"Jesus, not the cartoons again," McTavish sighed.

"Worse. I think Ruby wants to set you up with a lady friend."

"Ah, Christ," McTavish sighed even louder. "Guess this is the day for it."

"What do you mean?"

Hesitating, McTavish shook his head, "Ah, nothing, it's nothing."

"Obviously it's something. What is it 'the day for?'"

Realizing that his son was not going to let it go, McTavish sighed once more and said, "Apparently my love life is the subject of speculation at Lydia's too."

"Oh, boy," Noah said, relieved for some reason. "Have a seat. I'll pour you a drink and you can tell me about it."

Noah went to the cupboard and poured each of them a couple fingers of Bushmills. They sat in the kitchen rocking chairs for a quiet minute sipping their drinks.

After another few minutes, McTavish asked, "How's Louise?"

"She's fine, Dad. But don't deflect. What's going on?"

"I'm not really sure I want to talk about it."

"Sounds like you might be the only one in town who's not talking about it."

McTavish smiled and nodded in agreement. "So it would seem." He gave a brief account of the interactions he had with Julia Nisbett and Elmer Peterson.

"Julia's cool, but if Elmer is that guy I'm thinking about, the one who's got like five teeth and sits at the counter, then yikes!"

"Yikes is right."

"Well," Noah said hesitantly. "How do you feel about the whole idea of…someone else…you know, a lady friend?"

"To be honest, I can't say that I've thought much about it. I seem to be preoccupied with just trying to figure out how to live a life, to live my life, without your mother. She made everything seem so effortless…or maybe I just wasn't paying attention." Here, he stopped and took another sip of whiskey.

"And are you paying attention now?"

"Now I am. And it hasn't left a lot of time to think about…lady friends." The two men sat silently with this thought.

"How do you feel about it?" McTavish asked quietly.

Noah did not respond immediately. Though he suspected his father would ask his opinion, Noah felt unprepared. The jumble of thoughts and emotions all broke at the same time and he felt as if he was truly speechless.

"I don't know," Noah managed. McTavish nodded. "I mean, I really don't know how I feel, what I think…nothing. I guess I should say that I'm okay with it, you know, that it's your life and you have a right to be happy. You know all that Oprah bullshit. But I don't know, Dad.

I get this big lump in my throat when I think about it, when I think about Mom and all."

McTavish started to say something, but Noah rushed on. "And the weird thing is that I honestly think Mom would want you to, you know, to have a friend. She told me. Before she died, she told me that she hoped you would find someone to be happy with like you and she were, and she said you needed someone to help you, you know, to help you not seem like such a dope."

Father and son laughed.

"So I don't know, Dad," Noah said after a minute. "I know Mom loved you truly and you loved her back and, well, I guess I worry that you'll get hurt or disappointed or something if you don't find someone to be with who is like she was. You know? And then I wonder if maybe Mom will be disappointed too. Sometimes it's easier to just not try." Stopping again, Noah looked at his father, frustrated. "I don't know what the hell I'm talking about anymore. I want you to be happy, Dad. That's the bottom line. So, if you want to start dating, then…"

At the word "dating," father and son looked at one another and grimaced, shook their heads, and took long pulls from their drinks.

Grinning now, Noah raised his glass, "Here's to dating!" he said.

"Or not!" his father replied and they clinked glasses.

CHAPTER 15

Small towns, of course, can sustain multiple lines of conversation. McTavish's love future was one among many and this morning it was far from the most important. Sarah McAdams's Gazette story about the plan to open the Arvin Prize competition also took a back seat. A car-truck accident on Jenkins Hill between a couple of early-season tourists generated enough bodies and debris to keep the townsfolk occupied for a while.

Page one of the Gazette, then, featured the story and photographs of the accident rather than the big spread Robertay Harding expected.

The Arvin Prize story also missed page two of the paper as that spot was reserved for op-eds. Leading the page was the editor's column; letters to the editor occupied the rest. If the topic was hot enough, the letters spilled over onto—and sometimes filled—page three. The letters section covered several topics in this issue—the coming tourist season, the school board budget, and the Red Sox…always the Red Sox—but no issue predominated.

So at the top of page three, under the headline "Arvin Prize Rules Change," McAdams's story appeared. Any number of readers likely missed it as they went from the letters section directly to the high school sports page. Lydia's back table men and women didn't, though the grist of the Jenkins Hill wreck took a while to chew through first.

Given the short time to press and the energy she'd had to expend

GEOFFREY SCOTT

on the accident story, McAdams's Arvin Prize story was short and to the point:

> Robertay Harding, President of the Rascal Harbor Art Colony, announced that the Colony board has voted in favor of changing the rules of the Mattie Arvin Prize competition to allow non-resident artists to participate.
>
> According to Harding, this "bold" decision will "dramatically increase the quality of the work shown and gain immeasurable prestige for the Summer Exhibition." Harding also believes this move will promote tourism in the area and generate far more interest in the Rascal Harbor art show than in the annual Arts Festival held in Herrington.

McAdams had hoped to supplement the story with local artists' and town officials' reactions to the decision. Covering the accident, however, had taken her right up to press time. She didn't worry though as she had a hunch that this would be just the first of many articles on the Colony's decision.

Had Sarah McAdams asked them, Lydia's back-table patrons could have provided a range of perspectives on the Arvin Prize rule change.

At the men's table, a consensus formed, reformed, and then dissolved. Their peers on the other side of the hallway took longer to air their views, but they too eventually left the table without arriving at a common perspective.

The early consensus at the men's table developed around disdain for change in general, for changing the rules for the Arvin Prize, and for allowing non-residents to compete.

Ray Manley said, "Jesus, imagine the roadways! The idjits can't drive now without killin' each other. What's gonna happen when they start flockin' to town to win the Prize?"

"Be rock 'em, sock 'em robots meet the demolition derby!" Bill Candlewith added.

"Might be safer to stay on the water until the whole Exhibition is over," Vance Edwards said.

"Right. Unless they start runnin' into each other out there too!" Ray said.

Rob Pownall said, "Well, it might not be an issue on either the roads or the water. I know a couple of artists who are going to be pretty upset by this change. I wouldn't put it past them to put up barricades against the out-of-towners on land and at sea."

"Ayuh. And I know a coupla ladies who'd join 'em," Ray said emphatically. "They take their paintin' some serious and so they ain't gonna be happy to think some asswipe from Portland or Boston or New York City could waltz in here and walk off with the big prize."

Vance asked, "Do you really think artists are going to enter from that far away? Christ the prize can't be that much."

"I think it's decent sized. A thousand dollars or so," Rob said.

"Right, and I don't guess many of them artists would pass on a thousand dollar payday," Bill added.

Ray said, "Well, I don't like it. It ain't right to be changin' the rules after all these years."

"Specially since it's cuttin' out the locals," Bill added. His friends nodded.

A moment later, Vance said, "Well, technically, it's not cutting out the locals. It's just increasing the competition for the Prize. And, like Robertay says, it ought to increase the quality of the art."

"You ever actually been, Vance? To the exhibit, I mean," asked Ray.

"Well, no, can't say I have."

"I'd go if they had a bunch of pictures of that Robertay Harding!" Bill said.

"Here we go again," Vance said to Rob. And they did. Whatever merits the Colony decision had or didn't have dissolved into one of the boys' customary prattles about Robertay's chest.

Minerva Williams had hearing like a bat. And because she did, she became the official monitor of the men's table. Checking her watch, Minerva Williams said, "Christ, a new record! The boys went a whole ten minutes before Robertay's headlights came up."

"You're really not that much better, Minerva," June Pickering scolded. Her tablemates clucked in agreement.

Karen Tompkins said, "Let's not get sidetracked, ladies. This change in the Arvin Prize rules is starting to get a little ugly. I heard a bunch of artists who have been friends for years were yelling at each other over at Village Pizza yesterday."

"I heard that too," Geraldine Smythe added. "But then I heard part of the argument was over a rumor that the Summer Exhibition was gonna let crafts people show their work this year. And you know there's always been some kind of tension between the artsies and the crafters."

Minerva said, "Jesus, tell me about it. I know a coupla neighbors who ain't talked in five years cause one is a painter and the other is a knitter. Now you ask me, I think a good hand-knit sweater's just as much an artwork as some dumb paintin'."

Maude Anderson nodded in agreement. Her friend, June said, "Hell yeah, Maudie here knits them toilet paper cozies in all kindsa colors yet she can't get in the show. I mean who's to say what's art and what ain't?"

"Good point, June. Christ, what a tangle this could be," Geraldine said.

"I suppose," Karen said, looking at the article again. "But I have to say that it wouldn't hurt my feelings if the Colony event did get bigger than the one in Herrington."

"I agree," Maude and June said at the same time. Laughing, Maude continued. "Those Herrington—"

"Pukes?" Minerva suggested. "Peckerheads? Puss—"

"Okay, Jesus, Minerva, we get it," Geraldine interrupted.

"Well, just sayin'," Minerva said with a giggle.

Maude, blushing now, said, "As I was sayin', them Herrington people can be such la-di-dahs that it's a little hard to take."

"Givin' them a comeuppance with an even bigger and fancier art show might be kinda nice," June said.

"Maybe so," Geraldine said thoughtfully. "But I think the whole thing could blow up if folks start fighting amongst themselves. Mark my words, this thing is between residents and non-residents right now, but like I said a couple days ago, it could easily end up pitting long-time locals against the newbies. And then we'll be in a helluva fix as a town."

Jumper Wilson was an outlier in a town where the norms of acceptable behavior stretched pretty far. Questions about where he came from, how he arrived, and how long he intended to stay surfaced regularly. But it was Jumper's T-shirt designs that created the biggest buzz. Jumper could and did talk, but he preferred to make his observations on the current state of affairs apparent through the adages he repurposed on his hand-lettered T-shirts.

At the conclusion of the investigation into the theft of the Winslow Homer painting, Jumper created a shirt that said *God helps those who help themselves…find good lawyers.* As they were leaving Lydia's this morning, the ladies saw Jumper and waved him over.

"Whatcha got to say for yourself, Jumpah?" Minerva yelled, customizing the end of Jumper's name by replacing the "r" with an "ah" as is the Maine way.

Accustomed to such requests, Jumper turned to the women, pulled open his parka, and showed his work. The front of his shirt said, *If you can't beat 'em, let 'em join the competition.* Before the ladies could comment, Jumper turned around and pulled up his coat so that they could see the back of his shirt, which read *Better the devil you know than the out-of-towner you don't.*

Turning to her friends, Minerva said, "Guess old Jumpah's conflicted too."

CHAPTER 16

The back-table ladies had things to do that morning so they left before their male peers did. The men, by contrast, were hoping that Trudy or Julia would refill their cups once more as they had one more discussion item.

After the diversion of Robertay Harding's chest, the boys turned to a story about Hadley Cooper's traps being cut. The word was that two of Hadley's longer strings of lobster traps or "pots" had been cut the day before. Rob Pownall, who introduced the story, said Hadley professed to be mystified as to who or why.

"Hadley? Ain't that Jensen Cooper's boy?" Ray Manley asked. "I thought he was away."

Rob said, "Well, he is and he was. Guess he spent time sword fishing down to Massachusetts and chasing blue crabs down to Maryland. He's been around."

"But he come back up to lobster?" Bill Candlewith asked.

"Ayuh. His license was still valid even though he hadn't used it in a while," Rob said.

"Well, with all them guys on the wait list to get one, I expect that's where the culprit is," Ray said.

Vance said, "Maybe so, but if he's lost only a couple strings it could be almost anyone. Or even a boat prop or even a whale. You know they gotta use those weak-link fasteners now, so hard to tell who or what mighta cut the lines. Will he hire someone to go down and see?"

"Guess he's considering it. Think he's going over to talk with the police this morning," Rob said.

"Traps're expensive. Was me, I'd go down and see if I couldna find 'em," Ray said.

"You can't swim, Ray Manley! How the hell are you gonna go down lookin' for traps?" Bill spat.

"Simple," Ray said with a smile. "Just get an old inner tube, tie her around my waist, jump in, scout around, and when I was done I just blow up the tube and float to the surface!"

"Wait, what? You can't…hell, you can't…" Bill said, sputtering.

"Relax, Bill, relax," Vance said laughing. "Ray's just yanking on your bad leg!"

"Why's Ray yakking at Bill's bad leg?" Slow Johnston asked. Slow's real name was Samson and the size of the man supported that name. But it wasn't just his bulk: Samson approached life, work, conversations, and the like in a fashion that had earned him the nickname. Slow's slowness gained muster when the rap of a lobster pot upside his head had deafened him in one ear. Why he persisted in keeping that ear to the men's table conversation annoyed and frustrated his mates who had long ago given up trying to get him to turn his good ear inward.

Vance said, "No one's yakking at Bill's leg, Slow. Ray's talking out of his ass and Bill's moving in close enough to hear him." Everyone but Bill laughed.

Returning to the subject, Vance said, "Well, I just hope no lobster war develops. Most folks are skating a little close to the edge financially. If guys start cutting gear, then some 'em aren't going to make it."

Heads nodded at this conclusion. Lobster wars could start for any number of reasons and the results could be disastrous. Lobstering had operated for generations with rules largely unwritten. Unwritten, however, did not mean unimportant, nor did it mean unenforceable.

One of the biggest unwritten set of norms had to do with where one fished. To get or renew a state license, lobstermen had to declare their preferred fishing zones. After that, however, where they fished was largely governed by tradition. Like their homesteading brethren out west, lobstermen had always laid claim to particular waters over the ocean floor. Marking their preferred spots with cone-shape buoys displaying their license numbers and unique paint schemes and designs, lobstermen fished those territories with no expectation of interference.

Interference, whether premediated or innocent, was one of the most common causes of a war. Unintentionally setting one's traps in another guy's spot or letting one's buoy lines tangle with another's could cause a problem; deliberately doing so, or appearing to do so deliberately, almost always did.

The solution to such problems could involve a peaceable conversation and an apology over the transoms of boats, on a radioed call, in the Co-op parking lot, or at a bar. Angry words could be exchanged through all those means as well. Of course, angry words could also lead to punches thrown, pickup windshields smashed, or idle gear tossed off a dock into the harbor. These on-shore actions could be supplemented by another set taken at sea. There, territorial offenders might find their pots hauled up, cleaned out, and then thrown back with their bait bags missing and their trap doors open. More drastic action involved cutting the buoy or trap lines by which lobstermen locate and then haul their traps.

Pot buoy lines mattered. Buoys were twelve to eighteen inches long, bullet-nosed markers typically made of a dense Styrofoam. Running through each one, lengthwise, was a long piece of wood or plastic that functioned as a kind of handle when pulling up the buoys. Attached to the other end of the handle was the pot warp, a long piece of sinking line or rope. And attached to the port warp was a string of one to five weighted and baited traps that sit on the ocean floor luring in lobsters.

Cut buoy lines means no hauling and no paycheck and the expense of either hiring a diver to recover the old traps or buying new ones to replace them. So once the cutting of trap lines started, retaliation and escalation of the violence could run unchecked. No deaths from lobster wars had been recorded, but gun shots across bows or transoms did occur at sea as did the occasional knife and gunshot wounding on land.

Disputes over fishing territories started most lobster wars, but tit-for-tats could begin for other reasons as well. Arguments over spouses or girlfriends, over on-shore property rights, over alcohol-fueled slights—any and all of these reasons could precipitate trap cutting. To date, no one had heard of an incident caused by the long wait lists for obtaining a lobstering license, but every one of the men at Lydia's back table knew that it was a possibility.

CHAPTER 17

Hadley Cooper had a poet's heart, but he paid the bills by working the sea. With two sets of three-trap lines cut, paying those bills was going to be a challenge.

Born to an asshole father and a sainted mother, Hadley took his father's physicality and his mother's good-heartedness with him into the world. Between these poles, Hadley crafted an inner life that saw the world in poetics while his outer life saw it in the hard and dangerous work of fishing coastal waters from Maine to Maryland.

Jensen Cooper moved his wife Laura, daughter Nancy, and son Hadley to Rascal Harbor after his own father died. That father had fished the waters in and around Rascal Harbor for forty years. As an only child, Jensen inherited his father's small piece of property, even smaller house, a lobster boat with one hundred traps and the associated gear, and a license to fish. As a boy, Jensen's interests had been more mechanical than sea-bound, so he'd left home for work building ships at a contract-work boatyard. Having run into and up against a string of problems at his workplace, Jensen saw his father's death as an opportunity to recast himself as the captain and crew of a lobster boat. "Chance to be my own boss," he told a boatyard co-worker as he was leaving. "And fuck all you retards still workin' here."

So Jensen brought his small family, his rusty lobstering skills, and his short fuse to Rascal Harbor. There, he quickly wore out any good will his father had generated by bragging about his hauls, picking fights with other fishermen, and laying his traps in areas beyond where his father fished. Fishing too close to other traps earned him warnings, fishing so close that his buoy lines ensnared others earned him a couple of black eyes. Jensen avoided pissing off his peers to the extent that they'd cut his traps. But no one would have taken a bet that it would never happen.

Jensen Cooper's behavior had few repercussions for his wife and daughter. Laura and Nancy shared a sunny disposition that clouded over only at home and only when Jensen brewed up a storm. They suffered no physical abuse, but the pins-and-needles atmosphere around a temperamental man creates emotional strains hard to detect. Those who knew the family admired Laura's and Nancy's gracious calm and offered shelter should life with Jensen become unbearable. It never got to that point. Laura died in her early fifties and Nancy married a local lobsterman and moved out of the house at eighteen.

Hadley, a couple of years younger than his sister, suffered his father's ire and his classmates' aggressions. Always a strong, but quiet boy, Hadley had needed toughening up according to his father. The boy's penchant for reading, daydreaming, and, of all things, poetry drove his father to distraction. So Hadley was worked hard and cursed harder from age twelve on. Smart, dutiful, and compliant, the boy did the assigned tasks well. Still, his father invariably found fault. Though his own work barely meet the requirements of the job, Jensen was quick to point out his son's mistakes.

Hadley's teachers were kinder. But then they could be because the boy was a delight in class. Attentive, bright, and kind, Hadley Cooper was easy to like and the quality of his work was easy to praise. A good student and a good kid, Hadley found the school classroom a safe and welcoming place.

The school yard was a different story. Hadley was big enough and was generally well liked so he avoided a lot of the typical playground scuffles. But the mayhem that Hadley's father created trickled down

ISLANDS AND BRIDGES

69

to the playground. Most boys knew Jensen Cooper to be an all-around ass and they didn't blame his son. But when his father's more provocative actions enflamed the fathers of kids who liked to scrap, then Hadley ran into trouble.

Charlie Gibbons was the first to confront Hadley over one of his father's transgressions. Hadley had fielded some ugly looks from other fifth-grade classmates, but Charlie was the first to challenge him to a fight.

Mistaking Hadley's good nature for softness, Charlie charged Hadley as soon as both boys were out of the supervising teacher's sight. Charlie was a good-sized boy himself and he figured if he got in a couple good licks, Hadley would dissolve into tears. He was wrong on every count. Aware that Charlie was coming at him and knowing that his father's endless chores had built his strength, Hadley deflected Charlie's wild charge and his first punch. Then he turned Charlie around, wrapped up his arms, and held on. Charlie squirmed and cursed, but he could make no purchase against Hadley's bear hug. At the same time, Hadley talked quietly into Charlie's ear.

"I'm not my dad. I'm sorry for what my dad did, but I'm not my dad." Hadley repeated this mantra until Charlie exhausted himself.

Once released, Charlie rubbed his sore arms and said, "Your dad's a first-rate asshole, but I guess you ain't. We're okay, you and me." The boys nodded to one another and became as good friends as they could knowing that their fathers' animosity continued.

In fact, it was Charlie who, inadvertently, sponsored Hadley's interest in poetry. Much less academically able than Hadley, Charlie channeled a fair portion of his energies into misbehavior. "High-spirited" would be a generous interpretation; "unruly" was a more exact one. His high jinx typically aimed at the amusing rather than the destructive, but invariably they disrupted the class. Because he always got caught, Charlie's teachers had to be creative in their punishments. After a particularly silly prank, the seventh-grade teacher decided to get more bang for her penalty buck. The class was about to start a poetry unit so she assigned Charlie the task of locating a poem, memorizing it, and reciting it in front of the class.

Charlie immediately solicited Hadley's help. The boys trooped to the town library, located an anthology of poems about the sea, and began looking for a suitable piece. Within the first ten pages they found gold—a poem by Emily Dickinson entitled "An Hour Is a Sea." The poem read:

An Hour Is a Sea
An hour is a Sea
Between a few, and me—
With them would Harbor be—

A suitable topic, an established author, and fifteen words. Charlie smiled, stabbed his finger at the poem, and said, "That's the one!"

As his friend walked around the library reciting his poem, Hadley leafed through the rest of the anthology stopping wherever a word or title or phrase caught his eye. He had always been a reader and of some variety—he mixed in Steinbeck and Hemingway with Louis L'Amour westerns and Patrick O'Brian sea tales. He had no particular disdain for poetry, but neither had he much experience with it. So when he saw a short Langston Hughes poem with a provocative title, he stopped to read it:

Sea Charm
The sea's own children
Do not understand.
They know
But that the sea is strong
Like God's hand.
They know
But that sea wind is sweet
Like God's breath,

And that the sea holds
A wide, deep death.

The poem struck Hadley in a way that prose never had. He knew
all the words, most of which were but a single syllable long. Yet these
simple words, constructed in this way, seemed to say more than a hundred. He wasn't quite sure yet what they were saying, but he felt a
depth and an insight and a comfort lay behind them. Rather than tell
a single, straight-forward story, the poet's words seemed more like a
dream—pieces of an idea not yet put together. Later in life he would
come across this same analogy in quote by Adrienne Rich: "Poems are
like dreams: In them you put what you don't know you know."

Exactly, he thought.

The tug of this poem/dream idea kept him reading. He was finishing a Carl Sandburg poem entitled "Sea-Wash" when Charlie announced that he'd mastered his poem and was ready to leave. On a
piece of paper laying nearby, Hadley scribbled Sandburg's lines:

Sea-Wash
The sea-wash never ends.
The sea-wash repeats, repeats.
Only old songs? Is that all the sea knows?
Only the old strong songs?
Is that all?
The sea-wash repeats, repeats.

He stuffed the poem into his pocket and put the anthology back
on the shelf. Though he didn't ordinarily worry much about what others might think or say about him, he instinctively felt a need to keep
this poetry thing to himself. It wasn't for fear of being teased; he could
handle that. Instead, it was a sense of having been shown a passageway
to a land both familiar and strange. He might want to share it someday, but he wanted to savor the indulgence of a secret first.

GEOFFREY SCOTT

CHAPTER 18

Although Hadley and Charlie remained friends, Jensen Cooper continued to cause problems for his son. The next Jensen-inspired scrape didn't go as well for Hadley.

If Jensen had been able to fish as well as he annoyed, then he might have been a wealthy man. He worked hard and was, by most reputes, a decent lobsterman. But his inability to keep his mouth shut and his pots away from his peers' fishing spots continued to cause problems big and small.

One of the bigger ones involved Francis Dubois. Francis's family had lived and lobstered in Rascal Harbor for generations. One of the first French-Canadian families to take up permanent residence, the Dubois had suffered taunts and their boats and gear had suffered damage. Still, they persevered. They fought when they had to, but eventually gained acceptance through hard work, honest trade, and a willingness to help when needed. Yankee hardheadedness and hardheartedness can be slow to change—but they can change. Francis and his forefathers eventually moved from begrudged tolerance to general acceptance. To most, Francis was now just another lobsterman.

Why Jensen Cooper thought it a good idea to begin riding Francis Dubois, no one would be able to remember. They did remember the steady drum of how. Initial tavern comments like "Christ, they let Frenchies in here?" developed into Co-op barbs like "How are those

ISLANDS AND BRIDGES

French fries working for bait?" and then to parking lot taunts like "Hey, Francis! I heard a lobster pointed a claw at you and you surrendered!" Sometimes these jibes brought laughter, even from Francis. The second time he found Jensen's buoy lines crossing his, however, Francis had had enough. After spending an hour untangling the lines, Francis was in no mood to be poked. So when Jensen started calling him "Francine," Francis decked him. Francis was a big man and so Jensen wisely stayed down on the bar floor. But his mouth continued, and Francis suspected he had done little to arrest Jensen's abuse.

The first time that Francis's daughter Babette heard about the incident it was from a friend who had heard about it from her father. An attractive girl, Babette was physically as big an any boy in her class and she brooked no interference. Nor was she happy to hear about this event from a friend rather than her father.

Babette worked as sternman on her father's boat just as Hadley did on his father's. The captain of a lobster boat pilots the craft, gaffs the buoys, and uses a mechanical hauler to bring them to the surface. A sternman does everything else—from cleaning out the hauled traps and putting rubber bands on the lobsters' claws to filling bait bags and tying them into traps before they are cast off and reset. And all of this occurs on slippery decks in heavy waterproof overalls and boots and as the boat rocks gently or lurches violently depending on the sea's mood.

With years of sternman experience, sixteen-year-old Babette was as strong as her male peers. She had heard and tolerated Jensen Cooper's jabs and she had heard if not accepted her father's calming words. "Jensen Cooper is an ass, Babette," her father would say, all trace of a French accent gone from his rich voice. "He'll always be an ass. Everyone knows that. So we don't let him get to us. He can only make us feel bad if we let him."

Babette knew her father was right. She also knew that Hadley Cooper had no real influence over his father. Still, the day after her father had knocked his to the floor, Babette approached Hadley after school with a noticeable tone of menace in her voice.

"I know you can't control your old man," Babette said sternly. "But you know he's trouble and he's on a bad path." Not waiting for Hadley to respond, she continued. "I don't know what's gonna happen, but if he keeps messing with my dad or any of the really tough guys, he's gonna be history. You know I'm right, don'tcha?" Hadley nodded. "Now I'm not gonna beat the shit outta you like my dad did to yours, but I will if it comes to it. And you know and I know that I can cause you won't hit back. So I'm suggesting that you try to nudge that asshole father of yours closer to the middle. Do you understand me?"

Hadley nodded again, but when he started to speak, Babette held a finger to her lips.

"I don't want to hear nothing from a Cooper man's lips. You and me are not enemies, but we aren't friends. Remember that."

He did.

Given his father's troubles at sea, one might think that Hadley would want to avoid that environment. But it was just the opposite. The boy took every opportunity to sternman for his father, he got a job pumping gas into boat gas tanks, and he read all the stories and poems about the sea in the Harbor library. His latest walking poem—the poem he tried to memorize as he walked to school or to his job—was another by Emily Dickinson:

> As If the Sea Should Part
> As if the Sea should part
> And show a further Sea—
> And that—a further—and the Three
> But a presumption be—
>
> Of Periods of Seas—
> Unvisited of Shores—
> Themselves the Verge of Seas to be—
> Eternity—is Those—

Hadley suspected that some people would find the poem discouraging, reading into it a sense of endlessness, a vanishing and never-to-be-achieved destination. It didn't read that way to him. Instead, the sea and the farther seas called to him, they said to him that his own future was as vast as the sea and that it was up to him to sail toward his own destination. Hadley had no idea what that destination might be, but he knew that only he could set limits on it.

CHAPTER 19

Hadley Cooper wanted to work on the ocean, but he did not want to work for or with or anywhere near his father. He would take to sea, but would do so far from Rascal Harbor.

Jensen Cooper continued to be an annoyance to the other Rascal Harbor lobstermen. He never incited a lobster war, though he had come close a couple of times. And he had never been shot, had his boat wrecked, or had his gear thrown overboard. Still, his son worried about each of these possibilities and wondered if any more of his father's sins would blow back on him. He'd managed to stay friends with Charlie and a good number of other fisherman kids. He and Babette had maintained their détente. Hadley knew there were worse circumstances in which to live, but he also knew there were far better.

So the day after his high school graduation, Hadley Cooper packed his belongings, kissed his mother and sister, and told his father he was headed off to find his way. That his father only nodded convinced Hadley that he was doing the right thing—as long as his father was around, neither Rascal Harbor nor the Cooper house would feel like it provided a real home.

Hadley's teachers had pushed for college. He was smart and capable, they said, he could make something of himself. Hadley had every intention of the latter. But as his mother drove him to the bus station in Portland, he knew that the sea would be his college. His traveling poem, Carl Sandburg's "Young Sea," was a long one. But it spoke to the journey he had in mind:

Young Sea

The sea is never still.
It pounds on the shore
Restless as a young heart,
Hunting.

The sea speaks
And only the stormy hearts
Know what it says:
It is the face
of a rough mother speaking.

The sea is young.
One storm cleans all the hoar
And loosens the age of it.
I hear it laughing, reckless.

They love the sea,
Men who ride on it
And know they will die
Under the salt of it

Let only the young come,
Says the sea.

Let them kiss my face
And hear me.
I am the last word
And I tell
Where storms and stars come from.

GEOFFREY SCOTT

Hadley could have stayed in Maine for he knew well the lobstering trade and had passable knowledge of the shrimping business. He had even applied for and received a lobstering license. But he'd read a couple of articles about swordfishing and how the Gloucester fleet was one of the best in the world. So with his first bus ticket and his first trip outside the state of Maine, he headed south to kiss the face of the sea.

When Hadley got word of his father's death, he was a twenty-eight-year-old crabber living in a one-bedroom apartment in a small town on the Chesapeake Bay. He worked with an old crabber who ran long strings of trotlines. Previously he'd worked on larger boats that used dredging equipment and on smaller boats that fished with crab pots. His crabbing days came after a five-year stint in which he'd worked on sword and tuna fishing boats out of Gloucester. Feeling the pull of a different kind of fishing and a warmer climate, Hadley had moved to the Chesapeake region and hired on with whoever needed the help. It had taken ten years, but his education as an Atlantic coast fisherman was nearly complete.

Hadley met, romanced, and slept with a number of women since leaving Rascal Harbor. All loved, then tolerated, then hated the life he led. So when he got Nancy's message that their father had died, he grieved quickly and alone in a seaside bar.

As soon as she could, Nancy had married a lobsterman, Arnold Draper. Their mother had died five years earlier, so what to do with the family house and their father's business now became points of discussion.

"Arnie doesn't need any of dad's stuff," Nancy told Hadley after they had exchanged phone greetings a week after Jensen's death. "So we could try to sell it along with the house if you want. Don't suppose you'd want to come back…?"

"Truth be told, I'm not sure. Guess I didn't think the old man would ever die."

"But would you say you've made a real life for yourself, with the wandering up and down the coast? Isn't it time to come home?"

"Would it be 'home' though? It didn't feel like a home when I lived there. Dad's antics made that clear. We lived there, but I can't say it ever felt like home."

"I guess I can see why you'd say that. I expect it was pretty rough on you, not that you ever really let on. Arnie's told me some things. I'm sorry little brother."

"Nothing you could have done much about—"

"No, I know. Nor Mother, either. But we both know how hard Dad rode you and how much shit you probably had to take from the other kids because of him. But he's gone now, and folks aren't likely to blame you for his nonsense. Arnie says there might be a few hard feelings, especially from some of the guys who fished when Dad did, but, well, think about it. Think about coming back, Hadley. Tommy and Linda would like to see their uncle and, I think, it would be good for you to see and be with all of us."

"Probably so," Hadley said and sighed. This was not the direction he'd expected the conversation to take and yet he was not willing to dismiss it either. He knew that he had some thinking to do so he quickly said goodbye.

Over the next few days, Hadley's mind would not stop drifting to the possibility of returning to Maine. He really had enjoyed his years away, learning the trade of a fisherman. He had given himself to think that he might live this life forever. Why he'd never thought about his father dying, he didn't know: The old ass had to die someday. But to this point, Hadley had never really considered going back. Could he? Did he even want to?

Although Hadley had a poet's heart, he could also be practically minded. So five days after he and Nancy talked, Hadley sat down and totaled up his life. He had no outstanding bills and had even built up a decent-sized savings account for a fisherman. He had no outstanding fishing goals as he felt comfortable on any kind of boat and doing any kind of work. Moreover, he had no outstanding personal commitments. He made friends and courted lovers easily, but none tied him to this town or any other. He liked the life he led and he could see himself living it well into the future.

Yet, on the other side of the ledger were a similar number of reasons why returning to Maine could make sense. First, he did miss his sister and her children. Though he seemed to live a loner's life, in fact, Hadley liked people and he could see himself reconnecting with Nancy, Arnie, and their kids. Second, he did miss Maine. The rock-bound coast touted in tourist brochures actually did pull on Hadley's head and heart. The Chesapeake was a dynamic environment, but it interested him far less than did Maine's rugged shoreline. And third, he did see some opportunity to learn. Hadley's many fishing experiences had given him confidence in his knowledge and ability. The one thing he'd not done, however, was skipper his own boat. Running his father's boat would give him that chance.

Free to return to Maine, or not, Hadley worried only about any lingering messes his father left unresolved. But then he thought, "I've been walking through the shit my father caused all my life, at least I won't have to walk through any new crap." With a nod to himself and to the next phase of his life, Hadley called his sister.

CHAPTER 20

The Hadley Cooper who drove his well-used pick-up truck into Rascal Harbor on a late winter day did so with a bigger lump in his throat than he expected to have. To calm himself, he repeated the short Dickinson poem he had found for Charlie Gibbons those many years ago.

Pulling into his sister's dooryard, he put both the poem and the lump away. Kids, dogs, and Nancy rushed to meet him and within a minute he felt the closest to being home that he ever had. He smiled.

That smile both broadened and waned over the coming days. The home that Nancy and her family represented would sustain Hadley; other parts of his return proved less welcoming.

Previewing the mixed reception he would receive over the coming months was the conversation Hadley and his brother-in-law had that first night as they walked along the road outside the Draper house.

Arnold Draper's family came to Rascal Harbor shortly before the Coopers. Arnie's and Hadley's grandfather's had been friends and the two tried to be friendly even after Jensen Cooper began his tear through the Rascal Harbor fishing community. That tear had not much affected Nancy and Arnie's courtship. Jensen refused to go to the wedding, but that was hardly the worst of his familial transgressions.

Though a couple of years older, Arnie had known Hadley or known enough about him to feel badly about what would have been the boy's fate had he decided to stay in the Harbor. A burly man with rough features, but a ready smile, Arnie didn't exactly feel protective of his sister's brother, but he'd help him if he could.

"So you're thinking you might take up fishing for bugs?" Arnie asked using one of a lobsterman's pet names for their catch.

"Leaning that way. I've caught a lot of different fish, but lobster was my first and I guess you don't ever give up on your first."

"Well, Jesus, don't go all gooey on me now, Hadley," Arnie said and then laughed. "But I guess you ain't that far off." The men walked a couple minutes before Arnie continued. "So you'll be wanting to look at your dad's boat and his gear." Hadley nodded. "It's mostly okay. A couple of guys smashed up a few pots right after your dad died. But mostly folks are just glad he's gone. Sorry, no offense meant, but…"

Hadley held up his hand. "No offense taken. He was what he was and that was always a bastard. I expect a lot of folks wasted a bunch of time and energy wishing he was different. He never was."

"And I expect most of the guys will see it that way and cut you some slack. But there'll be a few that'll have a hard time with a Cooper being back on the water. But just so's you know, there'll be some others mad just because you coming back means they can't move off the wait list to get a license."

"Huh. Didn't realize licenses have gotten that tight. How long is the list?"

"Thirty-five, last I heard. And some're from old lobstering families including the Patch twins, Corey and Chance. Corey's ahead of Chance on the list cause he was born first by a couple minutes. But both have been working as sternmen waiting for the next license slot to come open. Tony Linden is ahead of 'em so I expect he'll get your old man's spot. But if you can't get your license renewed, Corey will want to grab it and Chance'll be right behind him."

"Good to know. Guess old Jensen won't be the only Cooper people will be mad at."

"Like most things, I imagine, it's how you go about it. There's ways and then there's other ways."

As he nodded in understanding and agreement, Hadley thought maybe I'm not the only fisherman with a poet's soul.

Early the next morning Hadley met Arnie at the Co-op or, more properly, the Rascal Harbor Lobsterman's Co-operative. "How'd you sleep?" Arnie asked his brother-in-law. Hadley had decided to spend his first night back in the Cooper house.

"Took a while," Hadley admitted. "Lots of thoughts had to race around in my brain before I could settle down."

"Imagine so. Woulda creeped me out."

"I had a lot of years there to work out the creeps," Hadley said with a weak smile. "Just kept reminding myself that the old boy was gone."

"And so he is." Arnie led Hadley to a pile of traps, lines, buoys, and other gear he had hauled upon Jensen's death. Arnie was good lobsterman and he and his sternman, Rachel Wright, had done a nice job stacking the equipment.

The gear appeared to be in decent shape. There was little evidence of vandalism other than the hand-lettered sign someone had stuck inside a trap that said, "So long, fuckhead!"

"Guess someone knew my father."

With that, the men walked down onto the Co-op dock, pulled over Arnie's skiff, and rowed out to the Cooper family boat. Unburdened with gear, Cooper's Catch rode high in the calm Harbor waters.

Tying up and climbing aboard, Arnie asked, "You gonna keep the name?"

There was no rule that a captain had to name his boat after a loved wife or daughter, but most boats sported such names. Jensen Cooper had more than enough strikes against him so his peers generally ignored his decidedly self-centered boat name. Still, behind his back, Cooper's Catch became Cooper's Cockbite. Hadley had heard the nickname on plenty of occasions and knew one of the first things he would do is rechristen the boat and give it a new name.

Hadley would do so even though he knew the sea fates might be angered. Renaming a boat is one of the oldest taboos in seafaring lore…unless done properly. Stage one is to remove every vestige of the old name from the boat's interior and exterior. Even logbooks with the vessel's name need to be dispatched and new ones appropriated. Once scrubbed of the old name, a new christening can be staged and the boat, should the fates agree that the new name fit, can then sail forth.

Had his sister not married, Hadley likely would have renamed the boat, the Nancy Ann. Arnie had appropriated that name when he'd had a new boat built five years ago. So Hadley needed to think of another name. Arnie's question forced the issue. Before he could demur, it hit him: Cooper's Catch would become the Emily D. When Arnie pressed for an explanation, Hadley simply said, "She's an old friend."

As the two men went through the boat, they discussed the value of Jensen Cooper's assets—house, furnishings, vehicle, boat, and gear. Hadley had no use for his father's beat-up truck, but he could use the rest. Arnie and Nancy had gotten fair market assessments on the estate and Hadley had readily agreed to pay his sister half.

It would take a couple of weeks to get his lobster license reinstated, but Hadley had plenty to keep himself busy in the meantime.

CHAPTER 21

As Hadley and Arnie finished looking over what would become the Emily D., Charlie Gibbons hailed them. Charlie rowed over from his own boat, the Princess Paulie.

"How they hangin', boys?" Charlie said, voice booming. Like Hadley and Arnie, Charlie was a barrel-chested man. Shorter than the others, he was even more powerfully built.

"Just above the water," Hadley said with a grin as he and Charlie shook hands.

Charlie said, "Heard you was comin' back and here you are. Think you can make Cockbite turn a profit?"

"Maybe once I change the name. What do you think of the Emily D.?" he asked, wondering if his friend would remember the poet whose work had gotten him off the teacher's shit list.

"Who's she?" Charlie asked, oblivious to the reference. "Some old squeeze?"

"Guess you could say that," Hadley said.

"Well, anyway, good to see you, Hadley," Charlie replied and the three men turned to talk of the trade.

After Charlie left and Hadley and Arnie finished going over the boat, the brothers-in-law rowed back to the Co-op dock.

"Let's go in and see if Tristan's around," Arnie said. Earlier, Arnie had explained the cooperative's organizational structure. Rob Pownall served as the elected president of the Rascal Harbor Lobsterman's Co-operative. Tristan Riggins worked as the hired manager. Pownall and the board met regularly to oversee the operation; Riggins made it work on a daily basis.

A tall, thin man, Riggins was talking with the outdoor restaurant manager when Arnie and Hadley approached. After introductions, Riggins said, "So you're the new and improved Cooper."

As Hadley nodded, Arnie said, "Tristan here come up from Portland 'bout five years ago so he only knew your old man for a short while. Still, long enough, right, Tristan?"

"Agreed. Wouldn't want to speak ill of the dead, but…"

"Everyone else does, so not to worry," Hadley said. "Still, I'm hoping to rebrand the Cooper name."

"I expect a bunch of folks will welcome that change."

"A lot will, but a lot won't either," said a voice coming up behind Hadley. Babette Dubois, now a tall, ruggedly-built woman, said, "Me, I'm not sure which way to lean."

"Hey, Babette," Hadley said, putting out his hand.

Looking down at Hadley's hand, but not moving to shake it, Babette said, "Maybe someday, Hadley, but not today." With that, she turned, followed by her sternman, and left.

"Not someone you want mad at you," Tristan said confidentially. "Babette's a helluva lobsterman, but she's got personality to spare. Best to stay on her good side."

"We've got a history," Hadley said obliquely. "But I appreciate the advice."

Arnie said, "I told Hadley here that there was likely to be some lingerin' animosities. Old Jensen ain't been dead that long and twenty years of asshole is hard to forget." All three men nodded. Arnie continued. "But I also told him that some of the younger boys might not be thrilled to see him either as they'll have to stay on the wait list. Tony's happy that he can move up with Jensen's license goin' back to the state. But them Patch twins are hot to do the same and I expect they figured one of 'em would get yours, Hadley."

"I'm happy to help you with the paperwork," Tristan volunteered. "You've got a right to reclaim your spot regardless of how long the wait list is."

Hadley said, "I appreciate that. I'll drop by tomorrow with the forms I've got." With nods and handshakes the group broke up. Riggins went off on another chore while Arnie and Hadley walked toward their trucks.

Arnie looked at his brother-in-law and said, "Tristan's a good man to have in your corner. But he's still new and, like I said, some of the boys on the wait list are from old fishing families who don't like the idea that their lobsterin' legacy ain't enough to get 'em licenses."

"I can't say that I blame them much, but I didn't make the rules."

"Rules only work when everyone abides by 'em. When they don't, rules don't mean shit."

CHAPTER 22

Hadley Cooper had expected problems; he hadn't expected to find his gear cut.

Despite Tristan Riggins's offer of assistance, Hadley anticipated some hang-ups in bringing his license out of state storage. That part turned out to be surprisingly easy to do so. A week later he had a new license to lobster in hand.

Jensen Cooper hadn't paid much attention to the need for paint, but he had kept his boat engine and hauler well maintained. Still, the boat had sat on its mooring for six months so Hadley anticipated some mechanical issues. Yet nothing serious had developed so far.

Hadley foresaw relatively few problems with his father's gear. Lobstering is a pretty low-tech process, gear-wise. About the only real changes over the past hundred years had been the move to replace wooden traps with plastic-coated metal ones, the required use of biodegradable escape panels, and the necessity of including weak linkage in all buoy lines. Metal traps were now best practice as they require less repair, they lasted longer, and they didn't get waterlogged as did their wooden predecessors. Escape panels allow lobsters to get out of pots that have been lost or abandoned. And the use of weak or breakaway links on trap lines is a concession to the safety of large water mammals that could get tangled up. Hadley had gone through all his gear in the time between his first trip to the Co-op and the time his license arrived. No problems there.

Not having a sternman might have posed a problem. Hauling, cleaning, and resetting lobster pots, especially on bucking seas, takes concentration and a measure of dexterity. It's doable with two hands; it's a lot easier with four. Hadley expected to be a little rusty hauling his first couple of sets, but he wanted to go through the entirety of the job by himself for a while before bringing on a sternman.

Figuring out where to set his traps also proved to be relatively smooth. Hadley had his father's set charts and Arnie volunteered to go out with him a few times to make sure he steered clear of any trouble spots caused either by the ocean bottom or by his fellow fishermen's lobstering grounds.

That none of the potential problems materialized still left Hadley with a tough nut to crack—his social entrée into the clutch of Rascal Harbor lobstermen who could become his peers, friends, and drinking buddies or his antagonists and enemies. On a good day, he might gain acceptance and respect as brother lobsterman; on a bad day, he might become a pariah and victim.

Having Charley Gibbons and Arnie Draper as friends would help. Both men were well established and respected members of the lobstering fraternity. But a common trait within that fraternity is a strong strain of independence in thought and action, and orneriness was a deeply held and accepted characteristic. By joining the Co-op, each of the members agreed to abide by a set of norms and expectations. How those norms and expectations were interpreted, however, was quite a different matter. The written rules of lobstering are few. The fishing trade works on shades of meaning and those shades could be variously interpreted.

So Hadley was ready for some Co-op members to react negatively to him. Though he hoped to win them over eventually, he expected that it could be a little bumpy until he did. Still, the bumps he expected—snubs, snide comments, even parking lot confrontations—were a far cry from cut buoy lines.

The first few days of fishing had gone reasonably well. Working alone, it took a while to load twenty of his traps on the Emily D., motor out to his identified locations, bait and set the traps, and then do it all over again until he had all two-hundred pots fishing. With that many traps out, Hadley figured it would take him four days to pull, clean, rebait, and set them all in rotation.

The first couple of hauls went about as expected. It took a while to fall into a rhythm and Hadley got tangled up more than a few times. "Glad I haven't hired that sternman yet," he said to himself. "Be embarrassing if he or she was better at it than me."

Exhausted at the end of each day, Hadley nevertheless felt the keen satisfaction of having put in a day's effort under his own direction. He might not be the best lobsterman in the fleet, but he was making gains.

And then one morning he motored to a string of three pots and he could find no buoy marking the set. He'd started the day pulling ten sets of single or two-trap strings. Approaching his first three-trap string and not seeing his green and white vertically striped pot buoy, he first wondered if he'd overshot the location. Checking the shore landmarks and the buoys of the neighboring lobstermen, he knew he was in the right place. He next wondered if he'd set the pot warp too short and so the buoy was just underwater. He slowly circled his boat looking over the side. No luck.

At that point, the sinking realization that the line to his traps might have been cut hit hard. He'd now checked every way that he could think of—reviewing the set markers on his nautical chart, verifying his land markers and the pot buoys of his competitors who were fishing nearby, and circling the area again in hopes that his buoy would suddenly surface. He even widened his circling area in case his line and traps had gotten tangled with another set. If that lobsterman had pulled up Hadley's traps and then reset them in a slightly different location, it would explain the missing buoy. No luck.

"Goddamn it," he said. As he steamed toward his next three-string set, Hadley reviewed the possible explanations. It might have been a deliberate cutting, but it also could have been the inadvertent result of another boat's propeller slicing the line or breaking away if the line got caught on a keel. He supposed a whale or dolphin might also be responsible. They could get sufficiently tangled to snap the break-away linkage and send the pot buoy out to sea and the pot warp to the ocean bottom.

These non-deliberate possibilities seemed more possible when Hadley saw the buoy for his next set. The likelihood grew as he found his next several sets intact. About to finish the day with a three-pot haul, the sinking feeling thudded hard when, again, he could find no sign of his pot buoy. He repeated all his earlier moves in hopes of keeping the loss down to only three traps. No luck.

"Goddamn it."

CHAPTER 23

The men at Lydia's back table were not the only ones to chat through Hadley Cooper's trouble. Cut buoy lines do not always result in all-out lobster wars, but they do often enough that it's big news. Small towns live on news, big or otherwise, and the brewing of a lobster storm guaranteed a full hearing.

The particulars of the story being told mattered, but equally important was who did the telling. Rascal Harbor residents got their local news from a range of sources.

Some folks could be trusted to report only what they knew to be true. What they knew to be true and what was true could vary, of course. But if a person had a track record of accurate reporting—"You know, Joe, he don't lie"—then he or she would generally be believed.

It was a small group, however, that formed this first category of reporters. A much larger group passed along as many particulars of a story as they had, but then felt obligated to offer invented details, new interpretations, or alternative perspectives in addition. Stories that passed the lips of these folks became more interesting, more exaggerated, or more crazy depending on the reporter's motivation—"That Lori, she can twist any story into a pretzel, heat and salt it, and then add the mustard."

And then there was Geneva Baxter. At seventy years old, Geneva was a community fixture. Seemingly always one of the first to get any bit of new information, Geneva made it her special mission to move stories around town. What complicated her role was that in and among the facts was a whole series of non-facts. It wasn't that Geneva manipulated a story or added her own spin. She reported any news in straight-forward, just-the-facts fashion. Unfortunately anywhere from half to three-quarters of those facts were problematic. Everyone Geneva interacted with knew this. They just never knew what percentage of her reports were untrue. As Minerva Williams once observed, "Geneva don't know her ass from a hole in the ground. If she ever saw a fact she'd wrassle it to the ground, spit in its face, and call its mother a whore!"

Geneva Baxter missed the initial scoop on the cutting of Hadley Cooper's trap lines. Instead, Rob Pownall was among the first sources as he was at the Co-op when Hadley steamed to the dock to unload the day's catch. Rob hadn't seen Hadley since he started fishing so he came down to the dock to help him tie up. Rob caught the full force of Hadley's building ire.

"They cut my goddamn lines, Rob," Hadley spit. "Someone cut my goddamn buoy lines." Hadley wasn't out of control, but he was mad and Rob understood it would take a minute for him to come out with all the relevant details. Once he did, Rob said, "Let's go see Tristan."

After talking over the matter with the Co-op manager, the three agreed that it would be best if Hadley went to see the police the next day.

After airing the story of Hadley Cooper's trap woes at Lydia's, Rob Pownall walked over the Rascal Harbor Police Department to see if he could help Hadley. As he did, each of the other back-table men began spreading the story to his various outlets. Vance Edwards went home and told his wife. Slow Johnston went to Village Hardware to tell his old friend, Ricky Baines, but got distracted and forgot to relay the story. Bill Candlewith and Ray Manley walked over Gary's Garage to meet with the regulars Alan Tuttle and Clint Evans.

At Gary's, Alan and Clint were in full chatter mode deliberating over who would have a better season—the Red Sox this spring or the Patriots next fall. They tried to enlist Gary in the debate, but Gary favored the Toronto Blue Jays so his opinion didn't really count. They'd also tried to engage Gary's daughter, Louise, again to no avail. Louise was a bookkeeper by trade, but her passion for and knowledge of cars made her indispensable when Gary got behind. Today, Louise was putting a new set of brakes on a Honda sedan.

Having gently rebuffed the boys' entreaties twice, Louise had had it. "If you gas bags are gonna keep at it, global warming's going to be here sooner than later."

"Jesus, Louise, if you didn't wanna talk to us, you coulda just said so," Clint said.

"Honest to Christ…" Louise said to herself as she went back to her brake job. Gary just smiled.

Clint and Alan smiled, in turn, as Ray and Bill entered the garage. The latter two had earned their livings at sea while Clint and Allan had worked as custodians at the high school. That difference aside, the four men shared a body type—short, spare bodies, with greying or gone hair, and work-toughened skin. They also shared a penchant for knowing and passing along the business of most everyone they knew and more than a few of those they didn't. Seeing Ray and Bill arrive meant, at minimum, some new perspectives on the Red Sox-Patriot debate. Even better would be fresh news. The garage boys were in luck.

Ray and Bill represented the embellishing type of reporter—more than willing to introduce a new detail or interpretation should the story need an extra bit of spice. So after they relayed the basics of the Hadley Cooper story, each added a little personal flavor. Ray picked up on Vance's thought that a whale might have broken the trap lines. In doing so, however, he advanced it more as a fact than as a possibility. Bill disagreed asserting that it was teenagers out joyriding in a borrowed outboard who bore responsibility.

ISLANDS AND BRIDGES

"You know how them damn kids are today," Bill said. "Crazy and horny and full of piss. Wouldn't surprise me if they was out runnin' over buoy lines on purpose."

Not being men of the sea, Alan and Clint both asked about the prospects of a looming lobster war. Neither man ever dined much on lobster unless they got some culls—small lobsters with only one claw—from a friend of a friend. But both were sensitive to the industry.

"'Spose it's possible," Ray said, "but if so, hard to tell why it might be brewin'." He explained that cut lines, if done on purpose, could have one of several rationales.

"Could be Hadley set too close to another guy or snarled the guy's lines and traps with his own. Or could be that it's one of the guys on the wait list hopin' to move up by pushin' Hadley out of the way. Or, one other possibility is that it's someone who hated Hadley's father and is gettin' back at him through the boy."

"It's a real mystery," Bill said with a solemn nod. His friends nodded as well. Close behind those nods were thoughts of who each man would tell next.

Alan Tuttle took the news over to Henry's Barbershop. He was due for haircut, but now he'd be able to command the attention of the fellows who made Henry's their local news station.

Henry was a tub of man, with height and width in similar measurements. His hairless head shone and was a continual source of joking by the customers who wondered how a bald man would know anything about cutting another man's hair.

"Hell if I know," Henry typically responded. "Sit down and let's see what happens."

Henry loved to gather the town news. Passing it along to his customers and the two or three men who typically hung around was second only to cutting hair on his list of passions. Unfortunately for Alan, the crowd had yet to appear. Disappointed in an audience of one, Alan nevertheless offered his best version of Hadley Cooper's problem. In his retelling, however, he forgot about the non-human possibilities for the cut lines, he concentrated on the probability of a lobster war, and he announced that Hadley was "Some kinda depressed" about the whole thing." He added, "Wouldn't be surprised if the lad gives up, sells his boat and gear, and heads back south."

After he closed up that afternoon, Henry headed over to Jimbo's for a draft. Jimbo's, once known as Jonathan Hannigan's, was an upscale restaurant now taking the turn toward seedy bar status. No one was quite sure when or how the renaming took place, but Jimbo's now seemed a more appropriate choice.

By the time Henry arrived at Jimbo's, he'd describe Hadley's trouble to a dozen men, though each time he did, the story gained a bit more intrigue and gravity. The account Henry offered up to the bartender/owner Arthur Yellen had lost all the alternative possibilities and now featured Hadley tracking down the culprits with murderous intent.

The story chain from Hadley to Rob to Ray and from Bill to Alan to Henry and then to Arthur was replicated all across Rascal Harbor. Hadley Cooper had lost some traps. From that one fact bloomed gossip roses of wide-ranging size, smell, color, and thorniness. Rascal Harbor had some news.

CHAPTER 24

Hadley Cooper's woes pushed most all local gossip to the side for a day or two, but the buzz around the decision to allow nonresidents to compete for the Arvin Prize continued.

By now the news had gone well beyond the Colony Board, the few artists who Board members had reached out to, and the back-table folks at Lydia's. In widening circles, people talked about the decision as a step into the future and a chance to put Rascal Harbor on the art world map or as a slap in the face of the past and a slight on the talents of every local artist from Mattie Arvin forward. Of course, those two perspectives simply defined the ends of a very long and complicated string of possible reactions. And so wrangling over the Colony Board decision continued despite competition from the Hadley Cooper story.

Richard Anthony Bates helped the wrangle continue. Bates was a slight man of average height and patrician features. A pastel artist, Richard leaned toward the sensitive side, his fine physical features seeming to play out in the fine rendering and shading evident in his muted work. Where Robertay Harding defined the bohemian stereotype of an artist, Richard Anthony, as most people called him, defined the refined version. And it was that refined element that stood in such contrast to his lobsterman partner, Babette Dubois.

The two met three years ago in Key West. Babette was vacationing with her Rascal Harbor friends, Mildred Sargent and April Hatch.

Walking along a public beach on their first day, Babette noticed a young man, fully-dressed, working on a drawing of the seashore. She gave little notice to the work, taken instead by the fact that the fellow seemed so obviously over-dressed for the beach. For his part, the man stopped drawing, captivated by this tall, strong woman with a face more handsome than beautiful. Babette's friends, Mildred and April, were also attractive, but the man could not go back to work until the tall woman was completely out of sight.

A similar situation unfolded the next day. This time, the man had been watching for the striking woman and her friends. As soon as he saw them, he stood from his small stool and watched silently as the women walked by. He observed everything about the tall woman's friends—their relative sizes, their gaits, their bodies, their faces. But it was the tall woman and, in particular, the tall woman's face to which he was drawn. Her untamed blonde curls framed a firm jaw, a strong nose, and tanned skin. But it was her eyes that gave life to each of these elements. Strength, intelligence, humor—all the finest human traits seemed to lie within them. He stared openly, appraisingly.

For her part, Babette stared back in equal measure. She took in the man's slender build and his beach-inappropriate long sleeved shirt and pants. When she turned to his face, she, too, found his definition. She began with his eyes—a kind mix of sophistication and naiveté—they centered a thin, aristocratic face and pale skin. She, too, examined and appraised.

Day three, they spoke. Then, it was a challenge to stop. Mildred and April tried to be mad at their friend who now spent most of her remaining vacation time with this man, Richard Anthony Bates. But their surprise and delight that Babette could be so captivated by someone so different enabled them to simply be happy for her.

And they were different. Babette's family worked and worked hard at the jobs they had and at gaining acceptance among Yankees who still found ways to stereotype and mock their French-Canadian neighbors. The Duboises had lived and worked in Rascal Harbor for generations and yet, they could still be perceived as outsiders.

Richard Anthony Bates's family had always been insiders. They arrived in the United States early on and spread throughout the new country. The family started in New England, but a large group migrated ever south until settling in Florida. The family businesses diversified over the years, but their work largely consisted of hiring and managing the work of others. Bates relatives in other parts of the country moved into manufacturing; the Bates family in Florida farmed. Richard Anthony's great, great grandfather began building an orange tree farm. His descendants extended that reach until they were among the most prosperous orange growers in the state.

Richard Anthony loved the orange groves, though more as an artist than as a grower. As a child he would walk the rows of trees fascinated with the way the strong southern sunshine played its way through the leaves, branches, and fruit. Given a sketchbook and artist's pencils for his tenth birthday, the boy spent hours sketching the patterns of light and dark, sunshine and shadow.

Though financially able to support his artistic intentions, Richard Anthony's pragmatic family found his pursuit frivolous. His father and mother indulged his fine art major in college, but expected him to return to the orange trade once graduated. He didn't. Instead, he made art, selling some, but mostly supporting himself with a variety of jobs and the small amounts of money that his sister would send him.

Having studied light and shadow throughout the state, Richard Anthony was especially taken with the way they played out in the Florida keys. Feeling restless, Richard Anthony had packed a small bag and his artist gear and driven to Key West to stay two weeks with a friend. His first day on the beach he saw Babette Dubois. He left for Maine when she did.

CHAPTER 25

From just about everyone's perspective, the Babette-Richard Anthony connection seemed an odd one. "Opposites attract," "Variety is the spice of life," and "Love conquers all" were some of the maxims Rascal Harbor residents offered up to explain this strange match. Even Jumper Wilson seemed to have an opinion. A week after the couple surfaced in town, Jumper could be seen wearing a T-shirt that said *Two is company, and good company at that.*

Try as they might, however, some dimension or another of Babette and Richard Anthony's differences struck the townsfolk as too odd to go unnoticed. Some folks focused on the fact that the couple seemed to swap gender roles. Babette's decision to follow in her father's lobstering boots had raised a few eyebrows. But many more shot upward when Richard Anthony's artistic inclinations were observed. "Guess Babette wears the jock strap in that family," one wag commented.

The differences in occupations seemed even more pronounced when the two were seen walking together. Though they were the same height, the fact that Babette outweighed her beau by twenty muscled pounds could not be ignored. "That boy never ought to cross Babette," one observer said. "She's just as likely to stuff him in a bait bag and set him out for the 'sters to eat."

And then there arose the worries about a working girl of the sea ever finding true happiness with a silver-spoon boy of the plantation. Coastal Mainers have seen more than their share of the ways of wealth. For the most part, they harbor their class envies silently. But given half a chance to castigate, swear at, or make fun of an out-of-towner "with more money than brains," Mainers won't hesitate. Once it became known that Richard Anthony "came from money," tongues clucked. "All's I'm sayin'," one local noted, "is that you can trust rich people…to trust rich people."

Babette and Richard Anthony knew that such talk would surface. But then each had encountered, been angered by, and long dealt with family members and others who balked at their choices. Babette knew that her chosen profession and her ethnic heritage would always be one joke away from surfacing. Richard Anthony's chosen profession and his walking away from the family fortune seemed like jokes both within and outside his family. That neither cared how they were perceived reflected their individual and collective will and the fact that love finds connections and bonds that are no less strong whether or not they are obvious.

Now three years into their lives together in Rascal Harbor, the couple no longer felt the town's scrutiny. Babette prospered as a lobsterman and Richard Anthony found some success selling his work in Maine and in Boston. Babette's days were filled with hard and dangerous work, worries about fluctuating lobster prices, repairs to her gear and her boat. Richard Anthony's days were filled with chasing light and shadow through his impressionistic pastel images of houses, wood trails, and harbor scenes. At the dinner table and through the night, their work talk rarely overlapped, yet each was fascinated with the other's account of the day's efforts. They lived quietly and peacefully, and socialized just enough to be considered sociable.

And then the Art Colony Board decided to change the entry rules for the Arvin Prize.

Although he was not one of the group surveyed by the Colony board members right after Robertay Harding pitched the idea, Richard Anthony heard about it soon enough. Another pastel artist, Janice Sewall, approached Richard Anthony and Babette during dinner at Lane's Wharf the next night. Richard Anthony had just received word of a commission by a Boston-area company and so the two were celebrating.

"I'm so sorry to interrupt," Janice started as she approached the table, "but, Richard Anthony, have you heard?"

"Have I heard what?" Richard Anthony asked. He looked up at the attractive, well-dressed woman. Janice's family summered in Maine for generations. She and her recently retired husband, David, moved to Rascal Harbor to live year round two years earlier.

"Well, it's all over the Colony. I'm surprised you haven't heard."

"Sorry, Janice, I've been shuttered away trying to finish a piece," Richard Anthony explained, trying to remain courteous. "What's all over the Colony?"

"Just about the most insulting news ever," Janice replied, her voice and color rising.

Sensing that this exchange might take a while, Richard Anthony asked, "Okay. Would you like to sit down and tell us about it?"

"Oh no, thank you," Janice said, suddenly looking abashed about her intrusion. "It's just that I wondered how you felt about it."

"How about you just tell us what the hell you're talking about," Babette said.

"Ah, right, sorry." Drawing herself up, she said, "Apparently, the executive board decided, well…Robertay Harding is pushing the board to decide…to change the rules for the Arvin Prize. They, but really this all sounds like her, want to allow non-residents to compete for the Prize. Can you believe that? I mean, it's just not fair! When David and I had a summer home and paid property taxes, I couldn't compete because we weren't considered 'residents.' It's just not fair!"

"Huh," Richard Anthony said as he processed Janice's information. "Did whoever told you offer any explanation?"

"Oh, there was some nonsense about elevating the level of the work submitted and bringing in more tourists. Like we need that!" Janice replied dismissively.

ISLANDS AND BRIDGES

"Hmm. I guess I could see that," Richard Anthony said, toying with the idea in his mind.

"Richard Anthony! I can't believe you would give this silly idea any credence at all! You have to see that this is just one more way for Robertay to pump up her self-image. Honestly, that woman would do anything to get a little more power and publicity."

"You may be right. But I guess I would like to hear more about the proposal before I decide what I think about it."

"Well! I can see that you will be no help in this matter. I'd have thought you would be a little more sensitive since you became a resident just a short time ago yourself." With that, Janice turned and strode back to the bar where her husband was waiting.

Startled for a moment, Richard Anthony turned to Babette with a what-was-that? look on his face.

"Jesus, what a terror that one is," Babette said quietly, but with a trace of venom. "She thinks mighty of herself."

"She does indeed, but what do you think of the news?"

"I'm not sure that I really understand the point." Through their conversations, Babette was learning the ins and outs of the art world, but much of it still seemed overly nuanced, petty, and vain. She had loved Richard Anthony's work from the beginning, though she would admit to Mildred and April that her infatuation with its creator probably helped. Slowly she was coming to see and appreciate differences in the media used, the images portrayed, and the notion of artistic vision. She found realistic work easy enough to value, but whenever she looked at an abstract piece, she would say, "That person needs some new vision!" It became their standard laugh line when confronted with anything that struck them as off-kilter.

"I'm guessing that this is a far more complex issue than Janice is portraying it, but the more I think about it, the more I can see the possibility of some angry artists."

"That's all I can see. I mean, why wouldn't all the resident artists be upset?"

"Maybe they will, but there must be nearly a hundred artists in the Colony. It's hard to imagine that they would all see the situation the same way."

"I don't see how they couldn't," Babette said firmly. "After all, why would they cut their own throats by letting outsiders in? And I'm surprised that you wouldn't see it that way now that you're a local." Babette squeezed Richard Anthony's arm.

"Ah, but am I?" Richard Anthony asked playfully. "After all, I've only been here for three years and you've not married me. And even if you do, I expect I'll still be 'that guy from down to Florida.'"

"At least you aren't a Masshole," Babette said to tease him. "But, yeah, you're a newbie all right."

"Well, I'm not sure where I'll come down on the issue, but I predict we're in for some interesting times."

CHAPTER 26

Babette and Richard Anthony's talk about the criteria that defined the residential status of a "local" percolated across Rascal Harbor. Those criteria seemed to vary, of course, depending on the discussants' domestic status and their views of the art world in general, the Rascal Harbor Art Colony in particular, and the actions of Robertay Harding specifically. A legal definition existed somewhere, but it was far more fun to debate the issue in light of this new controversy.

One of the few residents not interested in doing so was David Sewall. He knew his wife Janice was worked up about the Arvin Prize decision. But he did not look forward to the predictable melee. A former executive in a family-run corporation based in Connecticut, David had spent parts or all of every summer at the Sewall place on Harbor Point, an enclave of large, shingled, cottage-in-name-only summer houses owned by wealthy out-of-staters. He and Janice summered together as her family owned the cottage three dooryards away. Once married, trucking the kids, dog, nanny, and housekeeper up to the Point every summer had been, in Janice's mind, something akin to moving Sherman's army. But she and David loved their summer lives and the cottage they inherited when David's parents died. With retirement looming, the Sewalls hired a contractor to winterize the residence and looked forward to a Rascal Harbor life.

And Janice looked forward to competing in the Arvin Prize competition. She knew that some fine artists held memberships in the Colony and she knew the judges would not simply hand her the prize. But she worked hard at her pastels and harbored a small, but nagging grudge because she had been unable to compete in the past.

"I mean, honestly, David, if you totaled up all the summers I've spent in Rascal Harbor, I've probably lived here longer than most of the so-called residents. Think about it, someone could pack up her acrylics, move from Boston or Buffalo, live in an apartment for a year, and then enter the competition! Why is she a resident and I'm not? It's just not fair!" These points, expressed in numerous variations, had been Janice's mantra over the last few years before the couple moved north.

David clucked his sympathies in the time before the move. The morning they started settling in and unpacking, he'd hugged his wife and said, "And so the quest for the Arvin Prize begins in earnest!" Janice broke the hug with a fierce look and said, "You bet your newly-minted Maine resident ass it does!"

Janice wasn't on any of the Colony board member's first list of calls. Instead, she heard about the decision from a friend who had been surveyed by Toni Ludlow. The friend had a mixed reaction to the idea; Janice went apoplectic.

Fuming all day, Janice started making calls. Not being a member of the Colony, she didn't know a lot of the local artists. Still, she made sure that the half a dozen or so she called knew all about the travesty this decision represented. To her surprise, few felt as strongly as she did. Several bemoaned the decision, but chalked it up to "that bitch Robertay." Janice tried to incite a little passion in her respondents, and she got some. Still, the strain of languor she heard annoyed her.

"Don't these people know what's in their best interest?" Janice asked David, though it was clearly a rhetorical question.

"Maybe not, dear," David said diplomatically. "But I'm not too surprised that there are a range of perspectives on this decision. You artistic types are rarely of a single mind."

"David, don't patronize me!" Janice said sharply. "If anyone knows artists, it's me. What I just can't understand is why any resident artist would favor allowing in more competitors."

"But is that what they were saying, Janice? My sense was that several of the people you talked with were just apathetic."

"Apathy is the same thing as support in this case. If no one stands up to Robertay and the board, then we deserve to have outsiders come in and take the prize."

At this comment, David smiled inwardly. He thought , we've been here full-time for less than two years and Janice is now talking about others as "outsiders."

Janice was still wound up that evening when she spied Richard Anthony Bates and Babette Dubois dining at Lane's. She felt certain that Richard Anthony would see her point and join her cause. When he didn't immediately understand and embrace the importance of the situation, she realized that it would be a long hill to climb.

The next morning, Janice started the climb. Two of the six people she talked with earlier favored the board decision, so she concentrated on the other four. She invited them to come to a late afternoon meeting at her house to chat through the idea. Three of the four could make it, but each promised to bring at least one other artist they knew was uneasy about the decision. She also invited Richard Anthony in hopes of convincing him to join the cause.

It was a diverse group of ten artists who arrived at the Sewall cottage that afternoon. They differed in their media choices from painting to photography to sculpture; they varied in age from late twenties to early sixties; and they exemplified the range of "local" status ranging from a man whose family had lived in Rascal Harbor for six generations to a woman who moved to town just over a year ago.

After refreshments, Janice called the meeting to order. The discussion lurched awkwardly, however, as her interest in rallying the group

GEOFFREY SCOTT

to oppose the decision conflicted with the fact that most members simply wanted to talk it through first. Recognizing that she would make no headway until the group felt it had a full understanding, Janice acquiesced and pushed the group to construct a list of pros and cons. The result echoed much of the local buzz about the decision:

Pros
1. Better quality art work
2. More publicity for the Colony
3. More tourist money
4. More excitement about/interest in the Summer Exhibition
5. Outshining Herrington's art festival

Cons
1. Not Mattie Arvin's intention
2. More traffic
3. Less parking
4. Longer grocery lines
5. Divisive possibilities in the Colony and in the town

Janice scowled inwardly at the fact that the lists had the same number of items. She felt the con-side points held greater weight, yet several participants kept returning to the idea that an expanded Summer Exhibition could outdo the Herrington Festival.

"I'd love to see those Herrington jerks' faces when they see the publicity and attention the Exhibition will get," Janelle Hanson said. A sharp-faced woman of ill-defined proportions, Janelle was more or less acknowledged as the best pastel artist in the Colony.

"Me too," echoed London James, an oil painter whose entire physical description and artistic talent could only be described as modest. "It would be a real coup for the Colony."

"It might be," Janice said, trying to appear judicious. "But with these new rules then Herrington artists could submit their work just like any non-resident. How would you feel if one of them won the Arvin Prize?" From the ensuing silence, Janice felt she'd effectively undercut that item on the pro list.

"Mattie'd have a heart attack," Gerald Rimbaud said. Gerald, a gaunt man of considerable height painted in oils and had done so during the time when Mattie Arvin led the Colony. Janice and several others nodded vigorously.

Twyla Cameron said, "I agree, but my biggest worry is that this decision will create long-lasting divisions within the Colony." Twyla was one of two African-American artists in the Colony. A short, thin woman, she created assemblages of found wooden and metal objects over which some of the more traditional Colony members scratched their heads. "It would be really sad if, two years from now, we've bickered ourselves into dissolution."

"Twyla is exactly right. This decision could end up destroying the Colony," Janice said.

"Well, that's possible, but there are already so many differences and distinctions among us that I'm not sure one more would matter," Janelle said. The group laughed at the truth behind this statement.

Not wanting to lose the moment, Janice pushed forward, "So what should our next steps be? Shall we recruit more like-minded people? Should we try to meet with the Executive Board and push them to reconsider? Or should we generate a no-confidence vote in Robertay?"

At this point, Richard Anthony spoke for the first time: "It's not clear to me, Janice, that everyone is opposed to the decision. I, for one, am still thinking through the pros and cons." A couple of others nodded. Continuing, he said, "I really appreciate you pulling this meeting together, but it seems premature to take some of the actions you've just proposed."

"What would your idea be?" Janice asked, trying to keep the snarl out of her voice.

Richard Anthony said, "I would think a petition of some kind might be in order, a petition that calls for a general meeting of the Colony. Isn't there something like that in the by-laws of the group? That way the Executive Board and Robertay could present the issue and the rationale behind their decision and then take questions from the membership. I don't know if there is any such possibility, but I'd be surprised if there isn't."

"I can check," Twyla said.

"Sounds like a good plan to me," London said. The others agreed.

"All right," Janice said, silently acknowledging the shift in plan. "Let me know what you find out Twyla and I'll email the group. Then we can decide how to proceed. In the meantime, I hope you'll all talk with your friends and let them know what is going on and why this decision is probably not in the best interests of the Colony or the town."

Richard Anthony recounted the meeting to Babette later than evening.

"Janice was fighting hard with herself to seem open-minded, but it was a losing battle. She kept saying things that made it clear that she hates the Colony board decision."

"Well, is she wrong?" Babette asked. "I mean, really, wasn't the whole idea of the prize to honor a local artist?"

"I suppose, but wouldn't it be a greater honor if the Arvin Prize was a much bigger deal than it is now? That is, more prestigious because the competition was better?"

"So have you made up your mind to support the change?" Babette asked.

"No, but I can see the advantages."

"There's always advantages and disadvantages to anything, but I really wonder if this move is a good thing. I get it that this town makes its money on the tourists, but Jesus, do we have to let them in on everything? Can't there be a few things that are just ours?"

"So you're agreeing with Janice Sewall?" Richard Anthony said with a slight smile.

"Maybe with her goal, if not her reasons. I suspect she just wants to limit the competition. I think it's more about local pride and keeping some real connection with our past. Same purpose, but different intentions."

"I expect there will be a lot of purposes and even more intentions before this whole matter is settled."

CHAPTER 27

Twyla Cameron called Janice Sewall two hours after the meeting broke up.

"Sorry, Janice, it took me a little longer than I thought it would to find my copy of the Colony by-laws, but I did find them and there is a provision by which the membership can call for a special meeting 'to discuss matters arising.' Pretty vague, huh? Anyway, it was like Richard Anthony guessed, if forty per cent of the members sign a petition, then there can be a special meeting."

"That's great news, Twyla," Janice said excitedly. "Do you think I could get a copy of the by-laws? I know I have one somewhere, but I couldn't find it."

Twyla agreed to make a copy, then added, "It also says that the membership can recall the board members and even the president 'for deeds inappropriate to the health of the Colony.'"

"That's very interesting," Janice said with a smile.

CHAPTER 28

Trouble of a different sort was brewing at the Rascal Harbor Lobsterman's Co-op. Hadley Cooper's cut trap lines proved a trial for the organization.

Fishing co-operatives dot the coast of Maine. Beginning with the Pemaquid Fisherman's Co-operative in 1947, lobstermen have banded together in a range of loose organizations. Those organizations typically offer discounts on necessities such as bait and fuel by buying in bulk. They also offer members dock space, storage containers for their catch, and generally higher prices from wholesalers. As a group, co-op members share some of the profits of their collective labor.

These are substantial benefits; they come with a couple of substantial costs. One of those costs is the need for competent managers and staff.

Co-ops became an economic need, in part, because lobstermen found themselves increasingly at the mercy of wholesalers who colluded to keep prices down. The collective power of a co-op begins to level the field. But lobstermen work long, exhausting days and managing the diverse affairs of the co-operative necessitates a full-time staff and a capable one at that. Even with the bargaining power of co-ops, prices to the fisherman are far less than what the tourists pay, so many wallets benefit as a bug moves from trap to table. The co-ops that prosper are the ones that start by hiring a smart, honest manager who can keep the ledgers, negotiate deals, see to facility repairs, and manage the personalities of a couple dozen independent contractors. Other hires can be important, but it is the co-op manager who runs the show on a daily basis.

Many co-ops also have dining facilities, gift shops, and shipping services—all logical extensions of the lobstering trade, but all in need of workers and managers. These enterprises can generate as much money or more than the lobster trade itself. They can also generate headaches as the co-op members are ultimately responsible for all those salaries.

The other big cost that co-op lobstermen incur is time. Being at sea can be tiring even if one is not working. Hauling, cleaning, baiting, and resetting heavy traps while standing on the slippery deck of a pitching boat for eight or more hours is deep-bone exhausting. To then sit in long co-op meetings discussing this issue and that, all the while knowing that gear goes unfixed, suppers go cold, and beer goes undrunk is alternatively frustrating and annoying. Managers and their assistants tend to much of the on-shore operations of a co-op. Still, questions of all sorts need to be considered, chewed over, and decided and, in a collective, that takes time.

Having a strong board of directors and a good president helps. Co-op managers wield considerable power, especially over the day-to-day operations. Ultimately, however, the big decisions are made by the co-op board. It's useful to have board members who study the issues with a degree of wisdom and insight and who can weigh both short- and long-term challenges with a considered eye. It's critical to have a board president who can do these things.

The president of the Rascal Harbor Lobsterman's Co-operative could do these things. Rob Pownall was well respected for his brains, temperament, and diplomacy. And he called on all three in his effort to respect the members' various contributions while not letting their various limitations stall the organization's viability and progress. He was now nearing his second three-year term on the board and his fourth year as the elected president.

That Rob was a retired shrimp boat captain rather than an active lobsterman caused no particular concern. Rob lobstered for fifteen years before selling off his boat and gear and moving into the shrimp trade. Shrimpers generally use larger boats and trawl for their prey by dragging, hauling, cleaning out, and then resetting large nets.

Or at least they used to. As Rob contemplated retiring, the Maine shrimp fleet began downsizing. Maine shrimpers faced increased market competition from shrimp farmers from around the world. Shrimp raised on "farms" were more susceptible to disease than fresh caught. Still, the enormous numbers that shrimp farmers could raise in vast pools of circulating water outpace the product that shrimpers could catch on the open sea.

The bigger problem for Maine shrimpers, however, was the lack of shrimp. Beginning in the 1970s, the shrimp population began a slow, but very steady decline due to the warming of Maine's coastal waters. Entire shrimping seasons had been closed in recent years in the hopes that the crustaceans would rebound. Few observers were all that hopeful.

When he moved from captaining a lobster boat to a shrimp trawler, Rob retained his membership in the Rascal Harbor Co-op on the possibility that he might return to his lobstering roots. Might as well keep my hand in it, he'd thought to himself. So when retirement proved challenging for this hard-working and vital man, he turned his full energies to his position on the Co-op's board of directors. And when his peers on the board asked him to consider standing for the president's position, he'd agreed. The vote wasn't even close.

Rob and Tristan Riggins, the Co-op's manager, formed a good team. They liked and trusted one another. More importantly, each knew and did his own job and resisted the urge to meddle in the other's domain. They suspected they would need all their collective knowledge and skill to deal with the looming crisis that the cutting of Hadley Cooper's trap lines posed.

GEOFFREY SCOTT

CHAPTER 29

Word of Hadley Cooper's troubles blew through the Rascal Harbor Co-op like an angry wind.

From the teenager selling ice cream to the single mom who steamed lobsters and clams for take-out orders to the gift shop manager with a sick daughter at home, the talk about Hadley's lost traps hummed. Who could have done it and why defined the immediate conversational track. How and when it had been done followed soon after. Weaving in, around, and through every exchange was heated speculation about a lobster war. The longer the conversations lasted, however, the sooner the quiver generated by this prospect began to surge. A lobster war could prove disastrous for individual fishermen and the widening ripples could create problems all across the Co-op's business infrastructure.

The chatter about Hadley's misfortune, however, far outstripped the immediate actions. In fact, the only thing that happened following the incident was Hadley's trip to the Rascal Harbor Police Department to file a report.

Once he understood the situation, desk sergeant Andy Levesque introduced Hadley to Detective Dick Chambers. A tall, lean man in his middle years, Chambers had been the department's chief, and only, detective for the last three years. He had Maine roots through his mother's birthright, but he'd spent most of his life in Florida. He'd have remained there had a drug bust not gone bad. Chambers took a bullet during the botched raid and he used his recovery time as an occasion to weigh the merits of a warm climate versus life in the high-pressure environment of Florida's drug wars. He decided the temperate climate wasn't worth it. So he left Florida for what he thought would be a saner life as a detective in a small Maine town.

The volume of crime in Rascal Harbor couldn't compare with that in Florida, but life had been far from dull. Though unfamiliar with the term "lobster war," Chambers suspected it was more than a couple one-pounders snapping at each other in a salt-water tank.

Chambers knew the Cooper name because he'd been called out a couple of times to sort through incidents in which the elder Cooper had been involved. Chambers had not known about a younger Cooper until Hadley sat down in a chair in front of the detective's desk. As soon as they began talking, Chambers suspected this man reflected little of his father's jackass ways.

"Why are you here today, Mr. Cooper?" Chambers asked.

"Well, I seem to be having some trouble keeping my traps connected to my buoy lines," Hadley began. With that introduction, he told the story of inheriting his father's boat and gear, getting his license reinstated, and establishing himself as a Rascal Harbor lobsterman.

Chambers took in the narrative and then started exploring possibilities. The two men discussed whether the lines could have been cut accidentally (possibly, but unlikely), whether any of Jensen Cooper's actions were coming back to haunt his son (quite possibly), and whether Hadley had any known or suspected enemies (none that he knew of, but a fair chance of some with a lingering hatred of his father).

With little to go on, Chambers said that he would check around. He advised Hadley to keep his eyes and ears open, but to let Chambers know if anything came up rather than taking matters into his own hands.

"That last request might be a tough one, Detective," Hadley said honestly. "Losing those traps won't bankrupt me, but it puts a dent in my profits."

GEOFFREY SCOTT

"I expect that it does," Chambers said. "But best to work with us rather than pursue it on your own. If your traps really were cut, let us bring the bad guy to justice."

Hadley looked at Chambers a long minute. "You're going to pursue this matter for me? Even knowing who my father was?"

"I'd do it anyway, but you strike me as an all-together different kind of cat than your father." Pausing for a beat, he then said, "I won't make any promises about getting to the bottom of this. You know that fishermen can be a pretty tight-lipped crowd, so I might never be able to prove a case. On the other hand, this could be a simple matter of hazing the new guy. Might never happen again." Pausing again, Chambers continued, "But I do promise that I'll do everything I can to find out who did this and, if I can prove it, I'll see that he or she or they atone for the crime." With that declaration, Hadley stood and the two men shook hands.

Chambers broadened the gender of his pronouns because, even though common usage spoke of "lobstermen" and "fishermen," women increasingly took jobs in the industry. Chambers had met Babette Dubois and knew that a couple other women captained boats and that several served as sternmen. Fishing in general and lobstering in particular called for a tough disposition. If Hadley Cooper's traps were cut by a woman, Chambers expected no easier time in apprehending her than if it had been a man.

Detective Chambers drove over to the Co-op. He planned to talk with Tristan Riggins and Rob Pownall. He expected the former to be already at work and that the latter would be along after his morning chit-chat at Lydia's. Normally, he'd talk to the men separately. Doing so would allow him to compare their stories and see if the differences—there were always differences—might matter. Chambers suspected neither man of involvement, however, and believed that both would want the matter resolved as quickly as possible.

Chambers saw both Pownall and Riggins as soon as he walked into the Co-op office. They all shook hands and went into the conference room. Once settled, Chambers began. "Well, what can you tell me about Hadley Cooper's situation?"

"It's a potential shit storm, is what it is," Tristan began earnestly. "This thing's got the potential to destroy the Co-op."

"How so?" Chambers asked.

"Cutting traps is bad for the guy who lost them, but the ripple effects can be worse, especially if the responsible person isn't caught quickly. The guy wants to retaliate, but if he doesn't know who's to blame then all kinds of rumors start. Then the accusations fly and more traps are cut. These guys live pretty close to the edge financially. A war, especially if it's a long one, can tank some of the marginal guys. Course that's the damage that happens if the trouble stays between the guys who were involved originally. The real trouble occurs is when you get guys using the situation to settle old scores. And then—"

"What do you mean 'settle old scores?'" Chambers asked.

"Well, maybe a guy's been mad at another guy for years, but never dared to act. If a war seems to be starting up, he might decide to settle his grudge. If he acts then, folks might believe it's part of the original scrap rather than him settling some old beef."

"Yup, the guy sees it as an opportunity," Rob added. "He makes his play and it all gets assumed to be part of the original fracas as Tristan says."

"Jesus," Chambers said.

"Jesus was a fisherman, or so they say. But he'd have to do more than walk on water to settle a true lobster war," Tristan said with a wan smile.

"So best to try and wrap this one up fast," Rob said.

"I can see that, though we try to do that anyway," Chambers said.

The three men continued talking. Chambers wanted to hear their perspectives on how the lines might have been cut and why. The first topic took ten minutes; the second took far longer.

"So who should I be looking at?" Chambers asked, leaning toward the view that the buoy lines had been deliberately cut.

Rob said, "That's the hard part. I've been going through all the folks who fish and I can't come up with anyone who would have a particular grudge against Hadley."

Tristan added, "I haven't either. I've worked at places with a nastier bunch of lobstermen. This group is pretty low-key."

"Course you can't rule out someone having an unsettled problem with Hadley's dad, Jensen," Rob noted. "But if you made a list of those folks, it'd be a long one."

"So I understand, but anyone in particular have an ax to grind?" Chambers asked.

Rob said, "Ah, I hate to start throwing names around. Might be perceived in a bad way." Tristan nodded.

"I can understand that," Chambers said appreciatively. "So I guess I'll talk with every lobsterman in the Co-op. That way no one can feel singled out."

"That's a good plan," Tristan said.

"But I could use your help identifying any folks that I should be especially aware of while I'm talking with them."

"That makes sense too," Rob acknowledged. Pausing, he continued. "The fella who Jensen used to ride the most was Francis Dubois. You know Babette, his daughter?" Chambers nodded. "Well, Francis and Jensen got into a couple scrapes, always at Jensen's instigation, mind you. It's possible that Babette could be holding onto some anger." Pausing again, he said, "But one of the first people you ought to talk with is Arnie Draper. Arnie would know all the captains. He's Hadley's brother-in-law so I expect he'd have a good sense if there was any lingering bad feelings against Jensen that could get transferred to his boy."

Tristan said, "That's a good thought, Rob, but when you said that Arnie would know the captains, it made me think that you might need to talk with the sternmen too."

"Oh?" said Chambers.

"Yeah. You'd want to talk with them anyway as they can sometimes see and hear things that the captains don't. But more importantly, there's a bunch of them on the waiting list to get their licenses. I guess it's possible that one or more of them might see trap cutting as a way to move up." Tristan went on to explain the process by which the state distributed lobstering licenses, the fact that the demand exceeded the supply, and the tensions created by a long waiting list.

"Guess I better get to it," Chambers said.

"Don't envy you on this one," Rob said shaking his head. "But Tristan and I will do anything we can to help. We need this resolved."

CHAPTER 30

O n the way to his brother Mark's house for the monthly family gathering, John McTavish had a tumble of thoughts in his head.

At 55, McTavish was the oldest of Nadine and Malcolm's children. Five years younger was brother Mark, a computer salesman, followed closely in age by sister Ruth, a bookkeeper. Close in age mattered little between these two on the physical front—Mark's fleshy body doubled the size of the too-thin frame of his nearest sibling. On the emotional front, the two differed as well—Ruth was the worrier and Mark was the jokester. Giselle, the fourth of the McTavish children, resembled her brother John in looks and matched his temperament. Tall and lean of feature, these two siblings listened more than they talked and tended toward the ironic. Like John, Giselle had also spent time outside the state, though hers was a wandering journey of self-searching while he had gone directly to his mid-western college job. The one McTavish missing was the youngest brother, Daniel. Like Giselle, Danny had left Maine for college; like John he had stayed away. The best tempered and best looking of the siblings, Danny lived and prospered around the financial markets of Chicago.

For some reason Giselle's and Danny's out-of-state travels bothered the home-bound Mark and Ruth far less than that of their oldest brother. They adored Maggie and Noah, but they made sure that McTavish knew himself to be a scoundrel for leaving his home state. Fewer jibes came his way over the year since he returned. But fewer is not none, and so one of McTavish's tumbling thoughts centered on whether or not to ignore any barbs directed at him during this get together.

Another issue was the fact that Noah and Noah's girlfriend, Louise Park, were in the car with him. Noah arranged his summer job schedule at Lane's Wharf so that he could attend. Because it was Saturday and her regular day off, Louise had been able to go as well. Noah seemed to enjoy the last lunch gathering at Giselle's place and told his father he looked forward to this one. "I like the stories that they tell about you," Noah had said.

With Noah and Louise in attendance, McTavish figured less attention would come his way. He would get some as Mark and Ruth were still fascinated with his involvement in the theft of the Winslow Homer painting and the unfortunate events with Caleb Knight earlier in the spring. Still it should be easy to distract them with Noah and Louise.

Mark, his wife Amy, and their children lived in a suburb of Portland. Mark's work kept him on the roads around New England, still he made efforts to be home every night. "Can't rest until I'm in the bosom of my family," he said during one family luncheon.

Giselle said, "You get any fatter, you'll have bosoms bigger than mine."

"Said by a woman whose training bra just gave up!" Mark said with a laugh.

Ruth's head snapped up. "All right you two there are children around."

"Children who don't know what boobs are?" Mark asked in mock seriousness, but then held up his hands in surrender when Ruth's eyes flashed. He winked at Giselle who slyly gave him the finger.

And we're off, McTavish remembered thinking at the time.

This encounter and a dozen others crowded McTavish's thoughts as he turned onto Mark's suburban street.

Predictably, the clan surrounded Noah and Louise. Noah looked a little abashed; Louise handled the attention with grace and ease.

"And here we go," McTavish said to himself as he hugged Giselle and shook hands with her partner, Martin Mayberry.

"Nice move, brother, bringing along fresh meat," Giselle said quietly in McTavish's ear. McTavish pretended not to understand. Giselle punched him in the side.

"Don't think you're going to get out of here unscathed. I overheard Mark and Amy talking about how you 'need to find a friend,'" Giselle said.

"Damn."

"Fairly warned, brother," Giselle said and shrugged her way off to greet Noah and Louise. With a vague sense of dread, McTavish wandered around Mark and Amy's backyard greeting the rest of the assembled group.

Mark and Amy had rented a large tent, tables, and chairs so that the group could eat together and in comfort should the weather turn. Always the genial and giving host, Mark made sure that the tables sighed with food and drink.

As everyone found seats, McTavish saw that Louise looked as fresh as when he and Noah had picked her up that morning. Noah, by contrast, looked like he'd been through the wringer. The interrogation had been relentless as the who, what, when, where, how, and why of Louise and Noah proceeded. "Get used to it, son," McTavish said to himself.

With a dozen or so people of various ages and interests sitting around a large table, conversations proceeded along multiple lines. Mark and Amy's children prattled on about the latest iPhone with Ruth and her husband Ron's kids. Giselle, Ruth, and Amy thought of a few more questions to ask Louise. Mark, Martin, and Ron discussed the merits of Mark's new chop saw. Noah and McTavish talked quietly about running the family gauntlet.

"Wow, they can be pretty intense," Noah said.

"They can indeed, but they're that way because they love you. If they didn't, you'd know that too."

"Jesus, Mainers are pretty weird," Noah said softly. "The Indiana folks I grew up around just seemed so much more open and direct. You didn't have to guess what they thought about you."

"Yeah, but there's no challenge in that," McTavish said with a wink.

"Ayuh," Noah said in a weak Maine accent. "Guess you're right, mister man!"

Breaking off from his conversation, Mark boomed, "What're you two mid-westerners gabbing on about?" When neither father nor son spoke, Mark continued. "Well, I for one am glad to see that one of you has the sense to hook up with a decent Maine girl." Laughing with the others, Mark turned to Louise, "I give you credit, girl, for hanging around with these out-a-staters."

"Oh, they aren't so bad," Louise said with a smile. "Once they lose all trace of that Indiana accent and learn how to pahk the cah in the dooryahd…." This last part she said in her thickest Downeast accent. Everyone laughed.

Noah said, "It's true. I've been practicing, but….I do think I'm making some progress on putting that lost 'r' where it belongs—at the end of words ending in 'a' like pizza and Augusta." All nodded and giggled as Noah pronounced these words in true Maine fashion as "pizzer" and "Auguster."

The talk about Maine pronunciations quickly led to a free-for-all around unique Maine words and phrases: "ankle bitah"—small child, "beatah"—an old car, "cunnin"—cute or adorable, "finest kind"—very good, "gawmy"—awkward, "kife"—to steal, "right out straight"—very busy, "unthaw"—thaw, "wicked"—very, and "chupta"— what are you up to? and Maine expressions: "colder than a witch's tit"—damn cold, "since Moses wore knee-pants"—a long time ago, and "round Robin Hood's barn"—out of the way.

As the laughter ebbed, Mark turned to McTavish and said, "So what's the deal-e-o, big brother? Your son's found someone to hug. What about you?"

Ruth immediately said, "Mark! Stop your foolishness! John will find someone when he's good and ready." She offered McTavish a kind and knowing look.

"It's okay, Ruth. Seems like my personal life has become a topic of conversation wherever I go lately."

Mark said, "See, Ruth, I'm not the only one interested. Plus, I bet there's a line outside old John's front door."

"Not at this point," McTavish said, a little sharper than he'd intended. "But if one develops, you'll be the first one to know." McTavish hoped that this response would move his brother and the rest of the group onto a different topic.

Sensing the need to push past this awkward moment, Giselle said to the children, "Suppose Uncle Mark's got any cake laying around here or do you think he ate it all?" Their cheers signaled an end to the main meal and the move to dessert.

Though he wasn't a man to anger easily, McTavish now found himself in a stew. Probably could have handled that better, he thought to himself as he sat for a few minutes before getting up from the table and heading to the bathroom.

Taking a circuitous route, McTavish heard Maggie say, "You could have, John. But Mark's always been a nitwit. And this time, he's even managed to get on Ruth's bad side." McTavish thought Maggie right, though he had a stronger word than "nitwit" in mind for his brother.

As annoyed as he was with Mark, however, McTavish felt more annoyed with himself for not heeding Giselle's warning and preparing for the inevitable. Of course, Mark would push him, that's what he did. Introducing Louise to the family provided a perfect opportunity for Mark to ask about McTavish's relationship future. I've got to figure out some sort of a better response, he thought, hoping that Maggie might jump in with a suggestion. She didn't.

McTavish dawdled on his return to the table. He didn't understand Maggie's visits. He realized that they had come less frequently over the last month or so. He also realized that they never came in the midst of a truly anxious moment: In the times when he most needed her guidance, she remained mum. That absence angered him in the past, but now he wondered what it might mean.

Maggie had not a single mean bone in her body so not coming to his aid during tough times represented no vindictive impulse. Nor did Maggie play games. She wouldn't go silent to test her husband or to make him realize how much he needed her. Whatever the reason, he felt it lay just beyond his consciousness. Better give it some more thought, he resolved.

When he returned to the luncheon, the conversation had moved beyond McTavish's love life. Mark was playing the fool with the kids while Ruth tsk-tsked, but did so with a smile on her face. Martin talked with Ron and Amy about a house renovation he and Giselle had coming up. Noah and Louise walked along the back property line, holding hands and whispering.

Giselle sidled up to McTavish and gave him a big hug. "You'll get better at this human being stuff, big brother," she said softly. "I think—"

"Not a bet I would want to make," McTavish sighed. "I miss her, Giselle, somedays more than others, but I miss her."

"Maggie was a peach, John. You have every right in the world to miss her, but I can't see her wanting you to mope around."

"I'm not moping," McTavish said defensively.

"Yes, you are, John. I can see it, Noah can see it, even our dumbass brother can see it," Giselle said firmly. Pausing a beat she continued. "Look, no one expects you to run out and start jumping every woman you see—not even Mark wants that. Everyone grieves differently and you have the right to do it as you see fit. All anyone is saying, really, is to let yourself be open to the possibility that someone might come along who sparks you up."

Brother and sister looked at each other a long moment. Eventually, McTavish closed his eyes and nodded. When he opened them, he saw Giselle nodding and smiling. "We'll make a real human being of you yet, John McTavish."

GEOFFREY SCOTT

As they walked back to the group, McTavish and his sister could see smiles and hear laughter. "Wish the folks were still around to see this," Giselle said.

"We do have our moments," McTavish said and gave his sister a hug.

CHAPTER 31

On the drive back to the cottage, McTavish, Noah, and Louise debriefed their experiences with the family. Aside from the rough spot around McTavish's personal life, it had been a pretty good day.

Noah wondered what Louise thought of Uncle Mark. He liked his uncle generally, but felt that Mark had come on too strong today. And he was embarrassed for his father when Mark refused to let go of McTavish's love life.

"Jesus, Mark's a puppy dog compared to some of the uncles I've got," Louise said. Then, looking directly at Noah, she said, "Those guys have no boundaries at all. And they're some of the worst gossips I've ever met. My dad and I call them 'the Hen Club.' Course my mom thinks we're saying 'the Ben club' and then wants to know why since none of them are named 'Ben.'"

"Gossiping is bad enough, but Uncle Mark is just so loud and obnoxious sometimes. And once he thinks he's on something, he doesn't let go," Noah said.

"Noah," Louise said directly. "My Uncle Jacques has farted continuously for the last seven years. The doctors can't figure out why he's got so much gas or how to help him. So he toots his way around every family gathering. Most of the time, he ignores it, but when he lets go of a particularly loud one, he said, 'Sacre bleu, dar she blow!' Tell me that's not more embarrassing than your Uncle Mark!"

"Ah, you might have us there," Noah said with relief.

"What do you think?" Louise asked John. "Was this a typical meeting of the clan?"

"Pretty much so," McTavish said. "There's always too much food. Ruth always expresses a worry about something. And though Mark's target varies, it's usually Giselle or me."

"Giselle got him a good one with her bosoms comment," Louise said. Both McTavish men smiled and nodded.

Noah said, "Speaking of Aunt Ruth and worries, I heard Aunt Amy pressing her about going to the doctor. I couldn't tell what Amy thought was wrong, but she seemed pretty intent that Ruth needed to be seen."

"Hmm. Amy doesn't usually interfere, so it must be something. I'll give it a day or two and then email Ruth," McTavish said.

"You mean you'll call her, right, Dad? On the telephone? A real conversation, right?"

"Ah, yes, I suppose that's exactly what I'll do," McTavish said sheepishly.

After they dropped Louise off at her house, McTavish and Noah drove quietly back to the cottage. They unloaded the car and put away the remainders of the food and drink they had contributed to the meal. McTavish poured them each a couple fingers of Bushmills and they sat in the kitchen rockers.

"I saw you go off somewhere in your head, Dad. You know, after you and Uncle Mark had your little thing. Were you talking with Mom?"

"Not so much then, but when I went to the bathroom she certainly filled my ear."

Though he knew that Noah was aware of these conversations with his now-dead wife, McTavish felt uncomfortable talking about them.

Part of his discomfort came from the fact that he'd always been a skeptic of paranormal phenomenon. He didn't know what to think about this communication with Maggie; he just knew that he didn't want to give it up. A bigger part of his uneasiness, however, was a question Noah had asked him a few weeks ago. Apparently Maggie did not speak to Noah and the boy was hurt to know that she did so with his father. "Would you ask her to come to me?" Noah had asked. At the time, McTavish had said yes. He had yet to do so and he didn't know why.

"What did she say?"

"She just reminded me that Mark can be a nitwit and not to let him get to me."

"I thought she liked Uncle Mark."

"She did. Actually she's always liked him more than I did. She didn't like his bluster or the idea that he couldn't get over the fact that I'd left the state. But she saw below all of that, and what she saw was a kind-hearted guy to whom family means everything."

"Huh. I guess I can see that," Noah said. The two men rocked and drank in silence for a few minutes.

"So, did you ask her?" Noah asked hesitantly. Then he added, "And please don't tell me you don't know what I'm talking about."

Silence filled the space between them.

"Did you ask her?"

McTavish stopped rocking and sighed. "No, I haven't. I'm not sure I know why I haven't. But I haven't." Seeing the disappointment rise across his son's face, McTavish added, "Maybe I haven't been all that clear about what 'talking' with your mother means." He took a sip of whiskey. "It's not like we have conversations, you know back and forth dialogue. It's, well, it's more like she sees my thoughts and actions and she comments on them. She talks to me...hmm. I don't know, Noah, maybe I was wrong to imply that we 'talk.'"

Uncomprehending, Noah looked hard at his father. "But you said... I asked you if you still talked with her. And you said 'yes,' you said, 'yes, I do.' Were you lying?"

GEOFFREY SCOTT

McTavish hesitated before answering. "No, I wasn't lying to you, Noah. I can hear your mother and she tells me things. I guess that's talking, but it's not like, well, it's not like we discuss situations and events. I don't really know what it is or how to describe it because I never know when it's going to happen. In fact, when I most want to hear to from her—when I try to hear from her—she goes silent."

"I don't understand any of this," Noah said, his anger rising. "You talk with her, you don't talk with her, she comes to you, she doesn't come to you? What the hell, Dad?"

"I'm sorry, son. Maybe I shouldn't have told you. I certainly shouldn't have promised you that I'd ask her to come to you," McTavish said weakly.

"But you did. And now it feels like you're keeping her all to yourself. And that's just not fair, Dad. It's just not fair!" Noah got up from his chair, put on his coat, and walked out of the cottage.

"Goddamn it, Maggie!" McTavish heard himself say. "You know that Noah wants to hear from you. Why in hell won't you speak to him?" Only silence followed.

CHAPTER 32

McTavish sat in his rocker for a long time. Though he tried, his efforts to conjure Maggie to his conscious mind failed. After twenty minutes, he said to Maggie, "Well, fine, I'm just going to sit here until you answer the question!"

Five minutes later, Jimmy Park came through the kitchen door. Gary and Ruby Park's youngest child, Jimmy was a gifted artist. Nearly finished with his fine arts degree at the University of Southern Maine, he now spent most of his time in the Portland area after being falsely accused of stealing a Winslow Homer watercolor. Other than Noah, Jimmy was probably the only person who could pull McTavish out of a funk.

"How's it going, John? Have you recovered from my mother's assessment of your artwork?" Though he tried to keep the smile out of his voice, McTavish gave in and found himself grinning.

"Well, I haven't quit working, but I'll admit to having had a few doubts about my career path."

"Ah, you can't let that cartoon thing get to you. Mom says all kinds of weird shit."

McTavish nodded. "Well, as I said, I haven't quit working…but I haven't picked up those markers again either."

"Good. It's time you opened up your paint box. You've served your drawing apprenticeship. Time to put some real color back into your work," Jimmy said with a smile. After a pause, he said, "But actually I was wondering what you thought about the mess around the Arvin Prize."

"I'm not sure what you mean," McTavish said.

"Ah, right. You're still hanging out at the fringes of the Colony doings, I guess. I'm not as plugged in as I used to be, but even I've heard that the board voted to change the rules so that non-residents can have their work considered."

"Really? That's a pretty big change."

"Yup. And a fair number of people are up in arms."

"I'd imagine so," McTavish said. "I mean I can see why local artists might be upset if they think that outsiders could come in to win the Prize." After a pause, he continued. "Still, it would increase the competition and probably improve the quality of the work."

"Those are the main arguments people are making, along with a dozen others. I'm really surprised that you haven't heard anything. There's starting to be some talk about voting out the board and dumping Robertay as president. From what I hear, it was mostly her idea and the board vote was actually split. So the folks who hate Robertay are sharpening their knives."

"It's always hard to know what artists will get upset about, but I guess I'm not too surprised that this move would get some of their backs up. I wonder if anyone else will submit cartoons…?" Both men laughed, though Jimmy's laugh was stronger than McTavish's.

"Dad's worried that it's gonna have a ripple effect across town. The talk is all about locals versus outsiders. Guess there's even some thought being given to changing the property tax rates."

"The property tax rates? What's that got to do with the Colony?"

"There are some people saying that the summer folks who own property ought to pay a higher rate than the locals. Guess it's a new thing people are talking about up and down the coast."

"I thought residents already had a homestead exemption. I mean, it's not much—a couple hundred dollars off your property taxes."

ISLANDS AND BRIDGES

"Yeah, Dad said something about that. If I understand it right, this would be an extra tax on second homes or summer homes or ocean-front homes. I'm not really sure. Just that some locals think the out-of-staters ought to pay more."

"Jesus. Maybe we just ought to stop every car with an out-of-state license plate as soon as they enter the state and make them pay an entrance fee."

"That would raise some dough all right," Jimmy said. "Dad's worried that if we jack up taxes and such on the out-a-towners that they'll start looking for somewhere else to go and then we'll be in a helluva fix. I can see his point—tourists' dollars pay the bills around here. Still, the property values and the taxes are driving out a lot of local folks. Anyway, it'll make for an interesting town meeting later this spring."

"It will at that," McTavish said. "That's if the town hasn't torn itself apart with all this resident-non-resident animosity."

The two men were considering this possibility when Noah returned. He walked into the kitchen and saw Jimmy and his father in mid-conversation. Before either could greet him, Noah stared at them, shook his head, and then walked upstairs without a word.

Jimmy looked at McTavish. The latter shrugged and mouthed, "He's upset with me." Jimmy nodded and motioned that he would take his cue and leave.

Aloud, Jimmy said, "Well, if you hear anything else about the Arvin Prize problem, let me know. You know I miss the Colony gossip."

"Apparently you don't miss all of it," McTavish said, then added, "But I'll let you know if I hear anything."

After showing his guest out, McTavish returned to his rocking chair. He could hear Noah rustling around upstairs, making more noise than normal. "I guess he's trying to tell me he's mad," McTavish said to himself. He decided not to confront Noah, choosing instead to do some work at his art table.

Later, McTavish made a light supper of steak and coleslaw. Though neither McTavish favored the kinds of green salads Maggie had, they both liked coleslaw. As he was making the slaw, McTavish smiled. His brother Mark also loved the creamy mixture and had extolled its virtues at the last family luncheon held at Giselle and Martin's place.

"The cabbage, the carrots, and that velvety dressing, all mix together in pure delight," Mark had proclaimed.

"They all mix together in your belly and then it's gas city!" Amy had said.

"Yeah, watch out after Dad eats coleslaw," one of his children yelled out. "You could light a fire!"

"Now, now," Mark said, looking around the group. "I'll admit there's a small price to pay, but you gotta admit, all that fiber's good for the pooper!"

Grinning as everyone gagged, groaned, or swore under their breath, Mark farted loudly and said, "Let the coleslaw reign!"

Since then, every time McTavish and Noah had had coleslaw, they had clinked their forks and declared, "Let the coleslaw reign!"

The smell of the frying steak brought Noah downstairs as McTavish got out the dishes and silverware for the meal. Wordlessly, Noah picked them up, set the table, and poured glasses of water for each of them.

Sitting down to eat, Noah filled his plate with steak and coleslaw and waited while his father did the same. With a wan smile, he held up his fork for his father to clink. Each said, "Let the coleslaw reign!"

After their toast, the two McTavish men talked quietly about the change in the Arvin Prize rules. Noah had not heard much more than McTavish had so they worked through the likely pros and cons. As they began cleaning up the dishes, McTavish thought, if coleslaw can help an upset boy talk with his father, it really does reign.

CHAPTER 33

A lot of chewing goes on in a small town diner. About half the chewing involves the ingestion and digestion of food; the other half follows the same process, but the intake is gossip.

Small town gossips count themselves lucky when one meaty topic surfaces. They go a bit crazed when the number doubles. The back-table crowd at Lydia's had plenty to chew on regarding the Arvin Prize controversy. The addition of Hadley Cooper's cut trap lines added some extra spice.

Hadley Cooper's problems were topic number one at the men's table. With Rob Pownall as president of the Co-op board, his table-mates expected fresh and unfiltered news. Trudy had not even poured Rob's first cup of coffee when the questions and comments started.

"Think it'll be a war?"

"Seen any retaliation yet?"

"Is Hadley sure it weren't a whale that cut his lines? Or maybe a dolphin or one of them new type a submarines?"

"Anybody see where Babette was when the lines was cut?"

"Don't imagine it was one of them Patch boys, do ya?"

"Could be anybody, I s'pose, Jensen being the dick that he was."

"Or maybe it was some out-a-state yahoo speedin' around in his Cris-Craft and his prop cut them lines."

Rob tried addressing each submission in turn. No, he didn't think there would be a war as Hadley was a cool-headed man. No, he hadn't seen any evidence of retaliation. But then the questions came too fast and he decided to just wait them out. The boys weren't listening anyway. Rob had seen it before: Once something got stuck in their craw, they had to jump all over it for a while before a rational discussion could ensue.

At the ladies' table, the Arvin Prize mess took center stage and the discussion was already at the rational stage. The new bit, offered by Geraldine Smythe, was that at least one group of artists was considering a protest against the decision.

"What I heard is that a bunch of parallel, no, pastel artists met over at someone's house on Harbor Point. And they were pretty hot."

"Harbor Point? I thought those were all summer places," June Pickering said.

"Guess most of 'em are, but at least one of them is winterized now and the owners are living there year round," Geraldine said.

"Year round, 'cept during the winter, I bet," added Minerva Williams. "Them summer birds get a little taste a the cold and they motor on south."

"I don't know about that," Geraldine continued. "But the artist, Janice something, lives here now. She's some mad and I hear she's holding meetings to stir up a buncha the others."

June said, "Well, good for her. Somebody needs to stand up for the local folks."

"Weird that it's a newbie who's doing it," Karen Tompkins said.

"Well, she might be a newbie, but now she'll qualify for the Prize competition where she couldna before," Minerva said.

"You're right about that," Maude Anderson said.

"And if she's stirring up a shit storm for Robertay, then she's okay by me."

"You might get your wish this time, Minerva, I heard that there's something in the bylaws about special meetings and even a recall of the board members," Geraldine said.

"I recall that Robertay Harding's a first-class bitch!"

"She may be, but that doesn't mean that she's wrong about this decision to expand the competition. I mean, why wouldn't we want to see more folks coming to town. Plus, like Geraldine said last time, this would be a chance to get a leg up on the Herrington Festival," Karen said.

"Maybe so, but if it brings in that many tourists, how are we gonna get around town? Traffic and parkin' is already a nightmare most of the summer," June said.

"Yes, but more tourist dollars means more money for new parking spots and everything else," Karen said.

"True enough, but Jesus, ain't enough, enough? I wish to hell we could get our town back from all these damn newbies and day trippers and tour buses—"

"Well, we could if we wanted to roll up the sidewalks and close for business. The days of Maine for Mainers only are long gone. Farming and forestry are both drying up inland and fishing's been going up and down, but most down, here on the coast. If we don't have the tourist trade, all we've got to go on are our good looks," Geraldine said.

"Christ, that'd mean some of us would starve to death!"

"True enough," Minerva said, "though I don't eat much more than bird feed now, what with the little Social Security check I get." The ladies all nodded at the truth of that statement. "Well, if they got to be around, then maybe we oughta squeeze 'em a little more."

"Squeeze who?" Maude asked.

"The summer folk, Maudie! Jesus, keep up, girl!"

"All right, Minerva," Geraldine said sternly. Then she asked, "Squeeze them how?"

"Tax 'em higher on their lah-di-dah cottages, charge 'em an admission fee, I don't know, but something. If they're gonna be here annoying everybody, then they oughta pay for the privilege," Minerva said. June and Maude nodded in agreement.

"You've got to be careful with that strategy though," Karen said quietly. "You tax the golden goose too much and she'll lay her eggs elsewhere."

"Well, if she's layin' any around here now, I ain't seen any of 'em," Minerva said.

"Who's Minerva layin' now?" Bill Candlewith asked. Bill had been leaning his chair toward the ladies' table since hearing Robertay Harding's name.

"What's it to you, you old skunk?" Minerva yelled. "Ain't nobody laid herself down in front of you in a dozen years and then it was that old skank, Ginger Down, who'd lay with a corpse if it had a five dollar bill in its pocket."

"Jesus, Minerva," Geraldine said.

"Oh, you know it's true," Minerva replied. Then snapping her fingers, she said, "Jesus, there's a way to way to make some money for the town! Set up a booth down on the shore and charge the out-a-staters a buck to walk by and see Bill and Ginger goin' at it. Could call it 'The Rocky Coast of Maine Horror Show!'"

The ladies, even Maude, erupted in laughter. Realizing he'd been beat, Bill slunk back to his table.

The men were still jawing about Hadley Cooper and the possibility of a lobster war. They had yet to get to the Arvin Prize controversy. The ladies, however, had work to do, grandchildren to tend, and errands to run. They'd pick up the lobster war topic tomorrow, along with Minerva's ingenious plan to raise revenue for the town.

CHAPTER 34

The Arvin Prize controversy may have competed for attention with the Hadley Cooper incident at Lydia's. It didn't at the Rascal Harbor Art Colony gallery. There, the dispute over changing the eligibility rules for the Prize defined the conversation.

In another emergency meeting, the board members sat, worried about the possibility that the Colony could spin out of control. Robertay sat at the head of the table, doing a slow burn. She had neither called this meeting nor did she think it necessary. Her colleagues disagreed. They had demanded the meeting and they would have their say.

Jona Lewis started the discussion. "Robertay, I know you don't think we need to meet, but Toni, Regina, and I do." As Robertay cut her eyes toward Regina, who she had considered an ally, Jona continued. "Yes, even Regina agreed. This decision is creating all kinds of rifts among the Colony members and we think we need to take the concerns seriously."

"It's true, Robertay," Regina Baldo said in an uneasy tone. "Of course, not all of the reaction is against the decision. In fact, I've talked with a number of artists who are supportive. But there are enough who are upset that we need to think about how to proceed."

Pointedly ignoring Regina, Robertay fixed her eyes and her words on Jona and Toni Ludlow. "You are correct that I do not see a need for a special meeting when I could be painting. Moreover, you're all acting like

GEOFFREY SCOTT

the Colony is going to dissolve over this change. I'm not sure if you're just nervous Nellies or if you're actively trying to subvert a decision that was made by majority rule right here in this room." Still focused on Jona and Toni, Robertay continued. "Regardless, I will not stand for an insurrection within our own midst. We have too much work to do to be pulled into pointless meetings about an imaginary threat."

Toni said, "It's not imaginary, Robertay. Like Regina, I've heard from some folks who are supportive. But I've also heard from enough who are disgruntled to know that we can't just ignore the issue."

Jona leaned forward. "People are meeting in small groups and—"

"And so what?" Robertay said, leaning forward too. "Who cares if they have their little meetings. In the end, it will all blow over... because it always does." She took a deep breath. "Look, I know that change can be hard, but I also know that people can and will adapt to new conditions. They'll whine and grouse and complain along the way, but they'll adapt. And, in the end, the whole group will be stronger as a result." After another long breath, she continued. "Believe me, I have given this move considerable thought. And I have concluded that it is a move integral to the Colony's survival and prosperity."

"The Colony is surviving and prospering now," Toni said. "This decision, however, is driving a wedge between people. It might be a good thing to do—to allow non-residents to participate—but doing it this way, by fiat, well, it seems to be sowing some bad seed."

"And if those bad seed sprout into something like open rebellion," Jona said, "then the Summer Exhibition and the Colony are at risk. Look, right now, we're only a day or so into this thing. Before we do a whole lot of work and spend a lot of money promoting the change and get a whole lot more members riled up, then we ought to be sure that it's going to happen, that it's worth doing."

"Oh, it's worth doing and it's going to happen," Robertay said firmly.

Toni frowned. "There's talk about calling for a whole Colony meeting and even a recall of the board. I found my copy of the bylaws and saw that both things are possible." She hesitated. "Look I don't know what to do, but I think we ought to come up with some options. If we're proactive, maybe we can head off the worst-case scenarios."

"It would seem prudent to think and talk it all through," Regina said.

"What all of you need to think through is doing the jobs to which you've been assigned," Robertay said calmly, but with an edge to her voice. "We can and we will make this event a success and then we can all celebrate together, even the doubters." She swept her eyes over Toni and Jona, but keyed in on Regina who looked abashed, but said nothing.

With that, Robertay rose and said, "This meeting is adjourned. Come on, Thomas, we need to get some painting done before we waste the whole day." Without a word, Thomas rose and walked out with Robertay.

Toni, Jona, and Regina sat back in their chairs and wondered what had happened. No one had expected Robertay to take such a hard line.

"Is she just blind to what's happening?" Jona asked.

Regina shook her head. "She's very determined to see this through."

"No doubt about that. I just hope it doesn't bring down the Colony," Toni said.

After the three board members left the conference room. Larry Court tidied up the room. As he did so, he ran through the list of people he would tell about the nature of this meeting. Minerva Williams would not be at the top of that list. Larry liked Minerva, but she'd not seemed sufficiently grateful for the first bit of news. He could get her back by planting the story with a few others who would then pass it on to Minerva. Gossip of any kind was small town gold, but the value rose the closer one got to the source. Minerva would be ticked to learn about this meeting second or third hand.

More than one way to skin an old bat, Larry thought to himself and chuckled.

CHAPTER 35

After giving his report to Detective Chambers, Hadley Cooper went out to check his traps. He motored around to all his sets and was relieved to see all his buoys and traps attached to them in place. With the meeting at the police station and this survey of his equipment, Hadley chewed up a good chunk of the day so he didn't get to haul his normal number of pots.

I'm losing in two ways, he thought, those six lost traps will cost me as will the traps I'm not gonna get pulled today. He sighed and hoped that the following day would be better.

It was. The day dawned clear and crisp, a lovely spring day. Hadley started an hour earlier than normal in hopes of getting back on schedule and picking up his fifty traps per day. By five PM, he'd almost made it. Moreover, the haul was a good one, with most every trap having a lobster or two in them. Better yet, most were "keepers."

In order to keep a lobster, fishermen measured the back plate, from the eye socket to the beginning of the tail. Keepers measured between three and a quarter and five inches in length. Lobsters with shorter and longer back plates go back to the sea.

Fishermen also check to see if the bugs they haul are male or female. On those egg-bearing females, fishermen must cut a V-shaped notch in the second tail flipper from the right. Doing so marks them as breeders. By law, V-notched lobsters, whether they are "berried" or not, have to be returned to the sea.

Hadley's traps that day had a few berried bugs, a few more unberried V-notched, and yet a few more undersized "shorts." Still, it was a decent haul. He'd likely have had a very good pay day were it not for those six traps that continued fishing but without buoy and pot warps to pull them aboard.

Because he had gotten an early start, Hadley hadn't seen any of the other Harbor lobstermen that morning. Because he'd worked all day to catch up on his schedule, he got back to the Co-op late enough that few were around then. All of this was fine; he really didn't want to talk with anyone about his lost traps.

When he pulled into the dock, he saw Detective Chambers standing by a piling.

"When you get a minute, Hadley, let's have a chat. Come on over to the station when you're ready."

Hadley nodded and went about the business of unloading his catch, hosing down his boat, and stowing his gear. He then motored out to his mooring, tied up, and rowed back to the dock in his dinghy. He considered grabbing a sandwich as it had been a long day, but thought it best not to keep Chambers waiting.

Sergeant Andy Levesque was packing up his things when Hadley walked into the police station. They'd known each other in school, so greeted each other warmly. "Sorry to hear about your traps," Levesque said as he directed Hadley to Chambers's office and then left for the day.

Chambers and Cooper exchanged a few words about how the day's catch had gone and the latter confirmed that no more damage had been done to his gear.

"I wanted to talk with you about what I've learned so far," Chambers said. "I wish I could tell you that I've got the culprit in chains, but I can't. I talked with most of the fishermen and several of the Co-op staff."

Hadley nodded, but stayed quiet.

"You work with a bunch of pretty close-mouthed folks," Chambers continued. "Got mostly grunts and one-word answers from your

GEOFFREY SCOTT

peers until I asked about your father. Then I got an earful. None of it was all that helpful, but all of it was colorful."

"I could have predicted that. Did any of it connect back to me?"

"That's the thing that I couldn't quite shake out. Some folks are still pretty angry at your father, but I didn't get a strong sense that they blamed you. I want to keep pushing that angle though. The reactions I got were strong enough that it wouldn't surprise me to learn of a grudge or two that could surface in the form of a sharp knife.

"I'm going to catch up with the rest of the lobstermen tomorrow and then talk with their sternmen. I'm especially interested in talking to the folks who are close to the top of the line to get a license. I understand that driving you out would open up a spot and I hear some guys have been waiting quite a while. Could prove to be a powerful motive to cut trap lines."

"That it could. Anything I can or should do?"

"I don't think so. Common sense says to keep your eyes and ears open so if anything tweaks your sensibilities, let me know."

"I can do that, though I've been keeping a low profile up to this point anyway."

"Then don't change your behavior. People are going to be watching you, trying to see how you'll react. If you don't give them anything to react to, then they'll go back to their regular behaviors and then something might slip. Meanwhile, I'll keep pushing and hoping to create that slip."

"Okay," Hadley said softly.

"One more thing. You seem like a sensible guy, not a hot head like some of the guys I talked to today. But I want you to promise me that you'll come straight to me if you suspect anyone. Don't take on whoever it is by yourself. If you're wrong, you'll be the one landing in jail and, even if you're right, you might do something that will hurt your cause." Chambers stared at Hadley. "You understand what I'm saying, don't you?"

"Yeah, I do," Hadley muttered. "We done?"

"We're done."

But the trap cutting was not done. After hauling, cleaning, baiting, and resetting her first twenty-five traps the next day, Babette Dubois discovered that buoys marking her next three strings were gone.

"That fuckin' Hadley Cooper!" she shouted.

CHAPTER 36

In this week's issue of the Rascal Harbor Gazette, the twin controversies over trap cutting and art prizes featured prominently. Also featured was a new column by Toulouse Rustin, Nellie Hildreth's nephew and presumptive heir to the publisher's chair. Opinions are never in small supply in coastal Maine towns. With this issue of the Gazette, opinions ruled.

The letters to the editor section covered both topics and did so in a way that showed a consensus had yet to form on either issue. Hadley Cooper's cut buoy lines generated fewer letters than did the Arvin Prize controversy, but the diversity of points raised was just as considerable:

> To the Editor: I know the guys (and gals) at the Co-op and I can't believe any of them would be involved in cutting trap lines. They're good folks, hard-working folks, and they wouldn't take out their frustrations in that kind of way. It's got to be someone from outside, probably from Massachusetts!
>
> Lenny Cliff
>
> To the Editor: Please good fishermen of Rascal Har-

bor, do not let this incident around Mr. Cooper's lobster traps escalate into a civil war! Our town need not send signals to our summer visitors that we are at odds with one another.

Jennifer Lyndon

To the Editor: What is wrong with people? Cutting buoy lines just creates bad feelings all around. Stop it already! Think of what your mothers would say!

Lorraine Henderson

To the Editor: I can't imagine what sort of grudge would induce one person to harm another person's livelihood, but I expect our ready police force under the skillful leadership of Chief Miles will get to the bottom of it!!!

Mae Parton

Jerry Glenville went the short and sweet route: "Cutting trap lines? Pathetic!"

Though all the letter writers expressed concern about the trap cutting, questions about who was responsible, what effect it might have, and how it might be resolved were all points of contention.

The number of issues raised and opinions on those issues was even greater around the Arvin Prize dispute. Writers split over the same who, what, and how questions their trap-cutting-focused peers generated, but those interested in the Arvin controversy found more angles within each.

The question of who was responsible for the dispute focused on Robertay Harding individually—though without direct use of her name, Robertay and the executive board—again with no names attached, summer-time artists who had been excluded—referred to as "summer complaints," "summarians," and "touristas," and, according to Thurston Ring, the Russians.

The question of the lasting effect ranged from none—"Who gives a good g-d about art anyway?"—to some—"This thing will blow up and then blow over"—to major—"I can see the Colony collapsing"—to catastrophic—"The tourist trade will be destroyed!"

Views also varied on how the matter might be resolved—"Fire that Colony president," "Fire the whole Colony board," "Change the decision back, then fire everyone," "Learn to live with the decision," "Embrace the decision," "Stop belly aching about stuff that don't matter."

Other writers tried to offer solutions that would allow for the participation of both residents and non-residents. Alan Tuttle suggested that a lottery system could work where a small number of non-residents were randomly selected to participate in the Prize competition. Rodney Glazer wondered about the potential of reserving the Arvin for the locals, but scheduling a second competition for out-of-staters. Brandon Majors offered the idea that summer folks with property might participate, but those with no standing commitment to the town be restricted. And Vance Edwards said that, although he favored the idea, he thought that the decision ought to be put off for a year.

Although the letters section revealed a range of perspectives on the Arvin Prize issue, a new voice came down firmly on the side of maintaining the status quo. Toulouse Rustin, Nellie Hildreth's nephew submitted his first column under the banner, "Maine from the Outside In."

Raised in Boston by parents who left Maine soon after marrying, Toulouse knew Rascal Harbor as a summer resident. A product of New England prep schools, he spent his summers writing poetry and sailing, socializing, and sporting with other summer kids. Now in his mid-forties, Toulouse had decided to take up full-time residence in Maine. His poetry muse, which was fortunate to have a family trust fund to support it, pushed him northward to live in sight of the granite, the waves, and the fog of Maine's coastline. So Toulouse packed his notebooks and pencils and copies of the few books he sold along with his collection of poetry books and moved to the winterized family cottage. At the same time, he promised himself that he would leave for the family home on Florida's west coast during the worst of the winter months.

Poetry muses can be fickle and Toulouse's seemed more prankster than guru. After six months of producing work in dribs and of drab quality, Toulouse suspected his muse was toying with him. He buckled down, determined to assert his genius. His effort did produce a bit more volume, but he was forced to admit that it just didn't sing. As he contemplated his next move, the lingering thought of taking over the *Gazette* grew in appeal. Maybe an endeavor of a different sort, will help sort me out, he thought.

So Toulouse arranged a dinner with his aunt and together they discussed a plan by which Toulouse would gradually assume the publisher's mantle. His new column would be a possible first step.

Nellie adored her nephew, despite what she called his "fucktard" name. Not quite ready to give over the company reins, however, she approved of the slow transition. Nellie knew Toulouse to be a good writer, even if he wasn't a great poet. And she liked the idea of a column about Maine, but from an outsider's vantage. Given all the fuss about the Arvin Prize decision, she thought, this would be a good time to show the value of different perspectives.

But Nellie hadn't counted on the stance Toulouse took on the Arvin wrangle. She thought he agreed with her position that, though badly handled, the decision to expand the competition would be good for the Colony and the town. She had said, "Any chance to stick it to the Herringboners is a chance worth taking." Apparently Toulouse disagreed.

In the first couple of paragraphs, Toulouse introduced himself to the readership and explained that his now-regular column would "look at our community and our state with a fresh angle." He said that, like his aunt, he would not shy away from tough issues and that he hoped to "bring forward a clear-eyed account" to the readers each week. From there, Toulouse's editorial dawn began:

> It is from this perch that I turn first to the boiling controversy over the decision by the Rascal Harbor Art Colony Executive Board to revamp the entrance requirements for the Mattie Arvin Prize competition.
>
> Though one might assume my outsider status would bend me toward support of the board's decision, in fact, I oppose it. I do so for three reasons.
>
> Reason one—local matters. Today, we are urged to see ourselves as global citizens. That is a right and pragmatic view. But we live and act and thrive locally, in the areas where we know and are known. Those areas die if they refuse to let in any new ideas, but they die even faster if every new idea is embraced. If we do not support those good and well-tested ideas that have allowed us to prosper, then we will do ourselves in.
>
> Reason two—promises matter. Promises create an intimate bond between people. We look one another in the eye, we shake hands, we pledge to uphold the vows we make. In this fashion, we hold ourselves and one another accountable. A promise may need to be broken, but only under the most dire circumstances and with every recognition that this expressed pledge is being abrogated. We should never make a promise casually, but we should never break a promise unless heaven and earth demand it.
>
> Reason three—tradition matters. The current media-driven, cell phone-driven, fad-driven world is of

our own creation. Do not kid yourselves, friends, we are responsible for the crazed world in which we live. But that means we are equally responsible for holding firm to those traditions that matter to us. Supporting our local community and keeping the promises made are elements of a tradition that has well guided Maine folks for hundreds of years. Let others create—and abandon—traditions daily if they wish. Let us be willing to stand behind ours.

Individually and combined these three reasons tell us that the recent Arvin competition decision must fall. Mattie Arvin and the Rascal Harbor Art Colony she established made a promise to the local artists and the community that the prize named in her honor would go only to a Harbor resident. The tradition that promise created has benefitted all. The benefits afforded a change to that tradition do not out-weigh the costs. Let us keep the Arvin promise as well as the Arvin Prize.

When she first read the piece, Nellie hesitated. Was the boy deliberately disagreeing with her and the position the Gazette had taken thus far? Rich Reed handled the paper's editorials now that she focused only on obituaries. She and Rich had agreed that he would take a generally supportive stance on the Colony board's decision in last week's issue. Toulouse knew how she felt and the paper's editorial position and yet he'd contradicted it in his op-ed.

And then she smiled. Huh, might have a fucktard name, but the boy's got some balls. She emailed Rich to run the piece as is.

CHAPTER 37

"She feels bad, John," Gary Park explained when he called McTavish. "You know, about the 'cartoon' thing. I told her you weren't mad at her, but Ruby's, well, she feels bad so she wants to make supper for you, her famous poutine, ployes, and green bean casserole. Will you come?"

Taking a breath, Gary continued. "Jesus, you gotta come! She's drivin' me nuts. She goes from wanderin' around sayin' 'What can I do? What can I do?' to askin' 'Is he, John McTavish, still on the outs wit me?' Please come to supper, John, so she'll know you ain't mad at her."

Unsure Gary had finished his plea, McTavish hesitated. Unsure how to interpret the pause, Gary pushed on. "That is if you really ain't mad her... Are you mad at her, John, cause if—"

"No, no, I'm not mad at her," McTavish said quickly. "I was a little surprised by her comment, but I wasn't mad."

"I know, I know. Ruby's mouth gets as twisted up as her brain does and so you never know what's gonna come out. But she really didn't mean nothin' by it. She really likes you and just feels awful that she might have hurt your feelings."

"My feelings are fine. I'd be happy to come to dinner."

"Not 'dinner,' John, 'supper!' You're back in Maine now, mister man! You eat 'supper' at night and 'dinner' at noon."

"Ayuh. Roger that," McTavish said in his best Maine accent. Both men smiled.

"Oh, and bring Noah along. Ruby likes that McTavish boy too. Ruby checked with Louise and found out that Noah has the night off."

"Will do," McTavish said and hung up.

McTavish wasn't a fan of green bean casserole, the goopy dish made from canned green beans larded up with canned cream of mushroom soup and then baked under a sprinkle of bread crumbs or, more likely, french-fried onions. He loved Ruby's poutine and ployes, however. Those dishes, French-Canadian in origin, spoke to his philosophy of "eat for taste rather than for fiber." Poutine, Quebecois slang for "mess," consists of French fries, cheese curds, and gravy. Ployes are thin buckwheat pancakes cooked only on one side. They are covered with butter, maple syrup, brown sugar, or molasses and then rolled and eaten. His plan: Load up on the poutine and ployes and take only enough green bean casserole to be polite.

The green bean casserole would not be the only trial of the evening. McTavish knew Ruby could ramp up from miserable to maudlin in a matter of minutes, particularly if she'd been hitting the Manischewitz. He knew she'd begin by apologizing…and then apologize some more…then forget that she'd already apologized and start again. It was going to be a tough night, but McTavish genuinely liked Ruby. The thought that she might be feeling badly made him want to assure her that he was not upset.

McTavish needn't have worried about Ruby's mental state. She might have had a lingering worry about her comment, but it was quickly resolved with a welcoming bear hug and a "I really is so sorry for that 'cartoon' thing, John McTavish," whispered into his ear. Before turning to embrace Noah, Ruby smiled up at McTavish and said, "I have some making up to do and I have done it!"

Suspecting that she meant the poutine and ployes, he smiled back and said, "I can't wait."

The aroma of food that lacked any measure of good-for-you, filled McTavish's nose and he dared hope that the evening's only real challenge would now be the casserole. But then the doorbell rang. Ruby rushed to answer it as Gary handed Noah and McTavish glasses of an amber liquid McTavish hoped was Bushmills but was more likely

Canadian Mist. Turning toward the door, McTavish now saw Ruby embracing a woman who could be her twin.

"John McTavish, here is your make-up!" Ruby announced with a grin. "Let me introduce yourself to Miss Peggy Lavere!" The woman who now stood in front of McTavish had the same short, rounded features as Ruby Park. In fact the only difference McTavish could see was that, unlike Ruby's, Peggy's hair appeared to be mostly her own and a violet cast slightly less intense than Ruby's.

"I'm pleased to meet you, John," Peggy said warmly. "But from your expression, I'm guessing that Ruby didn't let you know that another guest would be joining the group."

"Ah, no, she didn't," McTavish said honestly.

Ruby began ushering everyone to the table, pointedly ignoring Louise's obvious entreaties to join her in the kitchen. Ruby said, "Here, you sit here, friend John and, let me see…let us put Peggy maybe right beside you? Yes, I am thinking that makes a good match-up."

Ruby directed a smiling Noah and a fuming Louise to chairs on the opposite side of the table from McTavish and Peggy. She pushed an anxious Gary down into his customary chair at the head of the table and headed to the kitchen to get the food.

"I'll help you, Mom," Louise said, rising from her chair and hurrying into the kitchen. Intense, but unintelligible words leaked out for several minutes. Eventually, Ruby emerged serenely holding a large platter of poutine. Louise followed with a chagrinned look and the green bean casserole. The ployes would come out later as dessert.

Ruby said, "There now, let us give some especial thanks to the God above and some hell to the Devil down below!" Everyone bowed their heads and Ruby offered a brief prayer in French. Then she called for the meal to begin.

The talk covered all things local. National politics, economics, and culture had no place at this table, though Louise did slip in a crack about the current President being a dope. No one disagreed.

Hadley Cooper's plight got some air time, though the principal theme was that it would be too bad if an all-out lobster war broke out. "Lot of folks would suffer. Hope they catch whoever did it sooner than later," Gary said.

Thoughts about the Art Colony board decision figured more prominently in the table talk. The announcement was only a week or so old, but the news had reached well beyond the Colony artists. Again, Gary wondered about blowback. "I might support openin' up the competition, I mean, competition's most always a good thing, right? But I gotta wonder if it won't pit the locals against the out-a-towners. We can't afford to get a reputation as bein' unfriendly to the tourists."

"I actually think it's a good move," Louise said. "Some of these locals think they're God's gift to art. Be good to bounce a few of 'em down the steps."

"Jesus, I just realized that I might not be able to enter the competition if the board changes their mind," Noah said suddenly. "I mean, I'm not a local, am I?" The question stumped the table for a couple of minutes. Louise put her hand on Noah's arm.

"Oh, I expect you are," Gary said calmly, "You're still a student so your permanent address would be with your dad, right? He's lived in town for a year so he's a resident. 'Spect that makes you one too."

"That sounds about right," McTavish added. Noah's face showed relief.

"Peggy, what are you tinkin' about the Arvin prize for artists?" Ruby asked. Before Peggy could answer, Ruby turned to McTavish. She smiled and said, "Did you know, John McTavish, that this Peggy is an artist also like you?" Before McTavish could respond, Ruby said, "Well, she certainly is so if you are asking me."

Peggy jumped in to say, "I'm not sure what I think about the board's decision. I can see Louise's point about increasing the level of the competition, but jeez, the prize has always gone to a resident so I'm not sure I agree that the rule should change."

"Well some of dem damn rules should be changin'," Ruby said loudly. "Dis is just not completely fair!"

"What are you talking about, Mom?" Louise asked.

"What I am talkin' about here is art!" Ruby said as if this declaration was all that was needed. It wasn't.

"What's about art?" Gary asked.

"Jesus, Mary, and Joseph! Dem rules about what counts as art and what is not. Tell 'em, Peggy. Tell 'em how you can't be in no competition that other artists can be! Is dat fair, I am asking you?"

The group's eyes turned to Peggy for some inkling into Ruby's rant. Peggy smiled, "What my good friend is trying to say is that she likes the work I do—I do cross-stitch—and she's thinks it's as beautiful as a lot of paintings she sees. Isn't that it, Ruby?" As Ruby nodded, Peggy continued. "So for years now Ruby's tried to get me to enter my pieces in the Arvin competition."

"Yes, I have done that," Ruby said. "But dem damn colonists won't let her. It's not fair!"

"I've tried to explain that it actually is fair. I do cross-stitch from kits I buy. The pattern is printed on the fabric and all the yarn is included. It's kinda like paint-by-numbers but with fiber. You just follow the directions. It's pretty easy."

"Well, art is art," Ruby said adamantly, her Manischewitz kicking in. "It isn't not fair that Peggy can't get in, but John's cartoons can…" With this last utterance Ruby's face went white, Gary's mouth dropped, Louise's head went into her hands, Peggy looked blank, and Noah bit the insides of his mouth to keep from laughing.

"Oh, shit Jesus," Ruby said with a gasp. "Here I am opening my big mouth with my foot again. I am so honestly sorry, John McTavish—"

"Really, Ruby, it's okay," McTavish said softly. "I think the point that Peggy's making is that, in order to qualify for the competition the piece has to be an original work." Peggy smiled and nodded. McTavish continued. "So…my pictures may be 'cartoons,' but they're original cartoons." He smiled and took Ruby's hand, sending a message of not to worry. "Maybe we could have the ployes now?" he added.

Without a word, Ruby rushed into the kitchen with Louise trailing closely. As before, the table guests could hear a blizzard of hushed words, but none were distinct enough to understand. A couple of minutes later, mother and daughter emerged with plates of the delicious dessert, though their smiles looked pasted on.

Not trusting herself to talk about art anymore, Ruby turned to Peggy's attributes and her availability. "Dis Peggy here is a very excellent cook and housecleaner," Ruby said, trying to regain her composure. "Her house is a sparkle and her apple pie, umm, the very best you can eat. But a'course she can't eat a whole pie her ownself cause she is widowed now five years. But she is liking to share her cookin'. Sometimes she share wit Gary and me, a'course, but she has plenty to share—"

"We get it, Mom," Louise said. "Peggy's got food to share—"

"Easy, Louise" Gary said. "Your mom is just—"

"She's just embarrassing John and Peggy, is what she's doing," Louise said. Then, turning to McTavish, she said, "Jesus, sorry about all this. Once Mom gets something in her head…" Turning to the table, she said, "Anyway, Noah and I have to go, we're off to the movies." To her mother, she said, "I'll empty the dishwasher when I get home." With that, Louise and Noah left the table and headed outside.

"I am sorry for that girl's bad acting," Ruby said, shaking her head. "I am having no idea what she's talking about."

"It's okay," McTavish and Peggy said simultaneously and smiled at one another. Both rose and started to clear the dishes.

After the two of them said their good-byes, McTavish walked Peggy to her car.

"I had a feeling Ruby was up to something tonight" Peggy said with a smile. "She's been trying to set me up with every available man in town for the last two years. Frankly, I came for the poutine and ployes. Ruby's a superb cook even if she's kind of ham-handed matchmaker." Sensing McTavish's relief, she continued, "You seem like a nice enough guy, John, but I'm not really looking for a relationship." Then she added, "It was an entertaining evening, though!"

McTavish had to admit that it was.

CHAPTER 38

For Rascal Harbor residents, the entertainment value of the Colony board decision continued to grow. No less than three different advocacy groups had formed, each with a different purpose in mind, but all with the mission to air their positions.

Janice Sewall's group was the biggest and probably the most well organized. After the first meeting at her house, the group had swollen to nearly twenty and now included oil and watercolor artists as well as sculptors and photographers. This broad representation, Janice believed, would be one incentive for the Colony board to pay attention to their demands for a reversal of the Arvin Prize decision.

A second incentive came in the unexpected form of Toulouse Rustin's three reasons to keep the Prize for local artists only. Janice had seen the Gazette's earlier editorial support for the board decision and had concluded the paper would not be an ally. She noticed that letters to the editor supporting her cause were printed, but she suspected that was done only to create the illusion of fair-mindedness and to sell newspapers. Rustin's clear, coherent, and convincing op-ed, however, gladdened her and she was pleased to get the attendant calls from a couple more artists interested in her group's effort.

A second group, a bit smaller than Janice Sewall's but equally avid about their cause, supported the board decision. This group consisted of Colony members who liked the idea of broadening the scope of the

Arvin competition, but hated Robertay. So they intended to support the decision, but planned do so independently of the executive board and its president.

The third group started as the most amorphous. Sitting around a table at Village Pizza discussing the Colony board decision were two knitters, a poet, a dance instructor, and a harpist. Their perspectives on the controversy ran the gamut, but they coalesced around the frustration that their arts lay outside those allowed in the Summer Exhibition. It soon became apparent that each knew several other people who could also be convinced to be disgruntled.

After word spread of this meeting, the following week twenty-five people met at the pizza shop and the owner had to bring in extra chairs from the back room. The group's catchy, but puzzling rallying cry became—"Add an S!" Whether or not the Colony allowed non-residents to compete for the Arvin Prize, this group wanted an "s" added to the word "Art," as in the Rascal Harbor Arts Colony and the Summer Arts Exhibition. Marie Townsend, a town selectman and an expert with crochet needles, promised to promote the idea among her town hall colleagues.

And so the decision become a debate which turned into a fracas. As a result, the implications of the decision expanded from one of resident v. non-resident to one about the nature and definition of art.

As various Colony members turned to their bylaws, they discovered the same thing that Twyla Cameron had—if fifty-one of the one hundred Colony members signed a petition, then the Colony board had to schedule a meeting. Because it was still several weeks before the tourist onslaught and because the artist community in Rascal Harbor was relatively small, it did not take long for Janice Sewall's group to organize a petition drive. Richard Anthony Bates continued to attend the meetings Janice hosted, but declined to sign the petition. Janice thought about berating him, but decided it might backfire. Besides the nearly twenty others in her group meant that she was nearly halfway to the mandated number. If each member got only one or two more signatures, they'd reach the goal.

In the end, sixty-five members signed the petition. Many of the signers supported reversing the decision, but not all. The Village Pizza group were not Colony members so even though a few signed the petition, their names were quickly invalidated. The pro-decision group all signed because they saw it as an occasion to stop the whining and move on with the planning. And artists who had expressed no public opinion about the matter signed because they were bored or they hoped to see a cat fight or they wanted to see Robertay get smacked down or a host of other, not-so-gracious reasons.

Whatever the motivation, legitimate signatures dominated the forms such that Robertay was forced to accede to a Colony membership meeting. Thomas Beatty got an earful that night.

CHAPTER 39

A storm of a different type brewed at the Rascal Harbor Lobsterman's Co-op. Babette Dubois was pissed.

As her heart raced and her mind reeled, Babette had circled her boat peering closely into the water in hopes that the first missing buoy might have been pulled just below the surface. It wasn't. She swore and then accelerated to the next buoy location. Seeing that it too was missing she went on to the subsequent set. Bile filled her mouth as she could not see her buoy with its distinctive red and blue markings. "That fuckin' Hadley Cooper!" she shouted.

Babette and her sternman, Davey Leonard, talked over their options. They could steam back to the Co-op and demand that Tristan Riggins and Rob Pownall "Do something with that fuckhead Cooper." Babette could put out a message over the radio that her trap lines had been cut and that there would be hell to pay when she returned to dock. They could try to track Hadley down on the water and…figure out what to do when they found him. Or they could finish checking this day's scheduled hauls and see just how bad the damage was. They opted for the last.

"But I'm gonna skin that asshole when I see him," Babette ranted as she got ready to haul the next set.

"Well, don't get mad at me, but what if it weren't him?" Davey asked.

GEOFFREY SCOTT

164

"I'm already mad and who else could it be? You know the history between my dad and his. And he and I had words back in school." She paused, then continued. "But I gotta say, I never thought he'd do something like this. His father, yes, but Hadley, no. Still, who else would do it. It's been years since we had this kind of trouble."

"You ain't wrong about that," Davey said. "Still—"

"Still…nothing. Let's get to work. Make something of the day, if we can."

Three cut strings defined the damage. Fishing two traps on each, Babette realized she'd lost the same number of traps Hadley Cooper had. Hard to imagine how that's a coincidence, she thought.

Although she'd lost her inaugural head of steam after checking her remaining sets and heading back to the Co-op, Babette regenerated it once she and Davey tied up. As soon as he'd made fast the docking lines, Davey looked at Babette and said, "Go." She nodded, bounded off the boat, and headed to find Tristan or Rob.

Instead she found Detective Chambers.

Chambers had been interviewing sternmen and was waiting for Babette's to come in. Before he could ask where Leonard was, Babette started.

"Where's Hadley Cooper?"

"I couldn't tell you, Babette. Why?"

"'Cause I think he cut my traps!"

"What? What happened?"

Though spitting mad, Babette told the detective about her missing buoys and her presumption that Hadley Cooper was behind the act.

"Why would you assume Hadley to be responsible?"

"I told you his dad and mine got into it. His father was a first-rate prick, always had it out for my old man and for no reason. I didn't have anything to do with cutting his traps, but I bet he thinks I did and went after mine."

"That's a pretty hard accusation. You know we cleared you because other guys saw you fishing off Knuckles Cove that day. So you couldn't have gotten over to Hadley's gear. You had an alibi for your time on shore so you're out of the picture as far as Hadley's traps are concerned. I didn't say anything to him about you because he never brought up your name. But knowing people, I've got to think that he heard that you were in the clear."

"Yeah, well, maybe, but that doesn't mean he didn't take advantage of the situation and cut mine, you know, for payback. Then he could blame whoever it is that cut his."

"That's possible, I guess. But Hadley just doesn't seem like the kind—"

"Anybody can be that 'kind,' Detective," Babette said.

"That's possible too," Chambers conceded. "But until I come up with something more solid, I want you to stay away from this. If Hadley is involved and you gum up a conviction, you'll be doubly mad."

"Well, then find the asshole!" Babette turned and stalked back to her boat.

By checking their GPS hauling records, Chambers confirmed that none of the Harbor lobstermen cut Hadley Cooper's trap lines, at least while using their fishing boats. Rascal Harbor had a lot boats, however, so anyone of them could have run out to Cooper's traps in a Boston Whaler or other small boat and cut the lines. Chambers was having Officer Artie Long run down the lobstermen's alibis for their on-shore time. He'd interviewed all the sternmen, but Davey Leonard, and he'd detailed one of the other officers to check on all of their alibis. Chambers was being thorough, but he wasn't expecting much. Most all of the men and women he'd interviewed had seemed surprised to hear that Cooper's trap lines had been cut. From all of his interviews, it was the Patch brothers who ranked highest as suspects.

Interrogated separately, both resisted giving a full account of their whereabouts. When he checked with others, however, both Patch boys' alibis held up. Yet neither could completely hide their frustration that Hadley Cooper's return had kept them from moving up the list to get a license. Wonder if there's something there, he mused.

News spread quickly about Babette Dubois's lost traps. She held her word to Detective Chambers that she would make no direct accusations of Hadley Cooper. Still, when others brought his name forward, she would not defend him. Left to their own interpretations, several Co-op lobstermen began to suspect Cooper, figuring that a bad seed father had produced a bad seed son. None would act against this new guy yet, but all would be more watchful than ever.

CHAPTER 40

Jona Lewis and Toni Ludlow were nervous…because Robertay Harding was not. Their phones, email, and Facebook accounts had lit up over the week since the announcement of the Arvin competition change. People seemed to be on every side of the issue and feelings were getting raw. Arguments over favoring locals v. outsiders, change v. the status quo, art v. the arts unhinged some people and good friends found themselves exchanging harsh words.

Jona and Toni reported these findings to each other and then to Robertay. Her response baffled them: All will be well. Assuming that Robertay hadn't understood the severity of the reactions, the two artists pressed Regina Baldo on what she had been hearing. Regina confirmed their suspicions that the Colony faced a crisis. Robertay remained unmoved. In an email to the three of them, she wrote, "Change demands courage and spine. The unenlightened will carp but, in the end, they will cave to the demands and the opportunities of the future. Hold fast, friends, and this storm will subside."

"She's nuts," Jona said to Toni over the phone. "Deluded, crazy, whatever you want to call it. She's lost touch with reality and with the membership."

"Or she knows something we don't. This thing seems like a train wreck, but who knows."

"Jesus, Toni, how can you even think that?" Jona asked. "You're seeing and hearing the same things I am. People are beside themselves over this issue. Are you trying to tell me that this is all part of Robertay's master plan?"

"I wouldn't go that far, but there has to be some reason for this calm she's exhibiting. I mean, you know her, Jona, she flies off the handle over the smallest thing. How can she be so relaxed about this mess? Maybe she knows something we don't."

"Can't imagine," Jona replied gloomily. "My worry is that she'll win the battle, but the Colony will end up being a casualty of the war."

"I guess we'll know soon enough."

The size of the Colony membership precluded meeting at the gallery, so the group met in the high school cafeteria. Being back in the school from which they'd graduated offered many of the local artists a chance to recall favored memories. They shared these thoughts with friends old and new as the hallway outside the cafeteria filled with happy talk about anything other than the upcoming meeting.

Much of that talk died down as Robertay walked through the group and into the cafeteria. Her determined smile and ramrod posture gave no doubt as to her intent to lead this group forward even if, as some of them suspected, that way might be over a cliff.

Once the Colony members took their seats, Robertay and the Executive Board members took seats together at a table in front of the crowd. Robertay rose and called the meeting to order.

With a beatific smile, Robertay began, "Friends, welcome to our membership-of-the-whole meeting. It really is wonderful to see all of you in the same room. I mean, think of the talent here, in the eyes, hands, and minds of this assemblage. It's really quite staggering—"

"Get on with it, Robertay," someone called out from the back. Titters rippled across the room. Robertay's smile broadened.

"Ah yes. Our Maine ways tell us not to fuss around the edges and, as you say, 'Get on with it.' And so we shall." Robertay paused here, looked from one side of the room to the other, then continued. "But first a bit of context. A week ago, your Executive Board of the Rascal Harbor Art Colony voted to expand the entrance eligibility requirements for the Mattie Arvin Prize. Doing so, of course, brings innumerable benefits in terms of prestige and exposure for the Summer Exhibition. That prestige and exposure will not be based simply on an enhanced PR campaign, but on the range and quality of the art entered into the competition for the Arvin Prize. Make no mistake— we will well publicize the event. Thomas has already put together an outstanding plan to do so. But you can't simply publicize your way to the top of the art world. There has to be some substance to publicize and this move to expand—"

"So what you're saying is that we aren't good enough for you," a man called out. "That's what it seems like to me." Several voices echoed agreement.

"Absolutely not, Carl," Robertay said with a bit of steel in her voice. "You know that I adore and admire the art that comes from our community hands. This decision has nothing to do with denigrating our individual and collective work. Instead, the decision enhances our efforts—"

Murmurs arose drowning Robertay's words. Someone whispered a little too loudly, "Horseshit," then added, "Sorry."

Robertay continued unfazed. "The fact is that we all need a push from time to time and this is the push we need right now. Moreover, think about it, if a resident artist wins the Arvin Prize, then that means she or he will have beaten out the very best. The Arvin Prize and its winner can claim to be second to none." Several heads nodded at this argument.

A woman artist stood and said, "Yes, but Mattie herself said it flat out—her prize was to go to a local. I don't care if you let the out-a-towners into the Exhibition, but I damn sight don't want them eligible to win the Arvin." More nods and echoes of support ensued. The meeting was on.

From her seat, Janice Sewall said, "That's exactly right. We local artists are the ones that Mattie Arvin cared about and wanted to nurture." Several people mouthed their agreement, though not a few looked at one another with the expression, "she's a local?" written in their eyes.

"I knew Mattie," an older artist said as he rose to his feet. "I knew her well. And, yes, she said she wanted her prize to go to a local, but she was not provincial. She was a forward-thinking gal of the first order. Otherwise she'd never have become an artist in the first place. She was adventuresome. Why I remember one time—"

"Get to the point, Thompson," someone yelled out.

"Right, right," Thompson Enders said smiling wanly. "As I was saying. Mattie cared about Rascal Harbor, but she really cared about art. And I think she'd support the idea that her prize go to the best artist who shows."

Robertay tried to hide her smile as several audience members purred agreement. "Well, if there are not more comments—"

"Wait a goddamned minute now, Robertay Harding," Richie Connor said loudly. "There are many more reasons for not making this move even if it was a good one, which it isn't. First, the timeframe is just too tight—there's no way that we can expand the Exhibition and the prize competition by God knows how many artists and still run a good show. Second, where the hell are all these folks gonna stay? The Exhibition is in the height of the tourist season already. How many more people can come to the Harbor and get rooms? And third, uh, third, well, what the hell was my third point?"

"Whatever it was, it was probably pointLESS," Thompson Enders said.

"Oh, go to hell, Enders," Connor snapped back. "You and your Mattie Arvin stories. I know for a fact that Mattie Arvin thought you were a hack."

"Richie, you don't know shit," Enders yelled, getting to his feet.

Pounding her fist on a table, Robertay quieted the two artists while friends around them pulled them back to their seats. As the chatter died down, Lynn Barnett stood. "I favor the decision to expand the competition, but that may not be our only problem. As some of you know, there is a group forming that wants the Colony to extend its membership to a whole range of other folks—dancers, poets, musicians. All kinds of other people in the arts and then there are craftspeople—you know, knitters and quilters and jewelers—who want in too. They've even got a slogan—"Add an S!"

"What does that mean?" Janice Sewall called out.

"It means to change 'art' to the 'arts' in the name of the Colony and the Summer Exhibition," Barnett explained.

"That's just stupid," someone called out to general agreement.

"Maybe so," Barnett said agreeably. "But they've got an argument: If we're going to let non-residents come in and compete for the most honored prize the Colony gives, then why not consider expanding the notion of what constitutes the arts?"

This question set the room abuzz. Allowing fellow painters, sculptors, and photographers into the Summer Exhibition was one thing, but knitters and poets?

Several voices sought the floor; none prevailed. Robertay pounded her fist for nearly a minute before the group quieted enough for her to be heard. But she did so with a slight smile on her face.

"It's very clear that the Colony has a wide range of issues to consider as we face the future together," Robertay said in a loud voice as the tumult among the group refused to quiet completely. "Please know friends that the Executive Board and your President have heard you and we will give every consideration to your viewpoints. So thank you for your input and your kind and generous support. This meeting is adjourned."

And with a wave her skirt, a toss of her head, and a firm hand pulling Thomas Beatty from his seat, she and he left the cafeteria.

The hubbub of voices and feelings and topics was such that only half the group noticed that their meeting had finished. For their part, Jona Lewis, Toni Ludlow, and Regina Baldo sat stunned.

John McTavish sat for a minute in his own same stunned silence. Turning to Noah, he then asked, "What in hell just happened?"

CHAPTER 41

As they drove home, McTavish was still at a loss to figure out what he had just witnessed. Over dinner, he and Noah had speculated about how the meeting might go. Neither was well-enough connected to the rest of the Colony to have heard all the different arguments. Still, they both knew enough about artists to suspect that the meeting could go awry.

"What happens next?" Noah asked.

"Hard to tell at this point. I suppose there could be a petition for another meeting or even a recall of the board members, but I wonder if there's much enthusiasm for either of those moves given the meeting we just witnessed."

"Huh. I see your point. Think there's any chance that the Colony would end up falling apart over adding in other kinds of arts?"

"I wouldn't rule out any possibility right now. Seems like a cluster is a'brewin'."

"A cluster fuck is what it was!" Janice Sewall stormed to her husband. "That goddamned Harding woman is a complete idiot and the board is worthless. They just sat there and let the meeting turn into chaos."

"Well, you know artists can be a little temperamental," David Sewall said gently.

"These people were just mental!" Janice paced the large living room floor. "We were supposed to be there to talk about the Arvin Prize decision, but that was less than half of the discussion. People were recalling the old days, picking at old grudges, introducing completely new and stupid topics—"

"Easy, dear," David said soothingly. "Don't work yourself up. Your blood pressure—"

"To hell with my blood pressure! I'm going to be in jail for killing some of these idiots!"

"They sound like idiots," Babette Dubois said after Richard Anthony Bates described the Colony meeting. "Sounds like they couldn't even agree on why they were there."

"That's about right."

"Maybe Robertay was right," Jona Lewis said to his friend, Katrin Stein. "She said this meeting was a waste of time." Shaking his head, he continued. "Nobody was listening to one another and so the couple good points that were made got lost in the noise."

"Is there any possibility of a good outcome?" Katrin asked.

"Depends on your position, I suppose. If you want us to reverse the board decision, I don't think so. There was no clear mandate. There was a good point or two about Mattie Arvin being a progressive and so even she might have supported the decision to open the competition to non-residents. But that idea didn't get developed either. It was like someone would make a point, then someone would make another

GEOFFREY SCOTT

completely different point. Then someone would call someone else a name. It was a mess. About the only thing there seemed to be agreement on was that the members are opposed to the idea of expanding its view of what counts as art."

"So my friends who are part of the 'Add a S!' campaign have got an uphill climb," Katrin said. Stein ran a yarn and fabric business.

"Up the hill, over the dale, and through the clam flats, I suspect," Jona said and sighed.

"But what if the town politicians get involved?" Katrin asked.

"That's all we need are for the fucking politicians to get involved," Nellie Hildreth said to Toulouse Rustin and to Sarah McAdams, the latter having attended the meeting at Robertay Harding's request. "I heard that Marie Townsend is rumbling around making noise about how the selectmen might try to force the Colony to start allowing dancers and musicians and, and probably bread makers and florists, into the mix. Hell, I guess we ought to get in as well, writers are artists too!"

"I believe you exaggerate, Aunt," Toulouse said, "but you're aren't wrong in thinking that, as mucked up as the Colony is right now, it will be worse if town officials become involved."

"Well, we may not agree on the Arvin prize decision, but we can agree on that," Nellie said.

"How could the selectmen tell a private organization what to do?" Sarah asked.

"They can't really, but they can yap about it during public meetings. Plus they can pull back on the little subsidy the Colony gets every year in the town budget. They can make enough of a nuisance of themselves that the Colony will feel the heat."

Toulouse said, "And stir up more animosity among the townspeople. It's bad enough now with the residents deriding non-residents. This business about forcing the Colony's hand on deciding which arts are the 'real' arts will pit neighbor against neighbor."

"As if that's not already happening," Nellie said.

"It's not happening," Robertay Harding chortled to Thomas. "The move to thwart us is over."

"Really, dear? Do you really think so?" Thomas asked, wide-eyed.

"Of course it is! And it happened just as I thought it would."

"What do you mean?"

"I knew that if we got everyone, and I mean everyone, in the same room that whatever points were going to be made against us would be drowned out by all the other nonsense and the other agendas that people have. Artists really are the best kind of people on the planet, but they couldn't organize themselves if their collective lives depended on it."

"But you seemed so against the idea of a general meeting when it was first broached."

"Well, of course! It was a waste of everyone's time. And now we're going to have to fight back against this bunch who want to expand the membership to include anyone who thinks he's got a talent," Robertay said, pausing before continuing. "But one battle at a time, Thomas, one battle at a time. We've won this one—the steam is gone out of the naysayers' sails so we'll move straight ahead with this year's Exhibition and then we fight the next battle when it comes."

CHAPTER 42

It's the rare group in which all members prosper equally. Lobstermen are no exception. A co-op equalizes some of the costs and ensures a more equitable price per pound. Still, fishing territories vary, fishing knowledge varies, quality of boat and gear varies...and luck varies. The result—some lobstermen do better than their peers. Tick Sherwood wasn't one of them.

Carter Holden set more traps this year in hopes of increasing his haul and his bottom line. But he could do so because he had the extra traps. Hadley Cooper was working without a sternman in order to improve his profit. And he could do so because, having no real family to go home to, he could work longer hours. Tick Sherwood had all kinds of family, not enough traps, and a generally useless brother-in-law as his sternman. Tick managed to keep his boat afloat, but his family and his finances floundered.

And so losing the first of what turned out to be his four of his longest strings of traps made his heart sink.

"Do you see the buoy, Bennie?" Tick asked anxiously as he approached the area where he should see his green and orange marker. Bennie Toms would take all day to bait and set a trap if Tick let him, but he had glasses and Tick didn't so Bennie often saw the buoys before Tick did.

"Nope, don't see shit," Bennie replied.

As the boat idled, Tick checked his tide chart. It was three hours to high tide so the buoy couldn't be underwater. Tick put the boat in gear and slowly circled the area where the buoy should be, his heart sinking further with each pass. This three-trap string had always been one of his most productive. He began calculating the loss if he couldn't haul traps and then had to replace them with new ones.

When the same result appeared with his second set and then his third and fourth, Tick lost it. He put the boat in neutral, leaned back against the shabby cabin, and cried.

Bennie, no pillar of emotional strength, tried patting Tick on the shoulder and telling him it would be okay. As the loss finally dawned on him, however, his own eyes reddened and he slumped against Tick.

"What the hell we gonna do, Tick?" Bennie asked plaintively. "We gotta catch bugs or we're gonna catch hell from Winnie." Winnie Sherwood was Tick's wife and Bennie's sister.

"We sure will," Tick said when he could find his voice. "We sure as shit will."

By the time Tick and Bennie finished their haul and arrived back at the Co-op dock, nearly all the Harbor lobstermen were there to meet them. Shock had been the first reaction. Tick was among the least offensive of the group, a quiet guy with too much debt and too many demands. Bennie was too lazy to inspire any animosity. Their colleagues didn't pity them; this was a group who believed you got what you worked for. But they also believed in luck and Tick, with or without Bennie, had little.

After shock, the next feeling expressed was confusion. The cutting of Hadley's and Babette's traps could be understood and explained, sort of, by reference to their fathers. But who would go after Tick's traps?

Lobstermen can be a loquacious bunch, but conversation was light as the group of men and women stood around waiting to get the story from Tick and Bennie.

Tristan Riggins had called Detective Dick Chambers as soon as Tick had radioed in the news. So as Tick and Bennie tied off their boat, Chambers approached to have a word. As he walked through the gathering, however, he found himself the topic of conversation both in murmurs and confrontations.

"Fucking cops always show up after the deal's done," Chambers heard one fisherman mumble to another, followed by, "He ain't done jack all."

"What the hell's going on, Detective?" Carter Holden asked directly. "And what are you gonna do about it?"

Chambers ignored the remarks until he had made his way through the knot of fishermen. Once he reached Tick's boat, he turned and addressed the group.

"I'll admit your tax dollars haven't gotten you much in the way of results, so far," Chambers began. Grumbles of "You got that right" and "Fucking A" surfaced, though softly. "So I don't blame you for being upset. I'm working the case hard, but I don't have anything tangible at this point. I've talked with all of you now and we've ruled out a few early possibilities. The fact that these attacks are continuing means you've all got to be vigilant out there and on shore. If you hear anything or sense anything that's off, you need to let me know. I'll track down every lead that comes my way, but it's pretty apparent that I'm not going to solve this thing on my own. I need your help and I need it sooner than later."

Chambers's words, calm and direct, soothed the raw edges of the group's exposed nerve, but that nerve still throbbed.

"Well, is it one of us or somebody from the outside?" Holden asked.

"I'm taking both possibilities seriously at this point. I can't afford not to."

"Well, I don't think it's one of us," Holden continued talking. He stepped beside Chambers so that he could see the group. "You all know I been strugglin' a little of late so I ain't afraid to say that this business has got me pretty damn worried. Tick here can't afford to lose no three or four strings and neither can I. So if, by chance, it's one a you doing it…" Holden hesitated, "Well, if it is, then you best watch your ass." Murmurs of agreement arose.

"I appreciate your words, Carter," Chambers said, stepping forward. "But it'll be best to let us handle it once a suspect has been identified. I get that you might want to settle this on your own, but I won't abide vigilantism. If you've got legitimate suspicions, call me."

Calmer, but far from calm, the group began to dissipate. Carter Holden called over his shoulder, "Tick, once Chambers gets done with you, you and Bennie come over to Jimbo's and I'll stand you to a beer before Winnie gets hold of you." A few laughs rippled, but most everyone knew that Tick's day was not going to be improved by a free beer.

Neither Tick Sherwood nor Bennie Toms could think of a reason why their buoy lines might have been cut. Though always on the lower side of lower class, both came from long-established Rascal Harbor families and neither could recall any bad blood with anyone much less other Co-op fishermen.

"Well, less you count Johnny Mitchell," Bennie said, musing.

"Can't imagine Johnny Mitchell doin' it," Tick said.

"Do you mean the Johnny Mitchell who just got out of Warren a month ago," Chambers asked.

"Yup, he's the one," Bennie said. "Johnny's a right asshole."

"Maybe so, but what beef would he have with you?" Chambers asked. Tick looked down at his boots.

"Well, Tick don't like to talk about it, but...okay if I tell him, Tick?" Bennie asked. When Tick nodded, Bennie continued. "Well, it was a couple years ago now, afore Johnny got pinched and went upta Warren. See we was all down to Jimbo's one night, that's me an Tick and Winnie. And Johnny Mitchell comes in all swaggerin' and shit and he sits down with us and starts sparkin' Winnie. He and Winnie used to be somethin' back in high school. Once he started gettin' in trouble though, Winnie dumped his ass, for sure." Bennie paused here to catch a breath and to pull up his pants. Continuing, he said, "Well, he—me-

GEOFFREY SCOTT

anin' Johnny—starts in with Winnie, y'know, 'Oh, Winnie, I still gotta thing for you after all these years… You was the best thing I ever had.' Just puke material. And there's me and Tick sittin' right there!

"Well, Winnie, she's tryin' to ignore him, tellin' him to quit it, but he won't go away. Finally, Tick says real quiet like, 'Johnny, Winnie don't want you here.' Well, Johnny gets this mad look on his face and gets right down and stares at Tick and says all growly, 'Don't you ever get in my way, Tick Sherwood.' Well, Tick, he don't want no trouble so he just looks away, then he gets up and goes to the bathroom or somethin'. When he gets back, he says, 'We gotta go Winnie, one of the kids is sick.' Winnie gets real concerned like and she stands up and Johnny stands up and, then, Tick just gathers up Winnie's arm and 'scorts her right outside."

"Next day I hear that Johnny's all mad cause when he goes out to his truck, he's got a flat tire and he's sayin' it's Tick what did it."

"Did you, Tick?" Chambers asked softly.

"Well, I ain't sayin' I did and I ain't sayin' I didn't," Tick responded with a half-smile.

"I suppose it doesn't matter a whole lot one way or the other," Chambers said shaking his head. "The real question is whether Mitchell's still got a beef with you and if he's got the means to cut your trap lines."

"Guess it's possible," Tick said, looking up. "He ain't got a boat, but his cousin, Wilber does."

"I'll check into them. But if you think of anyone else, let me know. I don't want anything happening to anyone's tires, understand?"

Tick nodded. Looking long at Sherwood's downcast face, Chambers asked, "Are you gonna make it, Tick? You gonna be able to bounce back from this?"

Tick, who had been staring at his boots again, said, "Can't see how."

By the time Chambers got back to the station, four anonymous calls had come in naming suspects in the trap cutting. None of the calls named the same person, but all expressed the worry that the cutting could continue.

CHAPTER 43

Fishing co-ops generally have a laissez-faire attitude toward one another. The fisherman associated with each organization work their territories within zones laid out by the state and everyone tries to make money. "Generally" only works generally, however, and the rivalry between Herrington and Rascal Harbor in high school basketball and the summer arts events carried over between the two fishing co-ops.

Any real tensions had gone by the board with Tristan Riggins' arrival five years ago. Riggins worked with the Herrington manager to negotiate better prices on bait deliveries for their respective lobstermen and that effort led to additional cooperative ventures. A year ago, Steve Putnam took over the Herrington manager's job and since then relations had soured.

What Riggins could not have imagined, however, was Putnam's plan to take over and absorb the Rascal Harbor Co-op. The Herrington outfit had always trailed their Rascal Harbor peers—fewer fishermen, smaller hauls, lower profits. But size and arrogance are not always related and the self-importance that Nellie Hildreth and others ascribed to the "Herringboners" was more real than imagined.

Unwilling to lag behind their rivals, the Herrington Co-op board sought out the most aggressive person they could find for the vacant manager's position. Steve Putnam's reputation seemed a good fit.

Putnam was a small, dark man. His facial features all conspired to create a scowl and his diminutive stature—he was barely five-foot-two—and hunched posture reinforced the expression. His physical issues aside, Putnam's brain was built for organization and manipulation. His talent for the first supported his passion for the second.

Within six months, Putnam had reorganized all the Herrington Co-op business efforts into a tight, profitable operation. Yet he could not expand the number of fishermen or their territories and so he and the board faced the fact that, unless something else happened, the Rascal Harbor Co-op would likely continue to out-produce the Herrington operation.

Putnam planned a two-pronged attack. The first was to drive out as many Rascal Harbor lobstermen as he could through intimidation and financial ruin. A lobster war can result in both. Putnam's second effort was to disrupt the faith in and the operation of the Co-op board and officials. Again, a lobster war can result in both. Putnam's two-prong strategy had a single ignition point.

The first part of the plan Putnam put together for a lobster war depended on intelligence, the second on disciplined action. The intelligence he needed consisted of information about which Rascal Harbor lobstermen were most vulnerable financially and what animosities could be exploited. To gain that information, Putnam needed insiders and he found two willing participants in the Patch twins. Both had more ambition than scruples and they soaked up the attention and promises Putnam offered as part of his pitch. That pitch was easy—the twins would get their lobstering licenses and, once Putnam had control of the Rascal Harbor Co-op, they would get cushy board positions. To add to the information gathered by the Patch boys, Putnam recruited one of the bait delivery men, Bob Morgan. Putnam had grown up with Morgan and knew him to be a weasel of the first order, but a weasel he could command.

With his intelligence sources in hand, Putnam built out the actions he would set in motion for the first prong of his strategy. Morgan would do the line cutting. Putnam wanted the Patch brothers to have solid alibis and he worried that they might go too far. He knew the boys, especially Chance, to be hotheaded so he entrusted the cutting of Cooper's, Dubois's, and Sherwood's buoy lines to Morgan.

Putnam had purposely selected these three—Cooper was new to lobstering and might be easily discouraged from continuing; Sherwood was on the brink of folding up anyway so a few cut traps would sink him; and Dubois was added to the list because cutting her lines would sow considerable confusion.

The second prong would come in time. Putnam figured that anger over the trap cutting would soon translate into frustration, finger pointing, and retribution. It would also induce turmoil and uncertainty among the Co-op's leaders. Here, the Patch twins could play a more active role. Their job was to stir the pot by spreading rumors and accusations and by questioning the Co-op management. They were also instructed to look out for other potential victims and for other potential allies once Putnam made his move on the Rascal Harbor Co-op.

So far the plan was working well. Cooper had been dealt a hard blow and he and Dubois had tangled through proxies on a couple of occasions. Putnam didn't think he could bring Dubois down— she fished a lot of traps and was well-established in the trade. But he thought Cooper was vulnerable, especially if he got hit again. Sherwood, of course, was easy. Putnam had thought about having Morgan hit him first, but decided that that might be too transparent a play. So Putnam planned the cutting order and Morgan had followed it to a T. "Six months at the most," Putnam said as he drove by the Rascal Harbor Co-op one evening. "You folks have got six months at most."

CHAPTER 44

Robertay Harding and the Executive Board of the Art Colony had less than six months to get their job done. But Robertay was every bit as determined to hit her goal as Steve Putnam was his.

And she, too, was having success. Within a week or so of the chaotic Colony meeting, the various chairs and committees were busy at their assigned tasks. Regina Baldo, head of the Events committee, had her group working to ensure that the Colony gallery would shine for the Summer Art Exhibition, that the exhibiting artists would be accommodated, and that the public would be impressed. Toni Ludlow, the Membership chair, met with her group to create a new membership category—with appropriate fees—for non-resident exhibitors. Jona Lewis, as Budget chair, worked largely by himself, but he found that he was much busier with Colony business than ever before as he checked the expenses his colleagues were tallying and then wrote the checks to cover them. The Administrative chair, Thomas Beatty, often seemed befuddled in daily life. Given an organizational charge, however, Thomas excelled. He developed the advertisements to induce artists to submit their work and a process for doing so. He also commissioned a graphic artist to design a reproducible poster to announce the event to the public. Finally, Robertay, queen of the Exhibition committee, made lists of tasks, got others to do them, and then checked them off with a smile.

Grumbles about the change in the Arvin Prize persisted; the formal resistance faded, however. There was much to be done and so the Colony members rallied around the work if not their president.

As the Colony artists turned toward one another in an effort to ensure a successful Summer Exhibition, the "other" artists continued meeting. Irritated to have their interests so blithely ignored, the "Add an S!" group actually grew in number and in intensity after the Colony meeting. It was a diverse group to be sure. Depending on their availability, musicians, dancers, and spoken-word poets drank coffee or wine with knitters, crocheters, and other fiber artists, and alongside jewelers, origami artists, and a small contingent of bread, pie, and cake bakers. A craft beer brewer and a clothing designer showed up from time to time.

The group meetings consisted of eating and drinking, scoffing at the hidebound "artistes," and strategizing. The last consisted of elaborate plans of both subtle and blatant varieties to push the Colony to expand their definition of art. It also consisted of even more robust plans to create a separate organization with its own catalog of events, should their attempts to join the Colony fail. In all of this work, the group pinned some of their hopes of support on local officials who saw an opportunity to expand the town's popularity and to stick a thin, but sharp knife into the inflated egos of the Colony artists.

Little of the "Add an S!" machinations reached Robertay Harding, however. Her attention focused exclusively on the Summer Exhibition. She felt fine about the way she quelled the Arvin uprising. Still, she wanted the summer showcase to so overwhelm the town that people inside and outside the Colony would forget a dust-up had ever occurred.

All was bubbling along toward that goal. She and the board and the various committees bent to the work and, thus far, had encountered no particular obstacles. They even developed a theme for the show quickly and with surprisingly little disagreement. Jona Lewis protested the Pencil-Paint-Paper title for a while arguing that it left out the sculptors. Robertay mollified him by saying that, as long as pieces incorporated one or more of those elements in reality or in representation, they would be accepted. She needn't have bothered as Jona's mind had already moved in that direction. Minerva Williams, on hearing the theme, suggested the Colony add a fourth "P" for "Pisspots."

The one thing that nagged Robertay was the selection of the Arvin Prize judge. As president of the Colony and chair of the Exhibitions committee, Robertay had always reserved for herself the choice of judges. To this point, she'd opted for well-respected, but retired local artists. Opening up the Arvin Prize competition, however, meant that she needed a big name. She thought she had the perfect one: Ransom Eldridge.

Ransom Eldridge was perfect. Born and raised in Rascal Harbor, Eldridge had shown early artistic talent, which his restaurant-owning parents nurtured. His ability was not scholarship worthy, but Eldridge made the most of his fine art major at a middling Ivy and went on to a respected, if not well-respected, career.

Though he rarely left his New York City studio loft for the coast of Maine, Eldridge's fame in the state ran deep. The long list of famous artists who worked in Maine carried names like Winslow Homer, Andrew Wyeth, Marsden Hartley, Edward Hopper, and Louise Nevelson. Few of these artists, however, had true Maine roots. Mattie Arvin did and so did Ransom Eldridge. Scoring Eldridge as the judge of the newly expanded Arvin Prize competition would seal its success, Robertay thought—a local boy who had made good and was now returning to bless the brilliance of her dream. It was a masterstroke.

Except she couldn't get Eldridge to answer her entreaties. Robertay had contacted his agent by phone, email, and text. The agent promised that she was forwarding the requests, but the great man had yet to respond.

"Perhaps if I could talk with Mr. Eldridge personally," Robertay suggested during one call with the agent. "I'm sure that, once he hears the outline of the project we've engaged, he'll be more than interested in participating."

Yet, neither that plea nor the offer of paid expenses and a generous honorarium could induce a response. And because she made such a big deal about why Eldridge would be the "perfect" judge, her reputation for sealing the deal was on the line.

Publicly, Robertay showed only a brave face: "The negotiations are underway," she told anyone who would listen. "There are multiple elements to the deal. Ransom Eldridge is a phenomenally busy artist and so the conditions must be finessed." Privately, she stormed: "What the fuck, Thomas! Can't this asshole simply respond to one of the hundred messages I've left for him?"

Thomas tried to soothe. "He probably is quite busy, dear. I'm sure your messages will be answered soon enough."

"They'd better be!"

CHAPTER 45

John McTavish was struggling, though less with his art work than with his life. Actually, that wasn't true—the struggles he had with managing his life were taking away from the time he could spend on his art. So he guessed he was having a tough time of it all around.

In the week or so before the Colony meeting and in the week or so afterward, he'd tried to avoid conversations about the Arvin Prize decision. He failed. As a rule, he didn't get many phone calls since he had only a cell phone and had given out the number selectively. Still, he had ended up on a couple of different email lists and the participants chirped steadily either applauding or denouncing the change. He didn't use Facebook or Snapchat or Instagram, but others reported the things they heard through those venues. The Letters to the Editor in the Rascal Harbor Gazette routinely overflowed their typical page two section. McTavish didn't read much else in the weekly, but he absorbed the obituaries, the op-eds, and the letters. "My guilty pleasure," he'd told Noah.

And then there was Noah. As the more social of the two McTavish men and with a summer job at a popular seafood restaurant, Noah got far more news and opinion about the Colony in general and the Arvin decision in particular. He seemed determined to pass along these insights to his father.

So while McTavish's direct connection with the Colony remained limited, he felt as embroiled in its dealings as he would if he were a board member.

"It's draining," he told Noah after listening to a few of his son's stories. "I'm not getting any work done."

"I know, I know," Noah would say, and then tell more stories of who said what to whom about whatever. The Bushmills didn't help.

McTavish hoped that, in the aftermath of the Colony meeting, the yip-yap would die down. Just as that seemed to be the case, however, he got an email reminding him that he'd signed up to participate on the Summer Exhibition planning committee.

Goddamn it, he thought, I forgot all about that commitment. He'd forgotten because, when he signed up, he hadn't anticipated having to do much. He knew that Robertay Harding ran the committee, made most of the decisions, and did a good chunk of the work herself. The Exhibition had run successfully for several years and the actual committee work, McTavish presumed, would be light.

Then Robertay and the Board changed the rules for the Arvin competition. The Exhibition committee was now in for some heavy lifting.

Over the course of the next three meetings, a range of issues were discussed and decided:

- Development of a theme—McTavish thought the Pencil-Paint-Paper idea a clever one as did most of the group. Still, they'd chew it over for a meeting and a half before recommending it for Board approval;
- Limits on the size and weight of the submitted art—paintings could be no larger than two feet by four feet, while sculptures could weigh no more than forty pounds;
- The number and value of the prizes, ribbons, and medals—McTavish had taken notes about that discussion, but could remember no details other than

that the check for the Arvin Prize grand winner increased to $1500;

- The age qualifications of 18-75 years old—the Exhibition was a "serious show," so the committee wanted no kids—a separate show for student artists was held at a different time—or old timers—a separate retired artists show had been discussed for years, but never staged;

- The number of submissions each artist could make, three, and in what format, digital, to the screening subcommittee. McTavish found out that he was on that group too.

In addition, another set of rules were discussed. Behind each proposed limitation was at least one recalled story that became the basis for the restriction:

- Abstract work had to be labelled with an "up" side— Someone recalled the time an artist had gone ballistic when he'd seen his abstract painting hung upside down. "Looked better that way," the story teller said.

- Works must be completely dry—Another committee member recalled the acrylic artist who rushed in with his painting at the last minute. When a busy staff member went to hang it, however, he discovered that the paint had yet to dry and that his handprint was clearly visible. In this case, however, the artist proclaimed the accident "A big improvement!"

- No kit-developed work—Chub Peters loved doing the paint-by-numbers kits his grandchildren gave him on every holiday occasion. The rule against kit-developed works had come about after Chub's third year of submissions.

And so McTavish's time for art became his time for gossip and committee work, and it unsettled him. If committee work was what I wanted to spend my time on, I would have stayed a professor, he thought.

The other drag on his time were the ladies. Since the dinner at Gary and Ruby's, he had been besieged.

"'Besieged,' John? Really now?" He heard Maggie giggle.

"Well, maybe not besieged so much as 'beset,'" McTavish responded weakly. He grimaced as soon as he imagined Maggie's smile broadening. "Ah, hell, Maggie, you know what I mean. I'm no good at this relationship stuff."

"No, you're really not, but you can be and you need to be. I have faith in you."

"But how do I do it?" McTavish asked. And received no response.

What McTavish referred to as being besieged or beset turned out to be three different invitations to coffee, a drink, and lunch. Two of the offering ladies had stepped forward due to Ruby Park's prodding; the third came forward because "My friend, Peggy Levere, she said that you could use a friend and, well, I thought, a friend might buy lunch for another friend. So would you like to go to lunch?"

McTavish begged off, pleading an overloaded work schedule—true—and an overbooked personal calendar—not so much. When Noah overheard this last excuse, he called his father out.

"'Overbooked?' Doing what and with whom? Are you going out with someone you haven't told me about?" McTavish thought he heard a trace of humor mixed with a tinge of anxiety in Noah's voice.

"No, there's no one. A little white lie. If I don't claim a busy personal and professional schedule, they start nibbling around for a free slot."

"So you've had more than one offer? How come I haven't heard about these?"

"I'm a man of mystery!"

"Man of mope, is more like it. You've got to get out there, Dad. You can't stay cooped up here in the cottage."

McTavish held his tongue for a moment. Wasn't this the same son who, just a few days before, seemed apprehensive that his father might become involved with a woman other than his mother? McTavish really wasn't all that interested in getting "out there," but he wondered just where Noah's head would be if he did.

To test those waters, he said, "Well, maybe you're right son. I'll give it some thought."

Noah flashed. "Dad, that's your problem—you think, but then you don't act. Be bold for once, take a chance. You know all the clichés… but, in this case, they're right."

Inwardly, McTavish sighed. Outwardly, he said simply, "Good advice."

Noah, knowing that his words would have little effect on his taciturn father, smiled faintly, sighed audibly, and said, "I love you, Dad, but you're hopeless."

CHAPTER 46

"Hopeless" defined the situation at the Rascal Harbor Lobsterman's Co-op. Or so it seemed to most of the fisherman, their sternmen, and a good number of the Co-op workers. The police were making no progress on any of the trap cuttings and the press coverage in the *Bangor Daily* and the *Portland Press Herald* was enough to make folks think that the tourist trade could be affected. Apparently some wars are better for business than others.

All of this attention weighed heavily on Rob Pownall, the Co-op board president. Pownall took his position seriously and he gave considerable thought to who might be doing the cutting and why. He trusted Tristan Riggins to manage the day-to-day operations. At the same time, Rob knew fishermen and he suspected that the longer the crimes went unsolved, the more likely the Co-op members were to take matters into their own, powerful hands.

And taking matters into their own hands was just what a small knot of lobstermen considered doing. Carter Holden, the Patch twins, and a few others sat drinking and discussing the matter at Jimbo's.

"Damn police ain't done shit so far," Corey Patch said.

"That's right," his brother Chance piped in. "I can't believe it's taking them so long. Hell, they solve crimes in an hour every night on TV!"

The group looked at Chance to see if he was joking. He wasn't.

Moving on, Carter said, "And now Tick's out and who knows who might be next. Lot of us are skating close to the margin. A couple of hits like Tick got would put me under."

"You ain't the only one," Sammy Hastings said. His sternman agreed.

Corey said, "Can't say we're getting much leadership from the Co-op neither. I mean I ain't a votin' member—"

"You will be soon. A bad break for Tick turns to be a good break for you," Carter said.

"Yeah, I know," Corey said, with a hint of humility. "Not the best way to come into it, but a man's got to take what he's given, right? I mean I been waiting for years to get my ticket. I didn't wish no harm on Tick Sherwood, but I ain't gonna let that license go by the boards neither."

"I was born two minutes earlier, it'd be my license," Chance said with a bit more growl than he intended. As the others looked at him, he said, "Just sayin'."

Looking sternly at his brother, Corey said, ""Well, my point was that I can't see that Tristan nor Rob have done a whole lot. I've heard a lot of yap, but I ain't seen much action."

Sammy said, "Rob and Tristan, they been talking with that detective. I gotta believe that—"

"No, you ain't gotta believe nothin', Sammy," Corey said. "That's the point. If those guys sit around talkin' and waitin' for the cops to settle this, then we'll all be waitin' for a long time."

"Well, what's your plan?" Sammy said in challenge. He hadn't been fishing as long as Carter, but he captained his own boat and he'd been on the water a whole lot longer than those snot-nosed Patch kids.

Corey said, "If it was me, I'd be on those cops night and day… but I'd also be organizin' the guys, not sittin' back and takin' it easy like Rob's doin'. How much longer's he got as president anyway?"

"Jesus, I think he just started his second term," Carter said.

"Well, like I said, I ain't a votin' member yet, but I'd be pushin' for some action. I mean, maybe Rob's tired, y'know, too tired to do the job."

GEOFFREY SCOTT

"Yeah, too tired," Chance piped in. "Like asleep at the phone."

"I heard of 'asleep at the wheel' and 'asleep at the switch,'" Carter said and smiled. "But I never heard of 'asleep at the phone.'"

Chance said, "Well, that's me, always thinkin'."

"Thinkin' of ways to be a dumb ass," Corey said with a bit of bite.

"Fuck you. Fuck you and your grandma too."

"Wouldn't that would be your grandma, Chance?" Carter asked smiling. He liked the boys, but knew they were several matches short of a full box.

"Ah, fuck it. I'm outta here," Chance said, throwing some money on the bar, and stomping off.

"Wound kinda tight, ain't he?" Sammy's sternman said.

Corey said, "He can be, but he's a damn good man on the water. Everybody knows that. Anyway, I'm just not sure that we got the right fellas in the Co-op leadership and I'm gettin' tired of waitin' around."

"Everybody's frustrated, that's for damn sure. Maybe give it a few more days and see if anything else pops." Then turning directly to Corey, Carter said, "Guess you'll be runnin' against Rob in the next election?"

"Me? Hell, no! I ain't no politician. You gotta be a politician in that job. All's I'm sayin' is that we need leaders. People who ain't afraid to step up."

"It's harder than it looks, being president of the board, but you're not wrong about needing leaders more than politicians. I always thought Rob to be a pretty good man and a damn good captain. You ask any of his crew. Still, just because a man's got talents in one place, don't mean he's got 'em in every place."

Corey nodded…and smiled.

CHAPTER 47

Corey caught up to Chance an hour later at the apartment they shared. He was not happy.

"You dumb fuck," Corey yelled at his brother. "You're gonna blow this whole thing with Putnam if you don't keep your trap shut."

"Fuck you. You're the one gettin' a license, and me I'm gettin' shit!" Chance had drunk as much or more since leaving the bar and, never a happy man, he got worse with drink.

"You'll get your license, Chance, but for Christ's sake, you gotta be patient and we gotta keep to the plan. We let Morgan do the dirty work and we stir the pot. Everything's working good right now. Don't fuck it up."

"Two minutes…" Chance slurred.

CHAPTER 48

When he did have a chance to work, McTavish felt his artistic juices flowing. He wasn't quite ready for the Arvin Prize deadline coming up in a couple of weeks, but he knew he would be.

McTavish had worked up drawings of most of the photographs he'd taken on his trip to northern Maine. In each, the "life amongst decay" theme appeared. And in each, McTavish used what he'd come to think of as his "cartoon markers" to highlight portions of the pictures. In one image, McTavish used a bright green marker to color a set of newly painted shutters against a paint-needy house wall. Another featured a bright red tricycle parked beside an abandoned, weed-covered car. A third showed a new wood addition anchored to a shaky-looking barn.

Yet the images to which McTavish kept returning and the ones he expected to submit for the Arvin Prize were the three colored drawings of crocus plants. As a set, he thought, they worked well—a full-on front image of the crocus, a side view of the plant, and an overhead view. Each image captured the same clump of flowers and the same shabby foundation wall. But taken together, they immediately conveyed the notion of perspective, for the vantage one took—front, side, and overhead—changed the image seen. One set of flowers, seen from three directions, seemed to become three different sets of flowers.

A sure-fire winner, he thought, if only in the cartoon category.

On the other side of Rascal Harbor, Detective Dick Chambers felt like a cartoon cop. All his interviews and investigations had netted him a big fat zero.

After his initial round of interviews, Chambers's early sense was that the Patch twins were involved. That thought fizzled. Both had small boats, but each also had strong alibis for all of the buoy-cutting instances.

So he'd then looked into Carter Holden. The fisherman's aggressive behavior on the Co-op dock seemed like genuine frustration. Some crooks tried to hide their misdeeds by shrinking from sight. Chambers knew, however, that others pushed themselves forward with the thought that being bold is a good way to throw off suspicion. Yet, Holden, too, had hard alibis and so Chambers went looking elsewhere for suspects.

Casting about, Chambers even looked into Arnie Draper. The fisherman, by reputation and interaction, seemed a straight-up guy and he was Hadley Cooper's brother-in-law. Far from disqualifying him, Draper's relationship to Cooper, actually made him a stronger potential suspect in Chambers' mind. He knew families to be a most complicated social institution and the ways that family members could screw one another were still being invented. Yet every angle Chambers pursued came up dry. It was what it was: Draper and Cooper were friends as well as in-laws.

All of this left Johnny Mitchell as Chambers's current and only real lead. Mitchell's record of mischief and mayhem might have put him on Chambers's list anyway. The incident with Winnie Sherwood and Tick's probable involvement in deflating his tire could cause a man like Mitchell to take serious offense. Mitchell didn't work in the lobstering trade, but he had in the past; he didn't have a boat, but he had

GEOFFREY SCOTT

friends who did. Chambers's preliminary findings discouraged the idea that Johnny Mitchell was any kind of criminal genius, but he reasoned that even a dim bulb like Mitchell might know enough to throw off an investigation by striking other fishermen's trap lines first.

So Chambers did his due diligence in tracking down Johnny Mitchell's movements and alibis and got nowhere. He and Constable Artie Long surveilled Mitchell for a week and discovered nothing relevant to the cut-trap crimes. Moreover, the deeper Chambers looked into Mitchell's background, the less convinced he became that Mitchell would have planned out two attacks before taking out his intended victim. Mitchell seemed like a straight-forward knucklehead: If he was mad at you, he came directly at you.

But once he pulled off Mitchell, Chambers had no other direction to pursue. There had been no other incidents over the past few weeks. Balancing that good news was the irritation that the crimes might go unsolved. Chambers got up each morning to put bad guys away. He would not let this case go, but until he developed another lead, he had other matters tugging at his time.

CHAPTER 49

A month later, the Arvin Prize selection committee met. Individually, the committee members had reviewed and ranked the nearly one thousand submissions. Now it was time to compare notes and chose the one hundred works that would make up the Summer Art Exhibition and the twenty-five pieces that would be judged eligible for the Arvin Prize.

Because Robertay Harding chaired the Summer Exhibition committee, she could not also chair the Arvin Prize group. Brenda Sharpe took on that task and she did so with a firm hand. That quality was not the only one she shared with Robertay.

A local of many generations, Brenda Sharpe was little enamored with Robertay's "flair." But she respected the latter's vision for the Colony and she had discretely worked the phones in support of the decision to expand the Arvin Prize competition. Had the membership meeting resulted in any sort of voting, Brenda knew that Robertay's plan would succeed.

A calmer presence than her loud and outspoken ally, Brenda nevertheless ruled over the selection committee. She had a good eye for interesting art and she knew it. Brenda could accept the fact that a lot of the membership's work was kitschy and anemic—sailboats and fishing shanties, lighthouses and pot buoys, and seagulls, lots of seagulls. All rendered with love, but much was without talent. Brenda was not

GEOFFREY SCOTT

averse to selecting some number of these works for the Exhibition. But she would make sure they did not make it into the competition for the Arvin Prize.

Allowing non-residents to compete for the Prize had not resulted in the thousands and thousands of entries Robertay envisioned—notice of the competition had gone out too late for that result. Still, the call for works had generated a nearly four-fold increase in submissions. Most came from east-coast artists, but Midwestern and Western pieces were in the mix as well.

The increase in submissions taxed the committee of ten. Only Brenda viewed all the works as she took on the responsibility of assigning them such that every piece was evaluated by three committee members. Brenda had experimented with different ranking systems over the seven years she chaired the committee. In the end, however, she reduced it to a three-tiered scoring rubric: 1-No way, 2-Okay for the Exhibition, and 3-Arvin Prize-eligible.

Past experience told Brenda that the first category would be the largest. She had an artist's temperament and appreciation for the many ways her colleagues could express themselves. Still, the "shit" that came in never failed to startle and, sometimes, annoy her. Fortunately, the shit made for quick and easy decisions, though invariably the committee would spend too much time arguing over whether a couple of "no way" pieces ought to make it onto the Exhibition list.

With the heavy volume of work to consider in the top two categories, Brenda expected fewer of those distractions, though she was under no illusions that the choices between Exhibition and Prize-eligible would be easy or quick.

A day prior to the meeting, Brenda received each committee member's rankings. She then compiled a master list of the works with their total scores. Even before finishing, she could see trouble brewing. There were twenty-five Arvin Prize spots, yet forty submissions had achieved scores of nine, meaning that all three evaluators ranked them as worthy of Prize consideration. Beyond that, three hundred works had scored well enough that, in the past, they would have earned one of the one hundred spots in the Exhibition. Hmm, she thought, we may need another round of rankings.

Thus, the selection committee faced a very different task than it had in years past. Then, the group had sometimes struggled to find enough good work to mount for Prize consideration. There had even been years when the committee had had to hold their collective nose to fill out the Exhibition roster. Brenda generally felt pleased with the Arvin Prize recipients, but she sighed more than a few times when reviewing the entire array of work.

Given the increase in the number and quality of the submissions, it was an excited group who met at the Colony gallery to review their selections and to make decisions about Exhibition and Prize worthiness.

McTavish knew several of the group assembled and most of the others by their work. It was a mixed bag in his view—about a third were excellent artists with the other two-thirds being strivers like himself. There were no shit producers in the group. Brenda appreciated every Colony artist's efforts, but she would not allow any hacks on her committee.

After introductions and a review of their charge, Brenda explained the "good problem" they faced—they had far too many quality works for the relatively few Prize and Exhibition spots. She quickly flashed through the forty top-rated pieces and the next one hundred fifty that earned scores of seven or eight from the reviewers. In past years, a score of six would have earned a piece consideration for a spot in the Exhibition. That would not be the case this year.

"We've some tough choices in front of us folks. I've been thinking about how to get from one ninety to the hundred and twenty-five slots we've got between the Arvin and the Exhibition. My suggestion is that we do the Arvin Prize selections first and then choose those for the Exhibition."

Brenda went on to propose another round of ranking where they focused first on the forty submissions that initially received top scores.

GEOFFREY SCOTT

To that list, Brenda allowed each committee member the opportunity to include one more piece that they thought worthy of Prize consideration. Once those choices were added to the mix, the group had fifty pieces to consider and they went to work.

McTavish was tickled to see his three pieces had made it into the field of one hundred and ninety, one of which got a top score. He was anxious to hear what the committee thought of the pieces individually, but he was even more interested to see what they thought of the collection.

A tight moment arose as soon as the committee began its deliberation when one member calculated the ratio of resident to non-resident works.

"Damn. Looks like about a two-thirds, one-third split," London James sputtered. "And it's the out-a-staters in the majority. Don't know what I was expecting, but guess I hoped it would be at least fifty-fifty."

Janelle Hanson agreed, saying, "We already know that a lot of members will be upset if their work doesn't make it into the show but, if the final roster is that heavily weighted toward the non-residents, their noses will really be out of joint."

"Nothing we can do about it. Our job isn't to make people feel good, it's to pick the best pieces for the Exhibition generally and the Prize in particular," Brenda said.

Janelle said, "I know, I know. Still, it would've been nice to have a separate category or something for the non-residents, maybe even for just this year."

"Water under the bridge," Brenda said firmly and pushed the committee on to consider the next submission.

Ranking efforts and discussion were followed by more rankings and more discussion. But by the end of the day, twenty-five works had been selected for the Arvin competition and another one hundred for display in the Exhibition. A few bruised egos could be detected, but no blood had been shed.

As the meeting wrapped up, a couple members congratulated

McTavish on having had two of his crocus works selected for the Exhibition and one for the Arvin Prize review. He mumbled some thanks, but one of the committee members noted a disappointment.

"Jesus, I'd be thrilled to get all my pieces in the show," he said to McTavish. "You look like you didn't get any in."

"Sorry," McTavish said, looking around the group. "It's just that, well—"

"Well, what?" Brenda asked.

"Well, the three pieces go together. I made them as a set. They're three representations—"

"Goddamn, I get it now!" London said. "They're the same clump of flowers—"

"Ah, I missed that too," another committee member said.

"Right. I wanted to show the same plant from three different angles, you know, to show that something can be the same and different depending on your perspective."

Janelle said, "Huh. That's pretty interesting. But they can't all be eligible for the Prize, can they?"

"No they can't," Brenda said. "It wouldn't be fair to push out two other pieces. So what do you want to do, John? What's more important to you—competing for the Prize or keeping your pieces together?"

"Maybe you want to think about it overnight?" one member suggested.

All eyes turned to McTavish. He thought he ought to take the suggestion that he deliberate about the decision but, to his and the group's surprise, he said, "Nope. I don't need the time. I've decided—I'll keep the three pieces together."

"So you want to pull your piece out of Prize consideration?" Brenda asked skeptically. "Are you sure you want to do that? Can't imagine too many people making that choice."

"Dumb, probably, but that's what I want to do."

Before any more discussion of McTavish's decision could follow, the committee room door opened and Robertay Harding rushed in.

GEOFFREY SCOTT

"I have terrible news everyone, just terrible news!" she said breathlessly. "I know I should inform the Executive Board first, but I just had to tell someone and I knew you were working here and—"

"What's the news, Robertay?" Brenda asked with a trace of impatience.

"Oh, it's awful, just awful—Ransom Eldridge will not judge our show! His agent just called to tell me. I can't believe it. I've been so patient, so accommodating. and then the ass wouldn't even call me himself!"

Murmurs of anger and disbelief circulated around the room. Several of the members knew Eldridge to be a self-centered boy and now a self-important man. Still, most thought he would recognize the importance of the event and the honor accorded to his selection as the Arvin judge. Local roots grow shallow in some people, however, and Rascal Harbor apparently had the shallowest of holds on Ransom Eldridge.

Robertay's problem, of course, became everyone's problem. The late date precluded the possibility of securing another big-name judge so the group proposed a host of other options—a well-liked state politician, a visiting movie star, a starter for the Boston Celtics. Though each of these suggestions offered a bit of cachet, Robertay and Brenda nixed them in turn.

"It's been a long day, Robertay," Brenda said finally. "How about if we send you our suggestions over email by tomorrow morning?" The committee members looked gratefully at their leader. Robertay, still seemingly in shock that someone would turn her down, simply nodded.

On his drive home, McTavish wondered what would have happened if he'd have put all three of his crocus images into one picture frame.

CHAPTER 50

After leaving the selection committee, Robertay went home and emailed the Executive Board. She explained the problem and called for a meeting the following morning. Robertay supplemented the email distribution list with Brenda Sharpe and a couple of other Colony members whose views she respected. She wished she had a good suggestion to put in front of the group. That way, they could simply ratify her idea and then move on. But no good solutions were coming.

With the group assembled the next morning, Robertay quickly called the meeting to order.

"We are facing a crisis," Robertay said matter-of-factly. "But we have some good news as well. We did the impossible by bringing together an amazing collection of work both for the Exhibition and for the Arvin competition. Tell them, Brenda."

Brenda gave a short report on the number and quality of the submissions. She finished by telling the story of John McTavish's curious decision to keep his three pieces together rather than keep one in the Arvin Prize group. No one was quite sure how to respond.

Robertay then asked each of the other committee chairs to give reports. When the last one finished, Robertay said, "As you can see, we are in excellent shape to stage the best Summer Exhibition ever. But we need a judge and we need one soon, especially if she or he is a high-profile person—we'll want to capitalize on her or his name. So let's go folks. Put your ideas out there."

After a brief hesitation, the group started. Some of the ideas repeated those the selection committee offered the previous day. Some were even less viable than those.

An hour later, Jona Lewis held up his hand and said, "Look, we're not getting anywhere. Having a big-name artist as the judge for the Arvin is a good idea, but it's just not going to happen this year. So I suggest we go back to our standard approach of having a panel of Colony members act as judges."

Though Robertay looked dismayed, nods of agreement appeared around the table.

Regina Baldo said, "Maybe we change up the panel. You know, maybe vary the group in a way to reflect the change in the competition."

"I'm not sure what you mean," Brenda said.

"Well, I guess I was thinking that we could have one or two judges be well-established local artists and another one or two could be non-residents. The idea, you know, would be to show a mix of old and new."

"I think that could work," Jona said hopefully. Again, nodding heads and voices seconded his comment.

Surprisingly, Robertay had stayed mum during this discussion. Toni Ludlow asked what she thought.

"Oh, I don't know, Toni," Robertay said and sighed heavily. "I was so invested in a high-profile artist like Ransom Eldridge that it's hard for me to think about stepping back to our old practice."

Thomas Beatty said, "But it wouldn't be exactly our old practice. Regina's idea about varying the composition of the judge's panel makes some sense and might calm any lingering anxieties."

"Oh, fine," Robertay said, throwing her hands up in exasperation. After a moment's regrouping, she called for nominations for the local and non-resident slots. Relieved that Robertay had not pitched a fit, the group quickly turned to the task. They soon generated names of seven local artists and five non-residents all of whom, they thought, would be available and interested in the task.

As the group tried to whittle the list down to first and second choices in each group, Toni said, "Wait! Don't we usually have an odd number of judges? You know, in case there's a tie?"

Regina said, "Oh, shoot, good point. But if we add either another local or out-of-stater, the balance will be off." Several others agreed, though it wasn't clear if they were agreeing that an odd number was necessary, that the local to non-local ratio needed adjustment, or both.

"So what do you propose?" Brenda asked.

Regina said, "Well, maybe there's a third category. Something like 'first-time contributor' or 'recently moved to the Harbor.'"

"You mean, like a 'newbie,'" Jona said.

"Exactly. A newbie," Regina said with a smile.

Toni said, "Well, if we go in that direction, John McTavish seems like a good bet. He's only lived full-time in the Harbor for a year. And, by his own decision, he's out of the running for the Arvin Prize."

"Good idea," Brenda said with a smile. "Sound good to everyone?" Everyone offered their agreement, though Robertay just nodded her assent. "Great, one down, four more to rank order," Brenda said.

CHAPTER 51

A month after the first trap cutting occurred, Detective Chambers was stymied. He'd tried, but he could not make any scenario work in which Johnny Mitchell committed the several crimes. Reluctantly he crossed Mitchell's name off his list of suspects. And then the buoys marking another three strings of Hadley Cooper's traps went missing.

Folks associated with the lobster trade had not forgotten the earlier trap cutting. Most everyone had a pet theory or two about the crimes and a short list of suspects, yet no one had any evidence. So as time passed, as no obvious culprits emerged, and as the cutting seemed to have ended, interest flagged.

And then Hadley's traps were cut a second time. Those who heard his angry rant over the radio to his brother-in-law Arnie Draper quickly radioed the news to their friends. By the time Hadley returned to the Co-op dock, most everyone knew of his troubles and either confirmed or revised their theories of who was involved and why.

Tristan Riggins had phoned Detective Dick Chambers to relay the news. Chambers met Hadley after the latter stowed his gear and squared up his boat. Rather than talk in front of the milling crowd on the dock, however, Chambers took Cooper to the police station.

"I don't know what to tell you, Detective," Hadley said as the men settled into office chairs. "I mean I'd almost come to think it was just some random kids screwing around. I mean, there didn't seem to be any connection between me and Babette or between us and Tick Sherwood, so it just seemed random. And then when it seemed to stop, well, I guess I was just trying to put it behind me."

"You haven't had any scrapes with anyone from the first cutting until now?" Chambers asked.

"I really haven't," Hadley said in a dispirited tone. "I mean that's the frustrating part. If someone was really mad at me, I think I'd know it. And if someone was still so mad at my dad that they'd take it out on me, then why did they wait so long between the two sets of cuttings?"

"Hard to say. I've got zero physical evidence to go on. I tried to convince the chief to hire a diver to bring up the traps so that we could look at the cut ends of the lines. But he wouldn't go for it—too expensive and too little chance of learning anything other than that the lines had been cut."

"Guess that makes sense," Hadley said. "Though woulda been nice to get my traps back."

"Will this latest attack put you under?"

"No. It's another big dent all right, but I can absorb it. Just not sure how many more I can lose before I'll have to quit."

"How many people know that?"

"Not many. Arnie and a couple of the other captains. I'm still feeling like an outsider so I don't socialize all that much."

"And no reason to think any of those folks would want to do you in?" Chambers asked.

"No. Like I said, I'd kinda come to the opinion that I wasn't really the target. Hate to think I was and that I let down my guard somehow and let it happen again."

"Well, that's part of the problem. There's no real way of keeping an eye on all the fishing gear out there. It's not like we could set up a stake-out or install surveillance gear out on the open ocean."

"No, don't guess there is. So what're you going to do?" Hadley asked.

GEOFFREY SCOTT

"Keep talking to people and hope that something leaks out. I'll start in with all the captains tomorrow."

The sad face of the fisherman sitting in front of him almost convinced Chambers to lie. He thought about throwing the man a bit of hope by promising that he'd get the culprit. But he had nothing to base that hope on and he increasingly wondered if this crime would ever be solved. In the end, he decided to play it straight.

"I'll do everything I can, Hadley," Chambers said, and hoped that that would be enough.

CHAPTER 52

Jumper Wilson's T-shirt read *Actions speak louder than words, but if buoys could talk...* The cutting of Hadley Cooper's trap lines was the hottest topic in town. But small town lives are no less complicated than their big city peers. No story has only a single narrative and the perspectives that those who hear and tell the story matter.

The men at the Lydia's back table could talk about nothing other than the trap cutting. Rob Pownall tried to answer his friends' questions, but frequently found himself unable to do anything more than shrug.

"Don't know what to tell you, boys," Rob said at one point. "I haven't got any better idea about this situation than you do."

Ray Manley said, "Well, guess it probably ain't no whale, though they say them things are damn near as smart as a man."

"Jesus, Ray, really?" Vance Edwards said incredulously. "You finally figured out that it's no Hadley Cooper-stalking whale?"

"Now Vance, ease up on Ray," Bill Candlewith said, defending his friend. "Ray was just advancin' a theory early on."

"Calling nonsense a 'theory' doesn't make it any smarter," Vance said.

"Was me, I'd look at them Patch kids," Slow Johnston said, surprising his tablemates. Slow might agree with a point made, but he seldom advanced a new one.

"What makes you say that, Slow?" Rob asked, happy to turn the conversation away from buoy-attacking whales.

"I seen 'em, them Patch kids kick a dog," Slow said. The other men looked at one another, not sure how to respond since Slow's point might be relevant or might be twaddle.

Always one to try and keep a discussion focused, Vance asked, "Well, okay, Slow, thanks for that insight. But what does that have to do with Hadley's trap lines getting cut?"

Slow, who looked as if he'd already moved on to the next topic, smiled at his friends as though they might be the thick ones.

"Simple. Anybody'd kick a dog would cut traps."

Toulouse Rustin, Nellie Hildreth, and Sarah McAdams discussed the trap cuttings in the Gazette conference room. Given the lull in the crimes and the lack of police progress on the case, Sarah had had little to report. The letters to the editor had declined as well. With this recent incident, all expected a bump in community interest.

Nellie asked Sarah to interview Detective Chambers and as many lobstermen as she could find. She also said she'd alert Rich Reed, her assistant editor, to plan more space for the inevitable increase in letters.

Adjusting his glasses, Toulouse wondered aloud about the angle his column might take. He'd written about a range of topics since his inaugural piece, but had yet to deal with the presumed lobster war.

"I've been doing some reading about past lobster wars and it seems that they end in arrests at about the same average as most crimes. They are essentially property crimes, though the gain is typically vengeance rather than financial. It's a relatively easy crime to commit given the access anyone with a boat has to the trap buoys. Still, it's also relatively rare."

"Thanks for the tutorial, nephew," Nellie said with a chiding smile.

"But what are you going to write?"

"I haven't quite decided, my dear aunt, but, as always, you'll be the first to know."

Carter Holden and Sammy Hastings settled into a different conversation about Hadley Cooper's troubles. The men were comparing the wildest theories they'd heard to date.

"One old gal told me that Hadley must have a water witch mad at him," Sammy said.

"What the hell's a 'water witch'?"

"No idea. And I couldn't get nothing more out of her. Pretty spooky though."

"Well, I heard that there must be a sinkhole right there under Hadley's trap," Carter said.

Babette Dubois, who had been listening in, walked over and said, "I heard it was either the aliens or the Russians or the Republicans that cut Hadley's traps. But the best one I heard was that Hadley cut his own traps."

"What? Why the hell would he do that?" Sammy asked.

"So's to get sympathy for being Jenson Cooper's kid. Then someone else said Hadley himself must have done it, but it's because he's got a worm in his brain," Babette replied.

"Jesus, ain't people peculiar," Sammy said and sighed. The others agreed.

"Yes, they are," Richard Anthony Bates agreed, after hearing Babette's recount of her chat with Carton Holden and Sammy Hastings. "But it's not just lobstermen." He then described the fracas around the

GEOFFREY SCOTT

Arvin Prize judging.

"Did you know this Eldridge fellow?" Richard Anthony asked Babette.

"No, he was several years older than me, but his family still lives in town. I expect they'll be mortified by him refusing to judge, but I think they're used to his antics. I heard he was a jerk when he lived here. Guess he still is."

"All in all, it does seem like a particular slap in the face to the community and to Robertay. I've heard that she is beside herself. I think she saw it as a chance to smooth some feathers over the Arvin Prize decision. You know, have a famous artist with local roots come back and add his blessing to the newly expanded competition."

"She's a shrewd one, that Robertay," Babette scoffed. "But I still think it was a dirty trick to invite in the outsiders."

"Maybe so, but the reports are that the artwork this year is several cuts above the pieces submitted in the past," Richard Anthony said. He added, "Except for the judging problem, it seems that Robertay's plan is working."

"Maybe," an unconvinced Babette said. "So there's going to be a panel of judges instead of just one?"

"Right. They've always had a panel, but it's been composed of Colony members since only locals could enter the competition. I guess they decided to keep the idea of three judges, but they've purposely chosen them to represent artists from three different constituencies."

"What do you mean?"

"One is a long-time local, one is from out-of-state, and the third is a fellow who just took up full-time residence. That last one is the reason I agreed with your colleagues' assessment that people are 'peculiar.'"

"Why's that?"

"Apparently the guy, John McTavish, had one of his paintings selected for the Arvin Prize competition. But he'd submitted two other pieces that he thought of as a set. So when the selection committee only chose one, he decided to pull it so it could be with the other two in the Exhibition."

"You mean he gave up a chance to win the Prize just so that his pieces would all be together?"

"That's it," Richard Anthony said shaking his head. "I don't know if it's dumb or noble or some combination, but it's definitely peculiar."

"He must be nuts," Janice Sewall said to her husband David. She, too, had heard about McTavish's decision and concluded that he was more than peculiar.

"There's no way I would have pulled my work from the Arvin competition. It was his first submission too. And he pulled it," she said in disbelief.

"Different strokes, dear," David said.

"Different strokes, my ass. He's got to be fucking nuts!"

"Jesus, Dad, are you nuts?" Noah asked his father.

"Probably."

GEOFFREY SCOTT

CHAPTER 53

"Jesus, brother, you must be nuts!" Mark McTavish boomed on hearing of his brother's decision. "I'll admit I don't know much about you art types, but that sounds like a dumb move. How can you win the prize if you take your piece out of the competition?"

"Guess I can't," McTavish replied simply. "Not this year anyway."

"Not this year or any year if you're gonna act like a pea brain!"

Giselle jumped in. "Mark, this family's only got one designated pea brain and that, dear brother, is you."

"Aunt Giselle just called Dad a 'pea brain,'" the younger of Mark's kids whispered to the older.

"Just wait. She'll call him worse than that!"

And so another gathering of the McTavish clan began. The hosting turn had come back around to McTavish and he'd made sure to lard the refrigerator and pantry with plenty of food and drink. He'd forgotten they were coming the first time the family gathered at his cottage and he'd been reminded of it more times than he could count. He'd not made that mistake again.

Noah felt badly. The news that his father had withdrawn his drawing from the Arvin competition had come from his lips, though he hadn't meant it as a criticism. In fact, in the time since his father had told him, he'd come to admire the move. He knew his father to be an odd duck at times. In this case, his odd action, however, seemed gallant somehow.

Sure it was self-sacrificing, but in a dignified, almost gracious way. Rather than whining or complaining, his father just decided that the integrity of the work mattered more than the chance to win a prize.

Of course Noah had had to figure all this out on his own. His father simply told him of his decision and then accepted Noah's immediate judgment that he was crazy.

And now he'd told Uncle Mark. In the course of describing his own excitement about getting a piece in the Exhibition, Noah began telling Mark about his father's decision. Mark instantly jumped to the same conclusion Noah had on hearing the news. And now Mark had used the information to dig at his father. To Louise who had insisted on coming to this gathering, he whispered, "Maybe Dad's right about not talking so much."

While Noah berated himself for not well explaining his father's decision, the rest of the family moved on to other topics. McTavish's sister, Ruth, and his sister-in-law, Amy, talked with Giselle about quilts they were making. Giselle's partner, Martin, described to Ruth's husband, Ronald, an elegant solution Giselle had devised to hide the plumbing in the house they were rehabbing. And Mark's children told their cousins about the old Playboy magazines they found in the attic over their garage.

Out of the spotlight finally, McTavish leaned over to Giselle and said, "You know, you don't always need to take up for me."

Giselle smiled. "For a smart man, John, you're dumb as a box of rocks when it comes to dealing with Mark. If you just snapped him back once or twice, he'd get the message."

"Are you sure about that?" McTavish asked with a smile. "Mark might not even notice 'once or twice.'"

"Ah, I'll grant you that, John. Talk about a box of rocks."

"Yes, but a heart of gold. If I were ever in enough trouble that you couldn't help, Mark's the first person I'd call."

"And he'd come flying, but then you'd have to hear about it for the next five years."

"Well, if I was in that much trouble, hearing about it might not bother me."

GEOFFREY SCOTT

Ruth and Amy called the group to eat. McTavish's dining area table had only four chairs so the group picked up their food and found seating wherever they could. The open design of the cottage, however, meant that everyone was within loud-talking distance.

And loud-talk they did, or they did after Ruth asked that they first say grace.

That request quieted half the room immediately. Religion of any stripe found barren ground in the household of Malcolm and Nadine McTavish and, to their oldest son's knowledge, none of his siblings had heard the call either. McTavish looked at Giselle and Martin, who both shrugged. Then he looked at Mark, who said, "Yup, Ruth has found the Jesus."

Ruth looked up, smiled beatifically, and asked, "Shall we bow our heads?" And so they all did. Ruth offered a mercifully short prayer and the meal and talk began.

Mark leaned over to McTavish and said quietly, "Ruth got the call about a month ago. It's not exactly clear what happened, but she's been all about it since then. Ron's not sure what to do about it so he goes along. Guess Ruthie decided to let the whole family in on it today."

All McTavish could think to say was, "I'll be damned." Sitting in such close proximity to Ruth, however, he decided to keep it to himself.

Mark seemed to see the thought cross his brother's mind, however, and said, "Yup, me too."

The meal passed with no additional surprises. Folks talked about the crazy ideas of the newly elected governor, the shortcomings of the Red Sox hitters, and the on-again, off-again lobster war.

"I hear the trap cutting is still occurring," Martin said.

McTavish nodded. He'd eaten breakfast at Lydia's that morning and heard the news about Hadley Cooper's traps.

"Thank God they've got those breakout sections on traps now so that the lobsters can get out eventually," Giselle said.

"Right," said Mark, grinning. "Otherwise their little lobster mommies would have to come visit them in trap jail."

"Hey, maybe the lobster mommies could bake them a cake with a file in it so they could break out sooner!" one of Mark's kids added.

Martin said, "Maybe it's the lobsters themselves that are cutting the buoy lines. I mean they're the ones who benefit most directly."

"Christ, they probably got a gang and that's one of their initiation rites," Mark said, laughing. Then he saw Ruth's face. "Sorry Ruthie," he mumbled. Ruth merely nodded.

"Anyway," McTavish said, adding the only bit of news he could. "Apparently the police are stymied and the mood among the fisherman is pretty tense."

"Well, it threatens their livelihoods, to be sure. I know I'd be upset if anyone messed with my plumbing gear," Martin said.

"What would you do? Try to get 'em into hot water?" Noah asked with a grin. His comment set off a flurry of attempts to top it with other plumbing references:

"Maybe you could elbow them out of the way!"

"How about flushing them down the toilet?"

Then Louise added, "Either that or you could call the coppers on them!" When silence followed, Louise said, "Get it? Coppers, like the police! Plumbers use copper pipes, right?" Everyone groaned, but decided that Louise's offering showed the most inventiveness even if they still weren't sure they understood it.

At that point, Mark tried to move the conversation to fart jokes, but Ruth and Amy moved quickly to shut him down.

"Oh, but just this one," Mark pleaded. "I just heard it and it's a great one." Before anyone could object further, he began: "An old couple go to church one Sunday. Halfway through the service, the wife leans over and whispers all anxious in her husband's ear, 'I just let out a silent fart. What do you think I should do?' The husband looks over at her and says, 'Put a new battery in your hearing aid!'"

As the laughter ebbed, Mark snapped his fingers and said, "Hey that reminds me…any news on the dating front, brother John?"

GEOFFREY SCOTT

Inwardly McTavish groaned, but taking his sister's admonition to heart, he resolved not to let Mark get to him.

"Nope," he said simply.

"Well, what about any prospects?" Mark asked, pushing.

"Cool it," Giselle said to Mark. "I'm sure that if and when John has something to tell us all, he'll tell you first so you can blab it all around. Honestly, sometimes I think you're the biggest nosybody in the state of Maine."

"You wound me, Giselle," Mark replied putting his hand to his chest.

"It'll take more than calling you a nosybody to wound you, Mark McTavish," Giselle said. She spoke calmly, but with an edge in her voice.

"Just trying to help our big brother get back on his feet. You know, get back in the game."

"Cut it out, Uncle Mark!" Noah said suddenly. "You know that you're just trying to poke my dad, because that's what you do. You think you're being funny, and sometimes you are. But sometimes you just push it too far. My mom's been dead just over a year—" Here, Noah stumbled, his breath caught, then he continued. "My mom's been dead for just over a year now. I know you liked her and she liked you, but give us some time. Just give us some time."

"Ah, Jesus," Mark started, "I'm sorry...I mean, I didn't mean—"

"Mark, probably best that you just stop there," Amy said, putting a hand on his arm. "Just stop there."

Watching all of this, McTavish thought he heard Maggie say that it's hard to fight your own battles when others are so willing to fight them for you.

CHAPTER 54

Dick Chambers sat looking out his office window wishing that his job looked more that the detective shows on TV. A crime is committed, the detective struggles for a bit, but then catches the bad guy after a moment of inspiration. An hour or so of drama, minus the commercials, and the crime is all wrapped up.

Chambers had had inspirations and had caught a bunch of bad guys over his career. But most of police work was a slog. That part about struggling a bit could take a whole lot longer in reality than it did on the cop shows. Worse, sometimes the bad guys got away. You could work and work and work and still come up short.

From the police shows, Chambers realized, that he should now be reaching for a bottle of whiskey in the bottom drawer of his desk. "Too bad I'm not an alcoholic," he said to himself with only a trace of irony. "Guess I could start up today."

Chambers's reverie began and ended with lobsters. The buoy cutting case was well lodged under his skin. He did the other work demanded of him. But he did so with only half of his mind on each task. The other half continued to push for a lead, any lead, on the cuttings.

And then a little something cropped up. Looking through the previous evening's reports, he noticed that the Patch brothers had been involved in a fight at Jimbo's. Chambers would have been sensitive to the involvement of any of the Co-op lobstermen, but the Patch kids had been on his radar from the beginning of the investigation. He knew them to be as brash and cocky as they were hard-working. This combination of traits defined most of the younger folks, men and women, who worked the lobster trade. The fact that both boys had had solid alibis for the first sets of cuttings took them off his immediate list of suspects. But something about the twins rubbed him.

As Chambers read Constable Artie Long's report, he began to doubt that rub yet again. The report described an incident between the boys and a Robert Morgan from Herrington. According to Arthur Yellen, Jimbo's owner and bartender, the three had been talking quietly at a corner table. The report quoted Yellen as saying that the conversation continued to escalate and he'd warned them to "Keep it down or move it out." The three seemed to heed the warning at first, but ten minutes later punches were being thrown.

What Chambers read next restarted the rub. He'd expected to read that the Patch boys jumped Morgan. Instead, Chance Patch was the victim having been assaulted by his brother and Morgan. Arthur Yellen had heard Chance make a loud remark just before the brawling began, but he'd not heard what it was.

"Next thing I knew, the three of them were scuffling on the floor with that fellow Morgan and Corey pounding the piss out of Chance," Yellen was quoted as saying. Yellen then said, "But after Chance was good and down, then Corey started punching Morgan."

Yellen had called the police as soon as the first punches were thrown. Constable Long arrived as all three men lay sprawled on the floor or sitting in chairs nursing cut lips, raw knuckles, and bruised ribs. No guns or knives surfaced, so Long separated the men and took their statements individually. Those statements proved largely useless; none of the three men had anything helpful to say about the incident and none would press charges against any of the others. Neither of the Patch boys offered any explanation; Morgan only said, "There was a disagreement." Constable Long dispersed the men and filed his report at the end of his shift.

Huh, Chambers thought, and made plans to talk with all involved.

CHAPTER 55

Steve Putnam did all the talking. With Bob Morgan on one side of his Herrington office and the Patch twins on the other, Putnam stormed at the three of them.

"Jesus Christ, I'm working with idiots," he yelled. Pointing at Chance, he said, "First this idiot goes out on his own and cuts Cooper's lines, then you two idiots start beating him up in public. What in hell is wrong with you? You're gonna pooch this whole deal. Jesus Christ!"

Morgan started to explain, but Putnam put up a hand. "Do I have to explain the plan again to you knuckleheads? Do I?" All three men, looking down at the floor, shook their heads. "No? Well apparently I do since we're in this mess now." After a pause, Putnam continued his rant. "Look, Bob does all the cutting, not you, and he does it when I tell him to." Again, pointing at Chance, he said, "You going out there and cutting Cooper's lines puts everything at risk. What if you were seen? What if you got picked up and couldn't establish a credible alibi?"

Chance looked up. "Sorry, Steve. I was just—"

"I don't want to hear it! You got antsy and you wanted to push Cooper out faster so you could get his license and so you went out on your own. You dumb shit, you just couldn't wait could you?" When Chance started to speak, Putnam said, "Shut up. You haven't got a single word to say that's gonna to help your situation right now."

Continuing, Putnam now focused on Morgan. "So I send you to

straighten out these numbnuts and you end up brawling on a barroom floor such that the cops have to come in and bust it up. Jesus Christ, I'm dealing with idiots!"

Morgan explained, "I tried to talk with these two, but as soon as Chance admitted that he'd gone out on his own, Corey started punchin' him and then I guess I did too. Corey and I both realized that Chance fucked up and, well, we kinda lost it. Then Corey sees that Chance is down and he starts wailin' on me and, well, that's when the bartender called the cops to come."

"Christ, I don't know who's the stupidest amongst the three of you!"

CHAPTER 56

As the Summer Exhibition drew near, McTavish found himself giving more and more of his time to the preparation of the show. The Exhibition and Arvin Prize selections had started to arrive and they needed to be logged in, labeled, and hung. Brenda Sharpe seemed to think he could be counted on to show up when scheduled and to work rather than indulging in the unholy trinity of gossiping, eating pastries, and drinking coffee. When she called and asked for his help, he'd agreed to do so.

McTavish understood that efforts like the Exhibition took a lot of work to stage. He complained to Maggie about the time it was taking away from his own art, but she'd chosen silence over commentary. During his time at the gallery, he worked diligently and, at the end of each shift, he admitted to himself that he'd enjoyed having a chance to look at the work being displayed.

Though he'd had a preview of the pieces through his participation on the selection committee, seeing them in person reminded McTavish of the difference between the representation of an art work and the work itself. It wasn't always the case, but some of the drawings, paintings, photographs, sculptures that he'd not much liked digitally had qualities he now appreciated. The pieces he saw were not all great art, but there were no obvious stinkers or "shit" as Brenda referred to it. He had yet to see all the selections, but what he saw convinced him

that he and the other Arvin Prize judges might well struggle to iden-
tify a single winning entry.

The Exhibition and the Arvin Prize entrants favored drawings and
paintings cast in a representational style. Toni Ludlow and few other
artists had abstract pieces in the show; some other works came from
the surrealistic camp; and there was even a sort of Cubist piece. Most
of the works, however, clearly and expressly represented recognizable
images—landscapes, seascapes, portraits, still lifes.

The photographs selected for the show seemed the least interesting to McTavish as only a few leaned away from the typical coastal
scenes. Those more ambitious photographers eschewed lighthouses
and sailboats in favor of more intimate and expressive images—the
shadowed face of a child, the close detail of a flower, and, of all things,
a pile of stacked wood.

The sculptors offered the most variety within their field. Several
works in stone ranged from abstract to representational. Other sculptures stretched the medium. McTavish was particularly struck by an
assemblage piece made up of artists' equipment—pencils, brushes,
paint tubes, palette knives, and the like—and a wall hanging in which
paper, canvas, cloth, and yarn were skillfully interlaced. McTavish had
never been tempted to express his ideas through any of these media,
but he appreciated the fact that some people could, and could do so in
a compelling fashion.

While McTavish quietly worked on the tasks Brenda Sharpe
assigned him, hubbub reigned. Much of it emanated from Robertay
Harding who seemed to butterfly around the gallery attending to details both big and small. Trailing behind her circled a knot of three
women whose sole job seemed to be to coo, awe, and applaud every
decision Robertay made. Robertay appeared to pay no attention to
their gestures, but McTavish noticed that she never moved too far
away from them either.

Also contributing to the hubbub was the arrival of the artists with
their works. Regina Baldo acted as the first point of contact. She greet-

ed each artist with a sunny smile, gave him or her a clipboard full of documents to read and sign, and then took charge of their pieces.

From his vantage, McTavish could see some artists blow into the gallery as if it was their own solo show being hung. They stood impatiently in the line to be checked in, they sighed loudly at the need to fill out the requisite paperwork, and they gave explicit and finicky instructions about how their work was to be handled, labeled, and displayed. Thompson Enders who worked with Regina on the check-in process would listen carefully, then turn and roll his eyes.

Other artists came in nervously, as if they were slightly embarrassed to have their work chosen for the show. They typically avoided eye contact, spoke only when spoken to, and mumbled their answers. When it came time to hand over their work, they did so in a way that suggested they were glad to be rid of it.

Of course, every manifestation possible between these poles presented itself as well. For every artist who crawled or blew in, there were others who simply brought their work to Regina's table, filled out the forms, and handed over their pieces with little fidget or fuss. McTavish supposed that this range of behavior likely mimicked that in other fields. Most historians he knew fell into the "basically normal" category, yet others stretched the limits from bombastic to timid. In fact, the longer he lived and the more experiences he accumulated, the more McTavish realized that humans were equally capable of both inventive and conventional behavior. The trick was to figure out how an individual would react in a given situation. He'd had a couple of psychologist colleagues who spent their academic careers creating models to better predict behavior. As far as he could tell, however, their explanations typically devolved to "It depends."

All of this musing made McTavish reflect on the past few months and the flap over residents and non-residents competing for the Arvin Prize. That division certainly could mean something, he supposed, but with so many ways to characterize and divide people, he wondered how useful geographic affiliation was. People argued, fought, spit, and

GEOFFREY SCOTT

swore over a whole raft of distinctions both more and less important than where they lived. In the end, McTavish supposed it was all about who was in and who was out—the classic conundrum of human society. The tendency to assign insider and outsider status seemed to define so much of what people did—trying to fit into a group, trying to push others out of a group, trying to get back into a group if they were pushed out, trying to start new groups if they didn't like any of the existing ones. It all seemed so pointless. People were similar and they were different, he thought. Does it really need to be more complicated than that? Why can't we just accept it and move along?

McTavish and Maggie had talked about these matters a number of times. As a high school English teacher, Maggie experienced them on a daily, sometimes hourly, basis. McTavish listened to her accounts of the tangles in which her students found themselves. Maggie described kids' abilities to accept and ostracize, to care for and criticize, to love and to hate, dramas that played out over weeks, across days, and sometimes in the time between class periods.

"It's just incomprehensible," he had said to Maggie on numerous occasions. "How do you keep track of it all. And, more importantly, why do you?"

Maggie would smile her knowing smile and say, "It's life, John, it's what people do. We've been doing it for thousands of years and we'll do it for thousands more. Next to feeding ourselves, living together might be one of the hardest things people do. And I'm not sure we're all that much better about it now than our ancestors were."

A common stereotype portrays the art world as more tolerant and inclusive than other social groups. And yet the Colony had just gone through a racking six months or so trying to figure out who should be in and who should be out and McTavish had seen and heard other artists express some pretty awful things. Now that the Exhibition was being mounted, however, most of that ill feeling seemed to have dissipated and the focus now appeared to be on putting together a good show. McTavish wondered, however, if the sour perspectives on all sides of the decision were really gone or if they lay below the surface waiting for a new situation in which to arise.

GEOFFREY SCOTT

CHAPTER 57

Detective Dick Chambers had never been to war and so wasn't sure what to expect when the Rascal Harbor lobster war ended. That it basically ended in a whimper, however, surprised him.

That whimper came from Chance Patch and it surfaced when he realized that, unless he cooperated with the police, the entire responsibility for the trap cutting would be laid on his shoulders. Those shoulders heaved a few times, then he caved.

But it took Chambers a while to get to that point.

After he learned about the altercation from Officer Long's report and a short conversation over the coffee pot, Chambers called the Patch brothers and Robert Morgan in to the station. In doing so, he arranged for the Patch twins to see but not to speak with Morgan before he had each of the three men assigned to an individual interview room.

Working on a hunch, Chambers decided to interview Corey Patch and then Morgan, saving Chance Patch for last. Each of the first two men repeated the non-committal responses they gave Officer Long the night before. Chambers pressed them, but they gave up nothing about the nature of the problem that lead to the fight.

Chambers waited another half an hour before interviewing Chance Patch, hoping that the time alone would agitate the boy. Like the others, however, Chance's initial responses were cool and largely unresponsive. Yet Chambers sensed a smugness behind the few words that he hadn't seen in the others.

Taking a gamble, Chambers said softly, "You know, Chance, Corey gave you up—" Chambers had thought about substituting in Morgan's name, but wondered if naming Corey might prove a more useful opening move. He purposefully left the accusation vague in hopes that the young man would take the bait.

"No he didn't!" Chance yelled, his arrogant expression still in place. "Corey would never give me up."

Sometimes a denial isn't quite a denial, Chambers thought. With his words, Chance denied the source of an accusation, but not the accusation itself. So Chambers pressed on.

"Chance, you interrupted me before I got to say that this fellow Morgan confirmed everything Corey said," Chambers said. Looking the boy directly in the eye, he added "You're cooked."

"The fuck I am," Chance blustered. "Those guys wouldn't say nothin'."

"Oh, they said plenty," Chambers said, still leaving the substance of any accusation unnamed. "They didn't have all the details, but they gave me enough." With that statement, Chambers abruptly got up and left the room. He knew that time had a way of working on a guilty conscience to good effect. He'd leave the boy to stew for a while.

Chambers didn't think that he'd get anything more from Robert Morgan. The man looked like he'd been around—he was middle-aged, brawny, and broken-nosed. He didn't look all that bright, but he appeared to be a tougher nut than the Patch boys. So Chambers decided to work on the other Patch twin.

"I'm not sure what you boys are up to with this Morgan fellow, but Chance is in there blubbering like a child," Chambers lied to Corey. "What do you suppose has got him so upset?"

"What? Chance ain't a crier," Corey said, rising to his feet. "What did you do to him that's got him cryin'?"

GEOFFREY SCOTT

"Sit down, Corey. I haven't done a thing," Chambers said calmly. "I just asked him what you two had going on with Robert Morgan and he broke down. He was crying so hard, he couldn't even make a coherent sentence. All I could hear were a few words—"Morgan," "fishing," "traps." Here, Chambers moved on pure instinct, throwing together words that he hoped Corey would interpret as meaning that he knew more than he did.

"What did he say? What did he say about 'traps?'"

"Can't say for sure. I mean he sounded like he was trying to tell me something, but couldn't get it out. You have any idea what he was talking about?"

"No! I ain't got any idea what he's mixed up in!" Corey said, giving Chambers another inkling that the twins might well be involved in more than a bar fight.

"Well, I don't know what he'd mixed up in either, Corey. But I will find out," Chambers said, adding an edge to his voice, but continuing to be vague. "Make no mistake. Not only am I going to find out, but it's gonna go a lot easier on some folks than others depending on who tells me what." As he did with the brother, Chambers suddenly stood and left the room allowing these words to gnaw on Corey Patch's conscience.

Chambers knew that he was close to something and he suspected it involved the cutting of buoy lines. But he worried about pushing too hard and too fast. After all, he'd brought the Patch twins and Morgan in under the pretense of finding out about the previous night's scuffle. They weren't under arrest and could decide to call his bluff and walk at any moment. "Keep the pressure on, but go slow," Chambers told himself.

Returning to Chance Patch, Chambers came into the room hard. "Goddamn it, Patch," Chambers said, full of bluster. "Tell me about the traps and tell me right now."

Startled, Chance showed a trace of panic in his eyes. "I don't know nothin' about no traps. Why? What did those guys tell you?"

The look in Chance Patch's eyes confirmed Chambers's hunch that he was involved in the trap cutting. But he also knew that Chance had solid alibis for at least the first three events. Still, that panicky look must mean something, he thought.

"They told me enough to think that I'm looking at a man who going to be doing some jail time," Chambers said authoritatively. "They tripped you up, Chance, and it's all gonna land on you. You're headed for the toilet, boy."

As Chambers talked, Chance's face screwed into a rage. "Those fuckin' assholes! They can't sell me out and think they're gonna get out of it. Fuck them!"

"Fuck them or they're gonna fuck you, Chance," Chambers said matter-of-factly. "Fuck them or they're gonna fuck you."

"Well, I can sure fuck them," Chance said sourly. He looked at the floor. Chambers couldn't tell what was happening until he saw Chance's shoulders shake. Then, looking up at Chambers with forlorn eyes, he said, "Let me tell you about Steve Putnam."

Chambers worried a bit about how to proceed with Chance Patch. He didn't want the boy to withdraw, but he also knew that he'd have to advise Chance of his rights. He did so quietly with Desk Sergeant Andy Levesque as a witness. When he got to the part about Chance's right to have an attorney, the boy waved his hand and said, "I don't want no fuckin' lawyer. I just wanta tell it."

Chambers smiled inwardly, but finished the Miranda warnings. He asked, "Do you understand these rights as I've read them to you and are you telling me and Sergeant Levesque that you do not want to be represented by an attorney?"

"Yes, I understand and, no, I do not want an attorney," Chance enunciated each word, but did so in a distant voice.

"Okay, Chance. I'm going to have Sergeant Levesque turn on a video camera and you and I are going to talk."

GEOFFREY SCOTT

CHAPTER 58

The break in the trap-cutting case quieted the talk about a lobster war. But it complicated the talk about the divisions between locals and outsiders.

Talk burbled all over town—at Lydia's Diner, at Jimbo's bar, at Gary's Garage, and at the town hall. Relatively few of the residents were intimately involved in the lobster trade, but lobstering was part of Harbor history and the lure of lobstering and all that went with it undergirded a big part of the tourist trade. The actual pulling of lobsters from the sea engaged a small part of the local labor force. Economically and socially, however, the trade surrounding the crustaceans mattered immensely.

But the trap cutting exposed a local/non-local fault line that no one anticipated. The Patch twins came from a lobstering family with deep local roots. Patch men had fished Rascal Harbor waters for generations. They had never made big money, but they paid their bills and kept up their boats and their gear. They'd been involved in their share of scuffles and scrapes, but none had ever cut a buoy line or had one of theirs cut.

To have two of the Harbor's own mixed up in a trap-cutting scheme created stress fractures that cracked in several directions at once.

Everyone could hate Steve Putnam, Bob Morgan, and the Herrington crowd. To Rascal Harbor folks, Putnam and his plan to overtake the local Co-op reeked of all things "from away." It was easy, then, to see the evil intent that drove Putnam's greed and, by extension, the ill will of the Herrington folks toward their more peaceable Rascal Harbor neighbors.

Except the actions of the Patch twins put the lie to the idea of a peaceable Rascal Harbor. Jensen Cooper had been such an all-round ass that folks had some trouble generating widespread and coherent animosity toward his son Hadley. No one wanted to see a lobster war, but the Cooper family were relative newcomers and Hadley himself had only recently returned to the Harbor after an extended time away. He had seemed a decent kid, but apparently he'd found Rascal Harbor wanting and so many thought he might never have returned if not for his father's early death.

Babette Dubois and Tick Sherwood were a different matter. Though different in many ways, they both came from good, if not great Harbor stock and had kept with the family business. They hadn't looked outward as Hadley Cooper. They had stayed in town, done their work, made a contribution. For them to be caught up in the buoy-cutting nonsense offended town sensibilities. Folks didn't exactly blame Hadley Cooper, but they were angry that his return had seemed to instigate the involvement of good folks like the Dubois and Sherwood families.

But the Patch twins—what to do about the Patch twins? Here a consensus view could find no solid ground.

Clint Evans might have been the first to take the news around town. Clint liked to hang around the police station and, as he was Sergeant Levesque's uncle by marriage, his hanging out was tolerated to a degree. Clint observed Robert Morgan and the Patch twins in motion and he saw anxiety and excitement alternate across Detective Chambers's face as he shuttled from one interview room to another. When his nephew passed him, Clint asked "What's up, Andy? Seems like big doings."

Sergeant Levesque shook his head, but nodded toward the room where Chance Patch sat and said, "Something big all right."

As Chance Patch unraveled and the air in the station grew increasingly charged, Clint's presence went unnoticed. He continued to hang around long enough to understand that the Patch boys were somehow involved in the trap-cutting business. Satisfied with that nugget, Clint waddled over to Gary's Garage where he found his gossip buddy, Alan Tuttle, being scolded, yet again, by Louise Park.

"I got some news today, old boy," Clint said as he entered the garage lobby. "It's them Patch twins that done the cutting."

"Christ, their dad will shit his pants," Alan said.

"Their whole family will shit their pants," Clint said.

"Who's gonna shit their pants?" Gary asked, coming into the lobby to get a cup of coffee.

"Clint says the whole Patch clan's gonna," Allen said loudly. "He says the Patch boys was mixed up in the trap cutting."

"Is that right, Clint?" Gary asked. When Clint nodded, Gary shook his head, "Jesus, that'll put some heads in a twist finding out that it was local boys involved. Wonder how the family's gonna manage."

When the news reached the Rascal Harbor Co-op, the initial talk focused on the Patch boys' involvement and the connection to the Herrington co-op. But the conversation then shifted to the implications for the Rascal Harbor organization.

"Think Hadley'll wanta take action against us, the Co-op, I mean?" Carter Holden asked Arnie Draper, Cooper's brother-in-law.

"Hard to say, but I wouldn't guess so. I mean it wasn't Co-op sanctioned or anything. I know Hadley was kinda upset that he didn't get much in the way of support from the guys. But mostly he laid that down to his dad being such a jackass. Still, I think it stung him some."

"Yeah, I s'pose it would," Carter admitted.

"Well, especially when Hadley could see that Babette and Tick were getting some consideration after their lines got cut. I expect that was the part that got to him most."

"I'da been pretty pissed had it happened to me," Carter acknowledged. "Guess we kinda blew it on that one."

At Lydia's Diner the next morning, the conversations erupted. As soon as one focal point emerged, another arose to challenge it for attention. Were the Patch brothers set up or did they help plan the attacks? Was Corey as culpable as Chance? Who did Steve Putnam and Robert Morgan think they were to interfere in Rascal Harbor matters? Who else in Herrington knew about the plan? Could the Rascal Harbor fishermen sue the Herrington Co-op for damages? In the end, however, all discussion resolved to the issue of impact on the town's image. Nearly all agreed that Rascal Harbor's name had taken a hit, though few agreed on how hard a hit it was.

Listening in on this babel, Toulouse Rustin considered the many ways to take his next column. Pulling out his pen, he scribbled the following on a paper napkin: "When communities war amongst themselves, no winners ever emerge."

CHAPTER 59

With the trap-cutting case in its rear view, townsfolk's attention, or a good chunk of it anyway, turned to the Summer Exhibition.

As it had among the artists, most of the residents' simmering animosity toward outsiders boiled off in the weeks after the Colony meeting ended. A few people, Larry Court most prominently, tried to keep the controversy going. But even he found himself drawn to other matters and, once the Exhibition mounting began, he got into the spirit of putting on a good show.

Unfortunately, that feeling did not last through the judging, either inside the judges' deliberations or outside among the viewers of the show.

That two-thirds of the selected pieces came from out-of-staters did not go unnoticed by the townsfolk. Some simply shook their heads at the injustice of allowing nonresidents to exhibit their work in what had always been a local show. Others nodded in support of the idea that the Colony regulars just couldn't compete with real artists "from away." Still others wondered if the ratio had been purposely tilted toward out-of-towners this time and would only increase in the coming years. Many of these observations and assumptions were expressed as unspoken thoughts or as quiet whispers to partners or friends. Others, however, became topics of conversations in kitchens, at bars, on Facebook pages, and during morning walks.

From murmurs to rants, these representations of the resident/non-resident fracas were fleeting compared to the sharp, divisive, and long-winded expressions that arose in the gallery office where the Arvin Prize committee sequestered themselves. And yet these squabbles touched only lightly on the decision to expand the Prize competition. Instead, the issues that divided the committee were far more complex.

John McTavish represented the newbie element on the Arvin Prize jury. Oil painter Thompson Enders stood for the locals. Enders was a tall and thin man, though his advanced years had stooped his shoulders and his large gray head and age-spotted hands showed the beginnings of Parkinson's. Representing the out-of-staters was Marguerite Jameson, a sculptor from Rhode Island. A woman of middle age, Jameson's colorful and flowing clothing masked her modest bulk.

As a member of the selection committee, McTavish had seen all the works selected for the Prize competition. Enders had helped display the Exhibition and the Arvin pieces so he had seen most of them, though he'd studied few. Jameson arrived in town two days before the winner was to be announced. She took the first day to carefully study all of the Arvin finalists, and to sneak a look at her own work which had been selected as part of the overall Exhibition works.

The twenty-five works judged worthy of Arvin Prize consideration tilted toward paintings. Most were oils, but acrylic and watercolor artists garnered space as well. In contrast to the Exhibition selections, which tended toward traditional scenes and subject matter, the Arvin Prize finalists were more diverse. Representational images, both big and small, still dominated the grouping, but abstract paintings were better represented than in the Exhibition selections. The themes expressed mirrored those in the Exhibition space—outside scenes of land and water, inside scenes of furniture and fruit, portraits of people

GEOFFREY SCOTT

and structures, images of flora and fauna. The photographs and sculptures, by contrast, seemed tamer, at least to McTavish's eye. All were well rendered, but seemed to lack the expressiveness of the paintings.

As the group sat down to their deliberations, McTavish wondered if this assessment might not be fair. He'd never acted as an art show judge before, but suspected that an open mind was important, especially early on. To dismiss whole categories of the works represented didn't seem like a good idea so he resolved to give each piece its due consideration.

Thompson Enders and Marguerite Jameson had both served as judges for juried shows, but Marguerite deferred leadership of the group to Thompson as a long-time Colony member. That bit of détente and good nature later appeared as the high point of the deliberations, however, as the two clashed on most every other point.

The fire began with the order in which the works were considered.

Marguerite began. "There are far fewer photographs and sculptures, so I think we should review them first so that they aren't bulldozed by the paintings."

"There will be no bulldozing, madam," Thompson said, bristling a bit. "Every work will get its fair attention."

"You know as well as I that works on paper and canvas always gain favor in shows. It's only fair that works in the other media get their due."

"And they will," Thompson said, voice rising.

"Maybe we could intersperse the works," McTavish offered, trying to broker what he wondered might be the first of many compromises. "You know, look at a couple of paintings, then a piece of sculpture, then another couple of paintings."

"That could work, I suppose," Marguerite said with a sniff.

"Done," Thompson said.. "Let's get to it."

Thompson proposed that they each rate the works independently on a 1-3 scale. One meant a piece that deserved top consideration; two meant a piece that a judge could live with as the Prize winner; three meant "not a chance."

ISLANDS AND BRIDGES

243

With agreement on that procedure, the group began work. They started by moving through the digital images of each piece talking about its relative strengths and weaknesses. Then each judge rated the piece on a tally sheet. Soon, however, the group decided to view the actual pieces thinking that the digital image obscured one element or another. So they gathered their tally sheets and markers and moved their operation into the gallery space.

McTavish found himself quite enjoying the discussions. With far less experience than his colleagues, he spoke the least. But when he did, Thompson and Marguerite seemed to listen to and take seriously his comments. By contrast, Thompson and Marguerite tried on their more erudite selves in the first few discussions, seeming bent on one-upping one another.

Looking at a pen, ink, and watercolor caricature of a fisherman, Marguerite huffed, "I just find work rooted in the New Objectivity movement of the Weimar period so terribly dated. Personally, I think Hitler did the art world a favor by banning it."

Thompson had his own moments of grandeur. Of the same piece, he said, "Oh, I don't know, Marguerite. If one sees the hint of Expressionism that I do, then I think we can agree that it is a decent representation of that movement."

McTavish knew something about Expressionism, but hadn't a clue what the New Objectivity artists did. What he saw in the piece was an adequately rendered image that was made "artier" by the addition of some squiggly lines. He marked it a three.

Marguerite and Thompson continued their one-upsmanship over the next few pieces. Eventually, however, they realized that neither intended to kowtow to the other so they focused on the technical and artistic elements of each selection that McTavish had been observing.

As they did so, the three judges' comments became more closely aligned. They all liked a beautifully rendered watercolor scene of a young boy walking on a beach, a finely wrought sculpture of an egret, and a surrealistic-style pastel of islands and bridges. And they each

GEOFFREY SCOTT

gave threes to a small abstract in oil, an oil painting of seagulls, and a photograph of stacked firewood. The drawing of a fishing shanty on a cloud seemed clever, but only just; the watercolor of lobstering gear was well rendered, but blah.

The biggest disagreement arose around a map of New England. Using thick slabs of oil paint, an out-of-state artist depicted five of the six New England states in a range of colors: Vermont in gold, New Hampshire in lilac, Massachusetts in tangerine, Rhode Island in rust, and Connecticut in amber. Canada was represented in aqua and the Atlantic Ocean was rose colored. Just off center, the state of Maine lay unpainted, the dingy white of the canvas showing through. There was a Jasper John quality to the work—the colors were variably applied and there was some blurring of the state lines. Still, the individual states were recognizable and the absence of paint covering the state of Maine caught the eye.

McTavish remembered the piece generated a lot of interest during the selection process. The sheer number of works to screen, however, prevented any sustained conversation. McTavish and the other committee members wondered about the artist's point, but didn't have time to discuss it.

The group of three judges had time, so discuss it they did—if raised voices, accusations, and swearing can be considered discussion.

"I can't believe this piece of garbage made it into the Prize competition," Thompson said as the group moved in front of the large painting.

"What are you talking about?" Marguerite said surprised. "I think it's terrific. I mean maps have been done before, but the way this piece is expressed seems quite profound. The interplay of color and bare canvas—"

"Exactly...'bare canvas'!" Thompson said, sputtering. "What the hell is that supposed to mean? Is he trying to say that there's nothing here in Maine or that we aren't worth painting? What the Christ is that supposed to mean?"

"It doesn't necessarily mean anything bad—"

ISLANDS AND BRIDGES

"Of course it doesn't look like anything bad to you. You're from Rhode Island. But it looks like a slap in the face to me. What's this jerk trying to say about the state of Maine? Does he think we're just a bunch of hicks?" Here, Thompson stopped his rant, paused for a moment, then restarted. "Goddamn it, I bet he thinks we're a bunch of racists! I bet that's what it's supposed to mean. A bunch of dirty white racists."

At the word, McTavish's mind flashed to the news about Lewiston, Maine. There, the settlement of a small community of Somali refugees created predictable results—a warm embrace from some residents and a wrathful scorn from others. Though little reported around the state, the story had generated some national coverage.

"Is that what he's trying to say? Is that what he means? A bunch of Africans gets called some names and now we're all racists? It's ridiculous!"

"Thompson, I've heard the stories and maybe that's what the artist is portraying, but there are other possibilities. Good lord, don't be so provincial," Marguerite said, her voice rising. "I mean you have to admit that Mainers have a long-standing reputation for frowning on all outsiders. You tease them, you mock them, you shun them. So it's no big surprise to learn that the Somalis would face discrimination here."

"Goddamn it!" Thompson said. "I supported the idea of allowing outa-staters into the competition and now I see it's coming back to bite us all right on the ass!"

"For Christ's sake, Thompson, grow up! I don't know what the artist was trying to say, but even if he was taking a dig at Maine, it's one man's opinion. You don't need to go off the deep end. And, if you want my honest opinion, if a piece of art can get you this stirred up, then I admire it even more than I did before." She then positioned her tally sheet on the wall and clearly marked a large number 1 next to the title of the painting. "You can wallow around here, but I'm moving on."

"Well, what about you?" Thompson now turned his attention and ire on McTavish. "You're supposed to be a Mainer now. Doesn't this painting get your goat?"

GEOFFREY SCOTT

"Not really," McTavish said calmly. "I understand what you're saying and it could be interpreted as a slight. But Marguerite's right—there are lots of ways to understand this piece."

"Bullshit. Name just one that isn't a slam on the state."

"How about the idea that the blank space represents a wide-open future. You know, literally a blank canvas. It could mean that folks in the other states are more staid—they're already colored in—but people in Maine are facing a future they can craft themselves."

"Interesting," Marguerite said. She'd moved to the next piece, but had been listening in as Thompson challenged McTavish. "So what you're saying is that, what looks like a white space could actually mean new possibilities. Maine could end up looking like one of the other states—you know, purple like New Hampshire or orange like Massachusetts—but it might also be lime or chartreuse or crimson."

"I don't know," Thompson grumbled. "But I concede the point. Maybe there is more than one way to look at it. Still—"

"Still more works to assess, Thompson," Marguerite said with a slight smile. "Mark your form and let's move it along."

CHAPTER 60

Tempers and disagreements flared over a couple other pieces, but the judges got through all the works eventually. Expecting more battles before coming to a consensus on a Prize winner, the group decided to take a dinner break. They'd be spending a lot more time together so they chose to separate and meet again in an hour.

"Well, how's it going?" Thompson Enders's wife asked when he bumped through the kitchen door. "Think you'll chose a winner tonight or will the puff of smoke not come till tomorrow right before the announcement?"

"Jesus, Minna, will you quit it with the pope allusions. We aren't electing a new pontiff, we're just choosing a piece of art."

"Maybe so, but I know you and I'm guessing you've got quite a bit to say about each and every piece. In fact I'm surprised you're home this early. You aren't really done, are you?"

"No, just taking a break for dinner. We evaluated and rated all the pieces, but we still have to decide which one wins."

"Got a few good ones in your sights, I suspect." After a pause, she asked, "How are the other judges? What's that McTavish fella like?

You know he was the one involved in all that mess around the stolen painting."

"He's okay." Thompson poured a liberal dose of scotch over ice. "Doesn't say a whole lot, but he makes his points."

"And how about the other one, the lady?"

"'Bout what you'd expect from an outa-stater. Got more opinions than sense. Honest to Christ, she can talk."

"What's the matter? She hog some of your talk time?"

"Oh hush, Minna. This gal can talk me right under the table."

"I doubt that, dear, so must be that she's making some of her own points. There's talking and then there's talking about something. You haven't said a thing about what she's saying so she must be saying something smart."

"You know, Minna, you really don't know everything."

"Oh, for Christ's sake, I do too! You're not a dumb man and I know three times as much stuff as you do!" Smiling at her husband, who knew she was right, Minna continued. "Now tell about all the things you're arguing over."

Marguerite Jameson drove over to Lane's Wharf for dinner. Robertay Harding and Regina Baldo had both recommended the Barlow House when she had checked in. She had listened to the advice but, more often than not, Marguerite found her own company to be sufficient so she'd opted for a different restaurant as a way to avoid Harding or Baldo "accidentally" dropping by to pump her for information.

Dodging the locals did not mean that Marguerite could avoid talk about the Summer Exhibition in general and the Arvin Prize in particular. She didn't engage in any of the talk, but it was all around her:

> "My lord, did you see that painting of a bare-breasted
> woman in the Exhibition? I swear to God, if that isn't

Robertay Harding, I'll eat my hat! Course the artist had to put a better looking face on her…"

"Far as I can see, half the paintings in the Exhibition ought to be competing for the Prize. They're a damn sight better than the Prize contenders."

"I still can't believe they're lettin' in outa-towners. Mattie A. would have a conniption fit if she was still around."

"Christ, you try to get through the grocery store since that art show got started? Every artist on the planet must be here and not one of 'em was in the deodorant aisle, though I dare say, a few of 'em shoulda been!"

"They say this new show is gonna put a lot of money in town folks' pockets. Wish to hell some of those pockets were mine!"

"Can you believe the locals around here? I heard there was a huge fuss about allowing non-residents to compete for the Arvin Prize. Since most of the pieces selected for the show were by non-residents, can you imagine how bad this show would be without them?"

Walking into his cottage, John McTavish expected to be grilled by Noah. But he had forgotten that Noah was working that night, so the house was empty. Anticipating a quiet dinner hour, McTavish went about fixing himself a simple meal—hamburger and home fries cooked into a hash, no vegetable need apply.

GEOFFREY SCOTT

As he did so, McTavish reflected on the whirlwind that had been his life since Maggie died a year and a half ago. First, he'd packed up their Indiana home and moved to the coast of Maine where he'd got mixed up in a fracas around a stolen painting. Soon after, he'd been involved in another mess involving a local tough who ended up committing suicide in McTavish's front yard. On top of that, his relationship with Noah had a stop and go feel. At times, he felt like they were making progress in knowing and understanding one another only to have that progress stymied over one thing or another. The same halting progress/non-progress seemed to be happening with the rest of his family. His relationship with Giselle continued to be the one solid element amidst a swirl of others. Mark couldn't stop being Mark, despite Amy's best efforts, and Ruth seemed to grow more pinched and odd every time he saw her. Beyond his human interactions, even his art work had pushed him up and down. McTavish had looked forward to a slow and steady track of relearning the basics of drawing before getting out his paints. But that plan had taken a couple of twists as he'd transformed his initial drawings of hands into actual pieces of art through the addition of some framing lines. And then he'd started his "life amongst decay" series only to have Ruby Park announce that they were little more than cartoons.

With Maggie around, McTavish lived at a pretty docile pace. He now realized how much Maggie shielded him from the buffeting of a full encounter with the world around him. He missed her for more than that shielding, but he often wondered if he was going to be able to make it on his own.

That admission carried with it its own tumult. Whether he welcomed it or not, his single status was prominent in a lot of people's minds and several of them seemed determined to see it end. It wasn't that McTavish was repelled by the idea of another loving relationship. It's just that he thought he ought to be the one to determine if and when it might happen.

At the end of his reverie, McTavish realized that he was engaged in another kind of turmoil, one he'd never anticipated. Thompson

Enders's vague accusation—"You're supposed to be a Mainer"—had annoyed him even if he wasn't quite sure why.

A Mainer by birth and by childhood, he had left for the mid-west as a young man, a move that still rankled parts of his family. Ironically, he'd felt like a Mainer throughout his life in Indiana, and now he was home again. But was he? He began to wonder if he was in some kind of no-mans-land.

"I am a Mainer," McTavish said to himself. "But I'm beginning to wonder what a Mainer really is. Maybe we're not all that different than anyone else." Geography and state affiliation might be one influence on a person's thoughts and actions, but he began to doubt whether it was all that important.

GEOFFREY SCOTT

CHAPTER 61

When the three judges reconvened, each entered with some anxiety about how long it might take to come to a consensus. Although no single choice for the Prize had arisen during their earlier review, their comments suggested that the field was narrowing. A narrowed field, however, still left plenty of room for disagreement and discord.

Once assembled in the gallery conference room, Thompson proposed that they list all the works to which they assigned the top mark. That proposal met quick acceptance so Thompson wrote the titles of the pieces on a white board. Each judge had given the top score of one to five different works. Once duplicate rankings surfaced, a final list of seven top-rated selections for the Arvin Prize emerged.

To be fair, Thompson asked if either of his colleagues wanted to make a case for another work to be added to the finalist list. Both Marguerite and McTavish demurred, so the group now focused at the list of seven pieces from which they would choose the winner.

"I don't know of any other way to start than to list pros and cons for each work," Thompson said.

Marguerite said, "We could do that, but we could also do another round of balloting to mark our top three so that we could eliminate some of the contenders."

"Well, yes, we could, but I'm not sure that would be that fair to all the ones that we ranked top-notch—"

"I understand that, Thompson," Marguerite said with a bit of an edge. "But if we get bogged down in listing pros and cons, we'll be here till dawn."

"If it's dawn, then it's dawn," Thompson said, voice rising. "The Arvin Prize is not a trifle and we ought not to short-change the process."

"For Christ's sake, we don't have a process! We're making one up on the spot!"

"Hang on, you two," McTavish finally said. "Let's try a different tack. Let's revote for the top three, but then if anyone wants to make a strong case for any of the other four, we'll do the pros and cons of that choice. Then we can revote if need be."

"Done," Thompson said.

Shaking her head, Marguerite said, "Done…Jesus!"

Thompson tore up and distributed slips of paper and asked the others to list the titles of their top three choices. After a couple minutes, McTavish and Marguerite folded their votes and slid them to Thompson.

After Thompson read the votes and marked the results on the white board, Marguerite said, "Well, that was a bust. I thought we might get lucky and all name the same three pieces."

"Not damn likely. And look, all we did was leave off one piece," Thompson grumbled.

McTavish agreed. "Yes, but we can see that there is some consensus around three of the pieces. The flag painting got two votes as did the islands and bridges piece. Oh, and the seascape also got two votes. So we didn't get a consensus on all three, but we've actually narrowed the list quite a bit."

"I guess you're right," Thompson said with a sigh. "So now let's see if anyone wants to make the case that one or more of the other pieces deserves to be in the final consideration." Each judge thought silently for a few minutes.

"I can live with the three that each got two votes," Marguerite said.

"Of, course, you can! Two of the three were on your list!"

"So are two of mine," McTavish said. "Don't you think—"

"Oh, never mind," Thompson said grumpily. "We can move on."

"Are you sure?" Marguerite asked directly. "Don't you want to make the case for one of your other choices? Because if you do, then do it now, because I don't want you to get all pissy about it later on."

"No. We can move on, but I'll tell you right now, I'll never vote for that goddamned flag painting."

"Well, you might not vote for it, but it might well be the Prize winner if we can't come to a unanimous decision," Marguerite said.

"All right," McTavish said, hoping to move the discussion along. "Let's state our pros and cons for the three pieces that each got two votes."

"Makes sense to me," Marguerite said. Thompson just nodded. "Okay. Well, we've already talked quite a bit about the flag painting. Is there anything else anyone would like to say?" Marguerite asked.

Both men shook their heads indicating they had no further comments. "Nor do I. It's a fine piece, but I made my feelings clear before. So let's move on to the seascape."

The seascape was the most realistic of the three selected images. Rendered in both fine and expressive detail, the watercolor evoked the danger and drama of breaking waves and the strength and resilience of the rocky coastline. What made the painting distinct, however, was the lone spruce tree growing out of the shoreline. Stunted and scraggly, the tree gave every indication of having developed and matured only through sheer determination. The artist, a non-resident from Delaware, captured the tree and the rocks around it right after a large wave had crashed over it and was starting to recede.

Marguerite said, "It's got a quality to it that seems just beyond words. I mean, I can name all the elements of the composition and each is nicely depicted. But there's something else to the piece that just speaks to me."

"Speaks to you, does it? What's it saying?" In a high-pitched voice, Thompson said, "I'm just like every other seascape every done, but please vote for me anyway!"

"Don't be an ass. If you don't like the piece then just say so, but be more instructive than just saying that it's a commonplace scene."

McTavish said, "I think you're right, Marguerite. It's well painted, but what I really like is the fact that the artist has captured a dramatic moment. Not the moment when the wave is actually cresting, but the scene afterward. Obviously this is not the first wave this tree has withstood. But now you have to wonder if it can keep doing so."

"Hmm…the story behind the scene?" Thompson asked, seeming more engaged. "That's interesting."

Marguerite said, "It is. Maybe that's what I was seeing, but couldn't name before. In any event, it's also interesting because it's the story that I see in the islands and bridges pastel that keeps pulling me in."

"What do mean?" Thompson asked.

"Well, I mean, look at. On the surface it just looks like a bunch of randomly arrayed island-like shapes kind of randomly sketched, drawn, and pasteled. And then there are the same sort of randomly sized and presented images of bridges between them. It's clearly intended to give a kind of child-like or surreal impression. What gets my attention, however, is the whole composition. The islands and the bridges are all different sizes and colors and depictions yet they're all connected.

"Huh. I see what you men. Seems like the artist is trying to show us that it's the connections between the islands that matter," McTavish said.

"Okay, but there aren't any people shown. It's only the island and bridge shapes…if that's what they really are," Thompson said.

"But maybe that's the point," Marguerite said with a dawning smile. "You know, it would be cliché to show people of different sizes and shapes to represent some kind of diversity. But if the artist is using islands as a metaphor for… Hmm. Remember the old saying 'no man is an island'? Seems like maybe the artist is playing off that notion and showing that, just like the islands, we are all connected."

"Interesting that it's a local artist who submitted the work," McTavish observed. "Richard Anthony Bates."

GEOFFREY SCOTT

In the end, the judges reached accord: The Bates piece depicting a surrealistic image of islands connected by bridges was named the Arvin Prize winner. Each saw something different in the piece, but all saw enough to call it the best in show.

Marguerite Jameson saw the artful use of pastels and the "no-man-is-an-island" storyline as the major selling points. Though not usually a fan of pastels, Marguerite thought this piece to be the most exceptional example she'd seen. Yet she wouldn't have voted for as the winner for that reason alone. Instead, it was the story that she saw within the work that excited her. We may be islands, she thought, but we are not completely independent. We are who we are, in part, due to the ways in which we connect with others. In her mind, then, Bates's image spoke to both her artist's mind and her human heart.

Thompson Enders voted for the Bates piece for different reasons. First and foremost, it was not the flag painting. He knew that art had a purpose to evoke passion; he just couldn't abide the thought that the work could demean the state he loved. So if his vote was going to count as it should, then he would cast his lot with the pastel artist Richard Anthony Bates. The second reason was that Bates was a local. Not a long-time local like Mattie Arvin or himself, but a local of a few years at least and one attached to a genuine local, Babette Dubois, who had deep roots in the Harbor.

John McTavish wrestled mightily with his vote. Like Marguerite Jameson, he was drawn to art that was both well rendered and suggested a story. In that sense, then, he could have voted for any of the three images. Yet the more he thought about the story he imagined to be behind the islands and bridges piece, the more it symbolized the drama of the last few months. People were islands, he thought, local islands and distant islands, new islands and old islands. Some were big and imposing, others small and seemingly insignificant. What made them islands was an individuality or disconnection on some level—

physical, emotional, social. It didn't really matter what the specifics were, people could either see or not see ways to disconnect with one another. The notion of being a local, a newbie, or from away could represent a significant disconnection. But so could the religious affiliations of Protestants, Catholics, Jews, and Muslims, the age categories of old, young, and middle-aged, and the career choices of historians, bankers, oil drillers, and farmers. The ways that we can divide ourselves, McTavish thought, are myriad. And yet we can choose—we consciously and actively can choose—to associate with one another and to build connections. Those connections can be fragile or strong, ever-lasting or fleeting, but the need to connect with others seemed as powerful a human impulse as the one to stand apart. I'm a Mainer and not a Mainer, he thought, and I suspect everyone else is too.

GEOFFREY SCOTT

CHAPTER 62

S ome blocs of viewers saw the same qualities that each of the three judges did when viewing Richard Anthony Bates's painting, *Islands…and Bridges*. Others saw the surrealistic images as an unfortunate rejection of representational art and thought the judges must have lost their minds. A different group liked the image, but wondered if Bates really counted as a local artist given his long Florida roots. And yet one more group, a small collection of Colony artists, thought the piece was fine, but felt the need to wrestle over the label terming the work a painting instead of a pastel drawing.

Most of Lydia's back-table patrons made time to take in the show. Slow Johnston missed it because he could never remember when the gallery was open. Bill Candlewith missed most of it because he couldn't move beyond the painting that depicted a busty woman who Ray Manley said was, for sure, Robertay Harding "with a different head on her."

For the most part, both men and women tablemates pronounced themselves satisfied with the winning piece and with the Exhibition as a whole. "Turned out to be much ado about nothing," Geraldine Smythe observed.

Minerva Williams said, "True enough, but that's only because it was Babette's boy toy who won."

For her part, Babette Dubois could not have been prouder of Richard Anthony, boy toy or not. She'd put up posters all over the Co-op advertising the show once she'd learned that Richard Anthony's work had made the Arvin roster. And when his victory was announced, she secured promises from all her fishing colleagues that they'd make time to see the Exhibition. "It'll do you boys good to get some culture," she said. No one contradicted her.

Islands…and Bridges struck Hadley Cooper the same way it had Marguerite Jameson. The "no-man-is-an island" connection jumped out at him and he looked up the phrase as soon as he got home. He learned that a British poet, John Donne, had written the phrase as part of a set of meditations and later as a poem:

No Man Is an Island
No man is an island,
Entire of itself,
Every man is a piece of the continent,
A part of the main.
If a clod be washed away by the sea,
Europe is the less.
As well as if a promontory were.
As well as if a manor of thy friend's
Or of thine own were:
Any man's death diminishes me,
Because I am involved in mankind,
And therefore never send to know for whom the bell
   tolls;
It tolls for thee.

GEOFFREY SCOTT

Hadley read himself into the poem. No island am I, he thought. Can't say that I'm thrilled by the idea that I'm diminished by my father's death, but if 'I am involved in mankind,' I suppose I am.

Robertay Harding and Thomas Beatty opened a bottle of fine single-malt scotch and toasted one another on the back porch of their house.

"You did it, dear," Thomas said.

"Thank you, Thomas, I did indeed."

Selectman Marie Townshend put together some notes for her colleagues in which she planned to ask for their ideas around expanding the Summer Exhibition into a true arts festival.

Toulouse Rustin co-wrote his column for the week following the Summer Exhibition with his aunt:

Provincialism's Quiet Death

On Sunday, August 21, provincialism and all its ugly siblings died…at least for a little while.

Rascal Harbor is not unique in having gone through a time where it turned on the outside world. The highly successful Summer Art Exhibition and Arvin Prize competition have obscured the fact that a few short months ago, we were a town at odds with those from away and, in turn, at odds with ourselves. We harbored mean thoughts, we said mean things, we committed mean acts. And we did all of this in the name of protecting ourselves and those for whom we care. We thought we were doing right, but we were fooling ourselves.

Every community tries to protect itself and its past in one way or another. What too often goes unrealized, however, is that the past will protect itself. If the past was once real and important, then it will continue to be so because it is real and important. Putting our past under glass and saying "look, but not too hard" may work in the short run, but it is a surefire way to undercut its value in the future.

The winner of the Arvin prize illustrates the truth of these claims. In his work, Richard Anthony Bates shows us that islands, like people, can be independent, but they can never be completely so. Our bridges today are to one another, to those who came before, and to those yet to come. Islands are wonderful places, but appreciating them means crossing bridges.

In our Summer Exhibition and in our Arvin Prize winner, we have crossed bridges and left them for others to use as well. Let's try to keep them well-maintained and operational from now on.

A week after the Summer Exhibition wrapped up, Jumper Wilson walked around town with a series of T-shirts. Monday's read: "You can't always get what you want…unless you build a bridge." Wednesday's shirt said: "Don't judge a man until you've crossed a few bridges with him." And on Friday, Jumper sported a shirt that read: "A journey of a thousand miles…will always cross some bridges."

GEOFFREY SCOTT

CHAPTER 63

John McTavish was relieved. He'd never judged an art show before and had only taken up art seriously for the last year. He'd made art while he worked as a historian and he'd read widely in the subject, but he knew himself to be a novice at best. Still, he felt pretty good about his participation on the Arvin Prize jury and, when he thought about it, the fact that he'd had all three of his pieces selected for the Exhibition. Best of all—no one else had called them cartoons.

Noah had also had a piece selected for the Exhibition. So in celebration of the McTavish men's accomplishments, Louise Park and her parents threw them a party. The eclectic crowd featured artists, lobstermen, mechanics, retirees, and a host of Louise and Noah's friends, most of whom worked tourist-trade jobs. The event doubled as an end-of-summer affair and most everyone was stumbling drunk by the time it broke up at one AM.

Fortunately, it was a short drive back to the McTavish cottage. Noah and his father made it without running off the road or running into a policeman. McTavish worried that he was setting a bad example for his son. But he reasoned that neither of them would remember the trip in the morning.

Entering the kitchen, McTavish felt a sudden weirdness come over him. The feeling was so intense that he sat down in one of the kitchen rockers.

Noticing, Noah asked, "You okay, Dad? You look a little shaky."

"I feel like I am. All of a sudden I felt light-headed so thought I best sit down."

"Are you going to be sick? I didn't think you drank that much."

"No, my stomach actually feels fine. Can't imagine what caused that sensation."

Pausing, Noah asked quietly, "Was it Mom? Did she come to you?"

Looking up at his son, McTavish said, "No, I don't think so. But I had an odd sensation of something there and then gone."

"And you didn't see anything or hear anything?"

"Nope. I definitely didn't see or hear anything, but now that I think about it..." He paused. "This is going to sound odd, but—"

"Go ahead, Dad. What were you thinking?"

"I'm not sure that I was thinking. It was more the perception that my eyes are now fully opened. That's the strange part—I had the sensation that my eyes have been half closed, that I could only see part of what was in front of me, and now I can see it all." McTavish paused and looked at his son. "Does that make any sense to you? That I could see before, but now I can see more?"

"No, it doesn't make any sense to me. And it's kind of freaking me out. What are you talking about?"

"I really don't know, Noah," McTavish said quietly. "But it's okay. Now that I'm a little more used to it, it feels okay, almost peaceful."

"'Peaceful?' Jesus, Dad, you really are weird. It looks like you're having a heart attack or something, then it looks like you're in some kind of fog, and now you've got a goofy, dreamy look about you. You're not flaking out on me, are you?"

"Actually, I feel quite good. I don't know how long it will last but, right now, I feel pretty good." Standing, McTavish reached out and hugged his son. "I'll see you in the morning."

GEOFFREY SCOTT

McTavish felt relieved to wake the next morning without the blinding hangover he'd expected. The bottle of ibuprofen on the kitchen counter suggested that Noah had not been so lucky and had sought chemical relief from his own excesses.

As he walked over to Lydia's for breakfast, McTavish worked to remember a dream that seemed to go on all night. He woke a couple of times during the night thinking about it, but once he woke that morning, it had vanished.

Walking along the narrow road with a warm breeze pushing him along, the dream slowly emerged. It did so in a series of disconnected images and impressions rather than a clear and coherent narrative. Maggie and Noah both appeared and faded, each saying things that now seemed just beyond McTavish's hearing. The other images—his cottage, the woodpile, his drawing table—also flashed and faded. They were there, somewhere, in his mind's eye, but he could not hold them still long enough to figure out what they meant. The impression left, however, veered toward comfort and security rather than anxiety and doubt.

Wonder what that's all about, he thought. More mysteries I suppose.

He'd just finished that thought, when a clear memory surfaced. He heard Maggie's voice in the dream image saying, "You'll be okay, John. You'll be okay." In this memory, Maggie repeated these words three more times. Once recalled, no other portions of the dream would come.

"Jesus, Mags, this is no time to go opaque on me," McTavish said with a hint of irritation. "What are you talking about? And while we're at it, why in hell won't you come to Noah?"

Walking farther, McTavish realized that Maggie had gone silent again. Annoyed, but used to her going quiet, McTavish's mind wandered. Nearing Lydia's, he began thinking about his next art project. He was finished with flowers and other vegetation images; he now wanted to focus on a different aspect of his "life amongst decay" series.

"Noah didn't need me, John," Maggie said into a startled McTavish's ear. "He never needed me like you did. He knows how to live on his own terms. And when he doesn't, he needs to talk with you. If he talks with me, then you two will never learn how to be with one another. Help him, John, and let him help you. You'll both be okay."

Maggie's voice interrupted McTavish's walk. Her words rooted him in that spot and it took him several minutes to regain his equilibrium. As he resumed his walk, he ran Maggie's words over and over in his mind—"If he talks with me, then you two will never learn how to be with one another. Help him, John, and let him help you."

Recovered enough to form a coherent thought, McTavish said to Maggie, "Once again, Mags, what in hell are you talking about? Why be so cryptic?" But even as he heard myself say these words, he sensed that these would be the last words he would hear from the woman he loved. He would never forget her, but she would be silent from now on.

As he walked up the steps to Lydia's Diner, an attractive, red-haired woman came out through the door. "You're John McTavish," she said bluntly. "I loved your work in the Exhibition, but I had a few thoughts about it…"

THE END

GEOFFREY SCOTT

is the pseudonym of **S. G. Grant**, a professor of history education at Binghamton University. Grant has authored or edited a dozen education-related books and numerous articles and book chapters. This is the third book in his series of art-flavored novels.

CPSIA information can be obtained
at www.ICGtesting.com
Printed in the USA
LVHW050132271221
707201LV00006B/56

9 781943 419883